CRITICAL
Alan S

Night Moves

'Mr Scholefield is a very fine story-teller – a writer impressively at home with character and passion and atmosphere.' *New Yorker*

'You can almost feel the tension crackling around the characters as they act their way through this seamlessly plotted novel.' *The Mystery Review*

Don't Be a Nice Girl

'A real original.' *Irish Independent*

'Seamlessly plotted, sardonically told, seeded with jokes and surprises that go off with bright lights and the smell of gun smoke.' Philip Oakes, *Literary Review*

Threats & Menaces

'Scholefield retains his place in the front rank of English crime writers.' *Publishers' Weekly*

'Scholefield serves up yet another wicked brew of sin and bitters.' John Coleman, *Sunday Times*

Night Moves

Alan Scholefield worked originally as a journalist but became a full-time novelist in the early sixties. He is now the author of more than twenty novels, one of which, *Venom*, was filmed starring Nicol Williamson, Sarah Miles and Oliver Reed. He has also written screenplays, a stage adaptation of *Treasure Island* and two thirteen-part adventure series for TV, as well as five suspense novels under the pseudonym Lee Jordan. He is married to the novelist Anthea Goddard and has three daughters.

Night Moves is the sixth novel in his series featuring Detective Superintendent George Macrae and Detective Sergeant Leopold Silver.

Alan Scholefield

Night Moves

A Macrae and Silver Novel

PAN BOOKS

First published 1996 by Macmillan

This edition published 1997 by Pan Books
an imprint of Macmillan Publishers Ltd
25 Eccleston Place, London, SW1W 9NF
and Basingstoke

Associated companies throughout the world

ISBN 0 330 34733 0

1 3 5 7 9 8 6 4 2

A CIP catalogue record for this book is available from
the British Library

Typeset by Intype London Ltd
Printed by Mackays of Chatham PLC, Chatham, Kent

For Tom Sharpe

My thanks for their help go, as usual, to Dr Robin Ilbert of the Prison Service, and Hugh Toomer, former detective inspector, the Metropolitan Police. And, as usual, any mistakes are mine.

Chapter One

Report 1/MSU/MS

SYMPOSIUM ON 'DANGEROUSNESS'
LOXTON SPECIAL HOSPITAL
CASE STUDY NO. 28

Malcolm Stephen Underdown
Date of birth 5.5.65.
Admitted under Section 37/41 Mental Health Act,
    1983.
Convicted at London Sessions for the following:
    Manslaughter x1
    Attempted murder x1
    Making a threat to kill.

FAMILY HISTORY
Mother, 64, retired airline stewardess. First husband
was in the navy. Marriage ended in divorce – infidelity.
Second husband was a farmer twenty years her senior.
He had a drink problem and was violent.
SIBLINGS: nil. Only child.

PERSONAL HISTORY

Born in Winchester. Could not recall much of early childhood, occasionally enuretic until seven or eight years, had nightmares and fear of the dark until about fifteen. Endured occasional physical abuse by step-father. Because of financial difficulties which followed his father's death, Malcolm educated in the State system. Continual difficulties. Considered a loner and would have been a natural target for bullying were it not for his large physical size. At fifteen he beat up another student in a rage. Considered to be bright and did enough work to be granted a place at Winchester University. Took part of a BA degree course in sociology but dropped out before completion.

OCCUPATION

Apart from occasional temporary work, has been unemployed since leaving university.

SEXUAL HISTORY

No girlfriends at school. First sexual experience was at university. Became infatuated with another BA student. She rejected him for someone else. Malcolm beat up her lover. His infatuation for the girl became obsessive. He began to follow her. Developed urges to kill whichever male she was with.

ALCOHOL AND DRUGS

Has abused cannabis, LSD, amphetamines and anti-depressants. Drinks in binges. Could not estimate his alcohol consumption.

FORENSIC HISTORY
1974: Cautioned for stealing sweets.
1978: Cautioned for violent behaviour.
1982: Cautioned for violent behaviour.
1988: Cautioned for making threats.

INDEX OFFENCE
Charged with and pleaded guilty to manslaughter.

PSYCHIATRIC HISTORY
Nothing known.

MENTAL STATE
Indifferent about events that have led him to present
position. Has no remorse about fate of his victim. Is still
obsessed about the woman. Talks of a shattered life,
broken promises, 'unfinished business'. Has a strong
hatred of confinement. Talks of 'moving', wants to
'move', but has no goal, no target to move towards.

INVESTIGATION
Physical examination – nothing abnormal discovered.
Blood profile – awaiting results.
Skull X-ray – NAD.
Chest X-ray – NAD.
Normal EEG.
HIV negative.

ADMISSION DIAGNOSIS
Borderline personality disorder.

FOR DISCUSSION
What is the diagnosis?
Is he treatable?
Morbid jealousy?
De Clerambault's Syndrome?

Chapter Two

Detective Superintendent George Macrae pushed open the door of Chief Superintendent Wilson's office and said, loudly enough for half-a-dozen detectives at nearby desks to hear, 'Scales can go and get stuffed!'

Wilson, on the phone, slapped a hand over the mouthpiece and waved the other angrily at Macrae.

'I bloody mean it,' Macrae said.

'For God's sake, George, close the door.' Then, into the mouthpiece: 'Yes, yes, of course I can remember. *Leg* of lamb. Not *shoulder*. All right. About seven.' He put down the phone. 'George, what the hell's the matter with you?'

'You know bloody well – or you should.' Macrae cast his eyes about the room, looking speculatively at desk drawers and cupboards.

'Not a drop, George. There's not a bottle in the room.'

'I'll be off to the pub in a minute then.'

'Don't tell me, I don't want to know. But I do

want to know what the hell this performance is all about.'

Macrae stood by the window. Cannon Row police station lay on the Thames, just to the east of the Houses of Parliament and Westminster Abbey, and commanded a view of the river and the Festival Hall. Wilson's office had a better view than Macrae's and indeed *was* a better office. Not that either was luxurious or even comfortable. Wilson's was just less bleak. He had curtains at the windows, Macrae had an old holland blind which was dark brown from exposure to the London air.

'George?' Wilson prompted.

Still looking out of the window at the grey winter river, Macrae said, 'Remember when we were beat coppers, Les? Remember those lovely days?'

'I remember.' Wilson's reply was guarded. He didn't like the tone of Macrae's voice nor the irony.

'How would you like to do it all again?'

'Do what?'

'Put on a uniform and go out on the beat like the wooden tops.'

'What are you on about, George?'

'I'm on about refreshing yourself, Les. Of interfacing with the uniformed branch, of going back to grass roots, of refamiliarizing yourself with the nuts and bolts of policing.' He paused. 'Have I left out any cliché?'

'I don't know what the hell you're talking—'

'Scales loves clichés. Not just the occasional one, but the whole bloody shooting match.'

Wilson decided to remain silent and Macrae turned back into the room. 'Because that's what he wants me to do – go back on the bloody beat.'

'What?' Wilson was aghast.

'You may well say "what". That's what I said to the miserable little shit.'

The Deputy Commander wasn't little; miserable, yes, in many people's opinion, but not little. In fact he was slightly better than medium height. It was just that beside Macrae, with his height and bulk and bullish – almost Minotaurish – proportions, he seemed small, which was why he had had his office chair heightened so that he could look down on people, and people meant especially Macrae.

Wilson, who had started his career in the Force at the same time as Macrae, did not now wish to journey down memory lane with him; his voice was too loud, his temper too volatile and Wilson had never learnt to control him.

'Did you know about this, Les?'

'About what?'

'About wanting me to go on the beat.'

'Of course not. You don't think I'd have let you go in there without telling you? Anyway, your rank doesn't do it.'

'Oh, yes it does.'

Macrae had said as much to Scales at the beginning of the interview, but the Deputy Commander had clicked his ball-point pen and touched the mat of sprayed hair covering his bald patch, and had then said, 'That's where you're wrong, George. Let me explain . . .'

And he *had* explained. He had used phrases like 'multi-skilling' and 'tenure programming' and 'flexible parameters' and Macrae had listened with growing anger.

'You see, George,' he had said, clicking the ball-point, 'it's people like you who are *needed* in the uniformed branch. It's you who have the experience and the expertise which *they* need. And it's only for a few months.'

'I'm not doing it,' Macrae had said. 'It's a bloody villains' charter. Who's going after them while people like me are on the beat getting cats out of trees?'

Click . . . click . . . 'Her Majesty's Inspectorate of Constabulary said—'

'Oh, fuck the HMI!'

Wilson broke in here. 'You didn't really say that, did you?'

'Aye, those very words.'

'Christ Almighty, George, have you gone raving mad? He's been looking for a way of getting you out, and now he's got it.'

'I smiled,' Macrae said.

'When you said "fuck the HMI"?'

'Well, it was a sort of smile. Then I told him that in one northern force eight hundred detectives were taking court action against the scheme and several other Chief Constables had thrown it out altogether.'

'Still smiling?' The thought of Macrae's smile caused Wilson to freeze.

'Not much. But Scales hates trouble, hates the thought that it might go down on his record. So he said, why didn't I think about it because it was a sure cure for stagnation.'

Wilson said, 'That's crap. The scheme was started to prevent corruption by moving detectives around and about.'

'I know that and he knows that, and I told him that a DI in East Anglia was suing the Police Authority in the Industrial Court and that there was a strong anti-movement right here in this station.'

'What did he say to that?'

'He clicked his bloody pen and stood up and said he'd talk to the lads. Christ, what a phrase! The lads! As though we were a bloody football team. But you could see he was scared. Suddenly there was rebellion in the air and he went pale at the thought.'

Wilson leaned back. He could see that Macrae was calmer. Had got it off his chest.

'You coming for a dram, Les?'

Wilson looked at his watch. It wasn't four o'clock yet and he shook his head. 'A bit early for me.'

'Well, not for me.'

Wilson knew that Macrae was drinking more heavily now than he had done for a long time and he knew the reason.

'Heard anything from Frenchy?' he said.

'Nothing more than the card at Christmas.'

'How long's she been gone?'

'Three months.'

Wilson took a pair of shoe brushes from his bottom drawer, leant down and began to polish his black half-brogues. It was a characteristic gesture by this neat and polished man.

'I know how you feel about her,' he said. 'And you'll think me a callous shit, but I have to say that once things settle down, I think you'll be glad. I know I will. She was bloody dangerous for you, George. Her being what she was.'

'Why don't you say it? She was a tart.'

There was renewed anger in Macrae's voice, with an undertone of violence, and Wilson said hastily, 'I don't mean anything derogatory. I liked Frenchy very much but—'

'Don't go on, Les.'

'OK, OK. It's just—'

The door opened on a knock and Detective Sergeant Leopold Silver put his head into the room.

'Guv'nor,' he said to Macrae.

'What?'

'Thought you'd like to know. Underdown's out.'

'Who?'

'You remember him. That—'

'Oh, yes. Aye. *That* bastard.' Macrae turned to Wilson. 'You remember him, Les, he—'

'I remember him.' It was Wilson's claim to fame

that he had a phenomenal memory and now he said, 'Murder. No, not murder. Manslaughter, wasn't it? Didn't he plead guilty?'

'With diminished responsibility,' Silver said.

'That's him,' Macrae said.

'It was one of the first cases you and I worked on, guv'nor.'

'No wonder I haven't forgotten it,' Macrae said dryly. 'But it's bloody soon to let him out, he's only been in two or three years, hasn't he?'

'Four. And they didn't let him out. He just walked out of the after-care hostel.'

Macrae turned to Wilson. 'He was a nasty piece of work. You remember what he did to the man? What was his name?'

Wilson paused for a moment, then said, 'Craig. Edward Craig.'

'What happened?' Macrae said to Silver.

'Remember Armstrong? He was with us that day and Underdown knifed him in the arm.'

'Aye, I remember.'

'He's just phoned. He's with the Hampshire force now. He wanted me to know in case . . .'

'In case what?' Wilson said.

'Underdown threatened me, too,' Leo said. 'Not only the woman.'

'Oh, Christ, they all do that,' Macrae said.

'He knifed a copper,' Wilson said. 'Not all of them do that.'

'What happened?' Macrae said again.

'He was in a hostel in Winchester and just walked out.'

'So he's likely to be off medication,' Macrae said.

'Well, thank Christ he's not our baby,' Wilson said.

'Can't say that, Les,' Macrae said. 'He was in our manor to start with and he'll be back. He was always moving, that bugger. They said so in court. Never slept in the same place twice. Well, he's moving now all right and he'll probably come back to London. I wouldn't want to be the woman. The one he was after. Joan?'

'Jane,' Wilson said. 'Jane somebody.'

'Jane Harrison,' Leo said. 'I wonder if anyone's got in touch with her?'

Macrae said, 'You can bet they haven't. It's only because of Armstrong that we know. This is where the whole bloody system breaks down, 'specially concerning the victim.'

'Or in this case the potential victim,' Leo said.

'No one gives a toss. No time, they say, no money.'

Macrae began pacing the small room. 'She wasn't much more than a child.'

'She was twenty-five, guv'nor.'

'Well, she looked like a child.'

Macrae was suddenly hurtled back in time. The blood, the terrified young woman. She had reminded him vividly of his daughter, Susan, and he didn't like the comparison. There had been something dark and sinister about it, as though it was a warning of what could happen to Susan, too.

'It's not really our job,' Wilson said. 'But to hell with that.' He turned to Leo. 'Go and ring her. And get the files.' Then to Macrae, 'We'd better do our homework, George. Sure as hell we're going to get phone calls.'

Suddenly there was a different air between the two men, the angry atmosphere had dissipated as the urgency of the present situation took hold. By the time Leo had come back with computer tearsheets and files the casual gathering had developed the tension of a formal meeting.

'Can't raise her,' Leo said. 'According to the files the flat was sold soon after the murder. Can't raise the present owner either but I'll go round. It's not far from my place.'

Wilson said, 'What was she like, George?'

Macrae paused. 'Good-looking.' Superstitiously, he erased Susan from his thoughts and said, 'Reminded me a bit of that actress, what's-her-name? Who was in that picture about Italy. The one where that stone statue bites her hand off, or you think it does. The one—'

'*Roman Holiday.*'

'That's it. Katherine Hepburn.'

'Audrey Hepburn,' Leo said.

'You sure?'

'Yes, guv'nor.'

'Aye. Well then, her. Didn't this woman remind you of her?'

'Not really.'

'What?'

'Well . . . sort of. It's a long time since I saw the film.'

'It was on the box the other night.'

'Is he always like this?' Wilson asked.

'It's his university education. It's called debating. They taught him that and speed reading and hair-dressing and—'

'For Christ's sake!' Wilson drew a sheet of paper towards him. 'OK, George, let's see. One: Location of Jane Harrison. Two: Panic button. Find out if she has one. Three: The escape – no matter what you call it that's what it was. Where? When? How? Anything else?'

The hour for the opening of the pub came and went, and the three men continued talking.

Chapter Three

'What sort of a day did you have?' Jane said.

Her husband, Michael, was reading *The Times* and did not look up. He was sitting in a grey recliner and behind him a big window looked out at the night. From this position on Hampstead Hill most of London lay below them, a million lights in black velvet.

It was an evening like many others. She had heard the automatic opening of the garage doors, then the sound of the Porsche being driven in, then silence, then footsteps, then the shower, then . . . then came his arrival in the room. Then the kiss on her forehead.

She lit a cigarette. It was now nine o'clock and he'd been home only half an hour. He'd had smoked salmon and brown bread and butter and a glass of Krug. Sometimes he didn't eat at all and she assumed he had had something at a restaurant after leaving his rooms, or the hospital or whatever court he had been appearing in.

'Are we talking tonight?' she said lightly.

'What?' He put down the paper.

'Talking,' she said. 'Are we?'

'Of course we are, why on earth shouldn't we?'

'I spoke to you a moment ago. Asked what sort of day you'd had. You hardly looked up.'

'I'm sorry, darling. I was concentrating on this case at the Old Bailey. You know the one?'

'No.'

'I thought I'd mentioned it. The man who killed that poor woman on the train to London. Just walked up to her and stabbed her.'

'Is he one of yours?'

'Yes, he's one of mine.' He smiled at her. 'You're looking tired,' he said. 'Were you at your mother's?'

She nodded. 'The house is awful. I had a surveyor in and he said it was structurally sound, but it's a mess. The deeper you go into the cupboards the worse it gets.'

He rose and put his plate and glass on a fine lacquered table and touched her hair before resuming his chair. She watched him as he tidied the paper. There was a time when he hadn't looked in his forties. He did now. Sometimes he looked fifty. The papers used to describe him as lithe. Now he was just thin and the mass of silvery hair of which he was once so proud was just grey hair. In spite of this he was still good-looking, especially with his tan, which gave the impression of someone who had just come back from Bermuda – which, indeed, he had. She wondered if winter conferences were ever held in places like Stockholm or Oslo. All the ones he went to seemed to be either in the West Indies in winter or near the Mediterranean in the summer.

'What are you going to do with the contents?' he said.

'Her body's not cold yet so it's a bit early to talk of that.'

'Her body's reduced to ash,' he said.

'That's true. Throw most of the stuff out, I suppose.'

'Not the porcelain, of course, nor the furniture.'

'Of course not.'

'What about the Hepplewhite table and chairs? And the Spode?'

'I'll have them auctioned. I'll get Christie's to have a look at them.'

'And Sotheby's. You should ask both.'

'I'm going to get professional cleaners in before I get either.'

'You should have it all valued. I'm sure your mother didn't.'

'I'll speak to her lawyers.'

'You want to check the insurance.'

'Of course I will.' She thought she might have been too sharp and smiled at him. 'You still some-times sound as though I'm your patient. I can cope, you know.'

'I know, my love. Forgive me. It's just that I like to look after you.'

'And never think I'm not grateful.'

The phone rang. She picked it up and a voice said, 'Could I speak to Mrs Stone, please?'

'Speaking.'

'This is the police. Is that Jane Harrison?'

The word 'police' had brought back the familiar feeling of emptiness. Now the use of her maiden name made everything worse.

'It's Sergeant Silver of Cannon Row,' the voice said. 'Do you remember me?'

She felt a twisting in her gut. 'Of course I remember you. Who wouldn't?' She could feel the sweat on her palm as she held the phone. She knew that this was the call she had always dreaded.

'I wanted to let you know right away,' Leo said. 'We've just heard that Underdown is on the loose.'

There was a long silence as she absorbed this and he said, 'Are you there?'

'Yes, I'm here.' She saw Michael staring at her. 'When did he come out?'

'Last night. Didn't return to his hostel.'

'His what? I thought he was in Loxton.'

'He was. Apparently he came up before the tribunal last year and they moved him out of Loxton to a regional secure unit. Then a week ago he was moved to a hostel in Winchester.'

'You mean they let him out?'

'Apparently it's the standard route. If the psychiatrists think he's made a good recovery they start the process of getting him back into society. So from a secure hospital like Loxton he'd go down one notch to a less secure hospital and then to a hostel.'

'And then?'

'Back into society and care in the community.'

'Oh, God!'

'I thought I'd better let you know.'

She couldn't think of anything to say except, why did they *let* him escape? And he would not be able to answer that.

'Are you there?' he said.

'Yes.'

'Look, they say he has recovered. Anyway, he doesn't know where you are or your married name. It took me some time to find it, and we have a computer. So don't worry. But just in case, and really to make you feel better, we'd like to put a panic . . . an electronic alarm in your house. You're not alone, are you?'

'My husband's here.'

'That's good. I'll need some details of your alarm system if you have one. The company's name.'

She gave it to him.

'OK, I'll organize someone to come round first thing in the morning. But don't worry, we'll get him before anything happens.'

'Will you?'

'Oh, yes, absolutely.'

She put down the phone and said to Michael, 'Underdown's out. Escaped.'

'Who was that?'

'The police. He escaped last night. He could be anywhere!'

Michael rose. He was the same height as Jane and he put his arm around her shoulders. She felt as stiff as a board.

'Tell me,' he said.

She told him everything Silver had told her. He did not interrupt and when she finished he nodded and said, 'Let me make a couple of calls.'

She watched him as he walked to his study. He looked so purposeful, so able to cope. Which was why, of course, she had let him cope in the first place, had been only too glad to have him as her bulwark. She lit another cigarette, closed the curtains and checked that the burglar alarm was activated.

Michael came back. 'I've phoned Sidney Michaelson.' She knew Sidney but hadn't heard his name for a long time. He was one of the consultant psychiatrists at Loxton, the special hospital. 'He says he only heard about Underdown a little while ago and was going to ring me. Bloody liar!' He took her hands. 'He says Underdown was making good progress, so you shouldn't worry too much.'

'If he was making so much progress, why did he escape then?'

'Escape's the wrong word. By law they couldn't hold him.'

'Why can't people do what they're paid to do?'

'What's that supposed to mean?'

'You know what it means! He's a murderer. He's dangerous. He's got unfinished business – he said so. And they let him go!'

'Well, first of all—'

'And you said he'd be in Loxton for life! You *said* it!'

'—first of all to answer your question: no matter what precautions are taken, someone, some time, is going to get out. And secondly, I assumed he would be held for a long time. I did not say for life. That's an assumption that can't be made and you knew that because I told you so at the time. You imagined it would be for life because that's what you wanted.'

She broke down then. The tears came in fitful bursts, like those of a terrified child. He held her close, as he had always done at the bad times.

'Dram and a pint,' Macrae said.

The phraseology was not commonly heard in Battersea, being more familiar in the pubs of Edinburgh and Glasgow and places north. But in the Blind Pig it was, when Macrae said it, perfectly well understood and even though the bar was crowded and a noisy darts match was in progress he did not have to say it loudly.

'Coming right up, Mr Macrae.'

The pint of best bitter and the shot of Famous Grouse were placed before him in a matter of seconds. The barman was already registering another order and only part of his mind was on his words as he said, 'Is Frenchy coming in?'

Macrae's glare was like paint stripper.

'Oh, sorry, Mr Macrae.'

Macrae watched him move off, raised the whisky, looked at the lovely light amber colour for a moment, threw it into the back of his throat, felt its resonance deep in his chest, then reached for the ale.

Why the hell was this bastard asking about Frenchy? He hardly knew her. Indeed Frenchy didn't much like the Blind Pig. She had once described it as 'non-elegant', with which Macrae had to agree. But it was the nearest watering hole to his house and as such was valuable.

People came in, crowding the bar. Macrae stood alone at one end, an expression on his face that Frenchy might have described as 'non-friendly'.

He was left alone.

Which was what he wanted.

If he couldn't be with Frenchy he didn't want anyone else, and this, when he first realized it, had surprised him. He had had woman trouble for a long time. Two ex-wives and now an ex-mistress. And that was a word that placed him in a time frame. People like Silver talked of partners. Macrae thought it sounded like a law firm or an office filled with accountants.

He drank his ale. Two ex-wives and an ex-mistress. Christ, he should be *pleased* she'd gone. No more complications, no more hassle. Yet he knew to the day how long it was since she'd left, the day he'd found the letter on the mantelpiece, the way they did it in junk TV.

'Dearest George,' it had said (and he still cherished the 'dearest'). 'I got to go. It's no good me telling fibs so I won't. I can't live no more like this. I got used to my own in-dependance moniwyse, so I am going to make some. I do love you George and I am sorry for what I am doing. Love, Your Frenchy.'

He could write it out word for word, even to the chronic punctuation and spelling.

Of course, Macrae being Macrae, he had thought instantly that she had been kidnapped. He had tried to analyse it: by whom? Well, by any of a dozen villains he'd put away or was threatening to put away. What for? Revenge. A not-so-subtle warning to lay off.

He had actually made a list of villains in and out of the nick who might want to do him a disservice, but had finally come to the conclusion that he was stretching things a little. First of all, kidnap wasn't a particularly British crime. Secondly, people were usually – not always, but usually – kidnapped for money. No matter how you read Frenchy's 'Dearest George' letter, there was no request for money. There was a sub-text called 'in-dependance' but he was used to that from Frenchy. No, when he came down to it, Macrae had to admit – after careful analysis – that she had buggered off and left him.

He'd gone to see her mother in Peckham Rye.

'Oh, it's you,' she had said.

'Aye, it's me all right.'

Mrs Pinker in her grey jump-suit, her blonde wig and her cigarette stuck in one side of her mouth was not the companion in misery he sought, so he came straight to the point.

'France,' she had said.

'France?' He made it sound as though it was some remote area in the Taklamakan Desert. 'What's she doing in France?'

'That's her affair.' Mrs Pinker twisted her face so the smoke didn't get in her eyes. 'She's never been abroad before.'

'But why did she go? And why France?'

'She said on the phone that's where she was going. Didn't say why, didn't say nothing more. Just going to France and I mustn't worry. Back in a few months.'

'A few months!'

'That's what she said.'

'What part of France?'

'Didn't say.'

That knowledge had come at Christmas. The card had said, 'Lots of love, George. See you won day. Frenchy.'

The postmark said 'Cannes'.

What the hell was she doing in Cannes?

Macrae finished his ale, bought a bottle of Grouse and drove home. There was a mist haloing the street lamps and when he got out of the car in his street he smelled the acrid but evocative – and illegal – smell of a coal fire somewhere nearby. That was how the street had changed, he thought, since he'd bought his house. Most of the fireplaces had been bricked up in those days. Now as the street had become gentrified the fires had been opened up. There was a fake carriage lamp on the house next door where once there had only been a rusty bulb holder.

The house was cold and smelled of unwashed dishes and old food. It was a smell he had smelled many times, usually as his life plunged into a phase of being without a woman. He gave himself a drink and went into the sitting-room. The curtains were still drawn from the night before and the room stank of cigar smoke.

'Home,' he said.

'Murdered?' Zoe said. 'Here? In Pimlico? You never told me about that.'

'That was before we met,' Leo said.

'Oh, those lovely days.'

Leo was getting out of his work clothes. He fancied himself in black: black brogues (expensive), black polo neck, black leather jacket. His hair too was black and sat close down on his skull like a cap.

Zoe stood at the bedroom door. She was wearing an apron and had a glass of wine in her hand.

Leo took his towel and went to the shower. She followed.

'Did you hear what I said?' she called.

Leo stuck his head out of the shower cabinet. 'Yes, of course. And terribly amusing. I must try and remember it. Pass the soap.'

'*Please* pass the soap.'

'OK. *Please* pass the soap.'

'No.'

He climbed out of the shower, took the soap from the wash-basin and returned.

'Well, go on,' Zoe said. 'This man, what's-his-name . . .'

'Underdown.'

'He killed the man but not the woman. Right?'

'He would have killed her too if a neighbour hadn't called the police. The neighbour heard the row when the two men fought. They were banging around all over the place and the woman was screaming and—'

'That's Jane?'

'Jane Harrison. Now Mrs Michael Stone. Her husband's a doctor.'

Leo came out and dried himself as Zoe watched. She was small and slight with high cheek-bones and dark hair and looked Spanish, which she partly was.

'That's what you should have been,' she said, following him back to the bedroom.

'What?'

'A doctor. Your parents would have loved that. Just think what your mother would have been able to say: "My son, the doctor." '

'My grandfather, her father, was a doctor.'

' "My son, the policeman." Not quite the same ring.'

'You looking for a fight?'

'God, no! *I* think you're terrific.'

'That's right. I am.'

They went upstairs to the sitting-room/dining-room/kitchen and Leo said, 'What's for supper?'

'Surprise.'

'Oh, God.'

'I'm going to ignore that. So go on, what's happened now? You don't tell stories very well.'

'Underdown escaped. All that means is he just hasn't returned to the hostel he was in.'

'And he might have come to London?'

'Might. The people at Loxton, the secure hospital he was sent to, don't think he'll be a problem.'

'They never do. You know, Leo, this care in the community business is hopeless.'

'Talk to Macrae.'

'No, I mean it. I read somewhere that one murder a month is committed by people released from mental hospitals into the community. One a month!

'The problem is, what do you do? Keep them locked away in those Victorian mad-houses?'

'You tell me. And tell me how you're going to

protect someone like Mrs Stone. What if he comes after her again?'

'I've warned her he's moving and we're going to put a panic button into her house.'

The phone rang and he picked it up.

His mother's voice said dramatically, 'Your father is crossing Oxford Street.'

'Now?' Leo said.

'Soon.'

'My God, south of Marble Arch! Have you got the water-bottles filled, and the pemmican?'

'Vot is pemmican?' Her Austrian accent was always thicker on the phone.

'Sun-dried beef. Just the thing to sustain you south of Oxford Street.'

'Don't be silly, Leo.'

'Me? Silly? What about Father?'

He could see his mother at the phone in the big old untidy flat on the wrong side of the Finchley Road in north London. Here his father taught the piano and his mother looked after his father.

He said, 'Can I ask what is causing Father to come south of Oxford Street?'

'Me,' Lotte said with satisfaction. 'The Graben Quartet is playing at the Queen Elizabeth Hall.'

'The Graben . . .?'

'From Vienna. When I was a little girl in Vienna my father used to take me to their recitals at the Musikverein. I said to your father, "I want to hear them again." He said we could buy a record. I said,

"Manfy, if you do not take me I go by myself and I get mugged and you can pick up the pieces. The police will telephone you and . . ." '

'For God's sake!' Leo said.

'Well, it is true. He never does what I want. He's always playing chess.'

'It's not his chess night, is it?'

'It was the only night I can get tickets. And you know what they charge? Better I don't tell you. You'll think we are Rothschilds.'

'I've never known him to miss a chess night.'

'The Mozart D major is better than chess.'

'How will you get there? You want me to drive you?'

'No, no, we take a bus or a tube.'

The thought of his father on a tube from north to south London was almost as bad as imagining Macrae making a similar journey – only different.

Barbara Spencer rang the door-bell of the house in Lambeth and the door was opened almost immediately by a young woman who said, 'I knew it was you, Mrs Spencer. Hang on a second and I'll fetch Hamish.'

She came back a minute later with a small white West Highland terrier in her arms.

'Everything all right?' Mrs Spencer said.

'Oh, he's no trouble, never is.'

'Well, he's getting a lovely present. One of those

big dog cushion things that he can get deep into. Hamish hates draughts. And it's being delivered this evening.' She paid for the dog's stay and said, 'Not next week, but the weekend after if that's OK?'

'Yes, that's fine. We're not going anywhere.'

She carried Hamish down to the car and put him in the passenger seat. 'You pleased to see me? Or were you having too much of a holiday?'

Hamish did not reply. He was a cross-looking dog and given to barking at anything that moved.

She drove back across the Thames and talked to Hamish all the way. She knew this was silly and tended to do it only when they were alone. But since Jeremy died she had no one else to talk to most of the time. So she told Hamish all about her few days in the country. 'Four widows playing bridge,' she said. 'You'd have hated it. And fields full of cows and sheep. Don't think you'd have liked that either. So we'll go to the square and you can have a lovely play there for a little while.'

Barbara Spencer didn't much like going to the square in the dark but she couldn't take Hamish home without giving him some exercise. The square was the size of a block, one of three which broke up the narrow streets of Pimlico. She hoisted Hamish out of the car, unlocked the gate of the square and let him in. It was beautifully kept, with a hard tennis court and small pavilion and gravel paths and shrubberies and a dozen great plane trees. In summer she often brought a rug and a book and lay on the lawn.

But now the square was deserted and dark and the trees were stark against the street lights.

'Come on, Hamish. Be a good boy and then we can go home.'

Hamish trotted off into the shrubbery and Barbara Spencer walked slowly along one of the gravel paths. You'd hardly believe you were in a great city, she thought, for the foliage seemed to deaden the sound of traffic.

'Come on, Hamish.'

She strolled along the path, swinging the dog's lead and told herself that if anyone tried anything she could lash out with it. The steel hook at the end was bound to do some damage. But would it be enough?

For God's sake, she told herself, stop thinking like that!

'Come on, darling.'

She could hear Hamish digging in some leaves to her left.

'Hamish!'

The great plane trees, even though they had lost their leaves, still broke up the square into places where shadows were impenetrable.

A bird suddenly rose in panic, and her heart almost stopped.

'Come on, Hamish, we'll come back tomorrow.'

But Hamish had not finished his explorations yet.

She stood on the path and called him several

times more, telling herself that if there was anyone in the square Hamish would have growled long ago, he was that sort of dog.

She decided to cheat. 'Here you are, Hamish,' she said. This was a phrase she used when she had a titbit for him, and it worked now like a charm. He came out of the shrubbery with an expectant look on his bewhiskered face and she scooped him up.

'I lied,' she said and made her way quickly towards the gate and her ground-floor flat. Sometimes she thought that with a dog she should really have had a basement with a small garden. But a woman living alone avoided basements.

She crossed the road and there, a haven, was her home. Her flat was dark and cold, but she was glad to be back. She closed the door behind her, taking care not to tread on her mail.

'Home,' she said out loud to Hamish.

Chapter Four

Report 2/MSU/MS

MEDICAL IN CONFIDENCE

The information in this report is provided in confidence
to assist the Court and Counsel engaged in the case.
No responsibility can be accepted if the report is seen
by the subject.

H.M. Prison, Stockwell
No: SVA 813   Surname: Underdown
Forenames: Malcolm Stephen

I have examined this man and have interviewed him at
length on four occasions during his remand. I have
observed his behaviour daily and noted the
observations of my health-care staff. I have discussed
his case on the telephone with the police at Cannon
Row. I will not replicate the details of Underdown's
social background as these appear in the probation
officer's report, except to reinforce its description of
a near chaotic childhood with lack of bonding and
of identity.

Since his arrival in Stockwell Prison he has been
introverted and silent. He has taken no part in the
activities allowed to remand prisoners, has not watched
TV. Nor has he had any visitors. He spends much of
the day walking. His movements are seemingly random
and I have estimated that he walks several miles per
day.

MENTAL STATE
In the interviews I have had with him he has cooperated
willingly but will only discuss the murder in general
terms. He has no evident remorse but this may be
hidden. He has not spoken of the woman he was
alleged to be obsessed with nor has he mentioned her
name and, when asked about her, has remained
withdrawn.

Underdown gives a clear account of the offences with
which he is charged and indicates to me that he does
not deny his acts. He has exhibited no serious psychotic
symptoms.

He states that the crime was committed under pressure
from a 'force'. He does not define this any further.

He indicated that a similar 'force' had been at work on
a previous occasion – no charges preferred – when he
assaulted the lover of the same woman at university.
Subsequent interviews, however, failed to illicit a
further reference to these 'forces'.

CONCLUSIONS
1 Malcolm Stephen Underdown is fit to plead within
   the definition of the Criminal Procedures Insanity Act.
2 He is not legally insane.

3 His upbringing, isolated background and escalating
   assaultative behaviour, together with elements of
   inappropriate understanding of relationships with
   women, lead me to conclude that Malcolm Stephen
   Underdown suffers from a serious disorder of
   personality corresponding to the concept of
   borderline personality disorder, i.e. a personality
   capable of suffering temporary collapse into frank
   mental illness if challenged or provoked in certain
   ways.

4 Within the meaning of the Homicide Act I believe it
   follows that at the time of the offences Malcolm
   Stephen Underdown's mental responsibility for his
   act was diminished to an extent which my colleague
   for the defence may well consider to be substantial.

5 It follows from this that within the terms of the
   Mental Health Act, I believe that Underdown's
   condition is amenable to treatment which could
   prevent further deterioration in his personality and
   which would offer help and hope of improvement.

6 If found guilty of the lesser offence of manslaughter,
   I believe Underdown should be admitted to a
   special hospital as an alternative to imprisonment
   under the terms of Section 37 of the Mental Health
   Act. A bed is available at Loxton Hospital if
   required. The learned judge may consider applying
   a restraint order without limit of time under Section
   41 Mental Health Act.

I am approved under Section 12 Mental Health Act as
having special experience in psychiatry.

M B LOMAX
Senior Medical Officer

Was he there, she wondered for the hundredth time. Was he down there somewhere?

She stood at the window of her study and looked out over the roofs of Hampstead and on past Swiss Cottage and Camden. On a decent day she could see the Telecom Tower, but not in the greasy, misty dawn now coming up.

Was he in a room down there? Dossing in a doorway?

She drank from a mug of coffee, the third she'd had since three o'clock that morning, and lit another cigarette. She had not counted those. Michael did not like her smoking but she was in her own study and she could do what she damn well pleased.

Her 'study' in inverted commas. 'Your own study,' Michael had said. He had one downstairs. Hers was upstairs. This, she knew, had been his first wife's study. This is where she had done her work. Jane had never asked about her work. It had been something to do with computers.

It had been redecorated, of course: desk, sofa, books. Her own books. Some of her father's, which he'd left to her. Some of Michael's because he had so many his own room wouldn't hold them. She looked at them now, squat, thick books, all with titles that seemed to have in them words beginning with 'psych'. She never opened them.

Michael called his study his workroom. And he did work there.

This was where she was going to work.

What work?

No one had ever answered that, including herself.

Her mother had echoed Michael and said she had this lovely room to work in. Oh, yes, it *was* lovely. It looked out on the garden and over London and it was really very lovely. Just the place to work.

Her mother would have worked there. She could have written her letters and her diary and made notes of things. That was *her* work. Well, she was gone now and Jane's work would be the dismantling of her house and the selling of it.

She moved restlessly about the room. Was he asleep? Was he awake? Was he moving?

That's what he was always talking about. Going somewhere. Not for any reason she could ever fathom. Just going. Once, when she'd been on holiday in America with her mother and step-father, she had stayed in a motel on the edge of Houston and the traffic had never stopped all night. Yet the road wasn't going anywhere, just round the city. She had realized that Americans, too, enjoyed moving. They wrote books and made movies about it. Underdown would have liked that. It was he, after all, who'd given her *On the Road* to read.

Was he moving now?

She thought: I must stop this! I have a whole police force to protect me!

She also had Michael. The police had guns. Michael had his brains. Between them they should be able to stop a person like Malcolm Stephen Underdown. The police might even have stopped him already. They were hardly likely to phone her in the early hours to tell her. And if they hadn't, they would. That's what people paid their taxes for, wasn't it? But they also paid their taxes to have mad people taken off the streets and locked up so they couldn't harm other people.

Didn't they?

'Darling? You all right?'

He put his arm around her shoulder. It felt good. It felt as it had in those early days, soon after it had happened. She'd left London and gone to stay with her mother and step-father. It was then she had met Michael. He'd been exactly what she needed. A rock with brains. Someone who knew the world that Jane had so briefly entered.

'Any coffee?' he said.

'I'll make some fresh.'

She emptied the *cafetière* into her wash-basin and put on the kettle. She felt slightly better to be doing something. Michael stood at the window. He was wearing a long, black and gold silk gown and might have stepped out of an opera. *Rosenkavalier*, she thought. He also looked what he was, a successful forensic psychiatrist.

'Couldn't sleep?' he said, and she nodded. 'Don't blame you. I couldn't either. That's why I went to the spare room. Didn't want to disturb you.'

'You wouldn't have. Anyway, I came in here about three.'

'Look,' he said. 'You're not to worry unduly. I'm not saying don't, of course you will, and so will I until he's back where he should be. But not unduly. The police are pretty good at finding people like Underdown.'

'Oh?'

'Yes, they are. We only ever hear about the ones they don't find. And they're coming today and putting in a panic button – didn't he say that?'

'Yes.'

'Anyway, they might have caught him already. And for goodness' sake, he doesn't even know where you are or what your name is now.'

He looked at his watch and went over to switch on the radio. 'There may be something on the seven o'clock news.'

There wasn't.

'That doesn't mean a thing,' he said.

'Michael, can you stay?'

'Here? At home?'

'Just for today.'

'I wish I could. But I'm giving evidence at the Old Bailey. The Woolwich murder. The one—'

'Yes, I know. But couldn't you postpone your appearance just for one day?'

'How? The whole thing's up and running. It would cost a fortune in fees to postpone.'

'You could be ill.'

'You know what they're paying me?'

'Does it always have to come down to money?'

'Look around you.'

'All right! Yes, I know! Without your work we wouldn't have the house in Hampstead or the cars or anything.'

'Jane, you know I have certain irreversible obligations.'

He was looking at her kindly and she wondered whether he was analysing her again.

'You do it all the time these days,' she said.

'Do what?'

'You know bloody well what!'

He paused at the door. 'I'm going to have a bath. You'll feel better in a little while. By the way, I meant to ask you. Was there any mail for me yesterday?'

'Nothing more than you saw.'

'I meant in the afternoon delivery.'

'Nothing.'

She heard him go into the bathroom, heard the water splashing into the bath.

The phone rang. It startled her. She thought: something's wrong with Mother. Then she remembered that her mother was dead. The thought that the caller might be Underdown came a moment later and she held the receiver to her ear, frozen, too frightened to speak.

A woman's voice she knew said, 'Hello. Anyone there?'

'Yes, Tammy, I'm here.'

'I'm sorry it's so bloody early but I thought you'd better know instanter. There's a piece in the *Mail*. Underdown's out. Escaped.'

'Yes, I know. The police phoned yesterday.'

'The paper says he's in London.'

Silence.

'Jane?'

'Whereabouts?'

'Thought you'd gone. Just London. It doesn't say more than that. Want me to come round?'

'Oh, yes! That'd be wonderful.'

'I'll be there in an hour.'

Macrae had once seen a film on television about a private detective in America. He didn't normally watch films about private detectives in America, or anywhere else, but he remembered the beginning of this one when the man, living in squalor, had to go to his kitchen rubbish-bin to find used coffee grounds to make the morning cup. Macrae hadn't become quite so reduced, but as he surveyed the grisly kitchen and scraped the last instant coffee from a jar, he realized that soon he would become like that man. Linda, his first ex-wife, had told him, when Frenchy was clearly not returning, that he should get someone in to clean the house. She knew what he was like on his own. Les Wilson had said the same. Maybe they were right. But how did you find someone? He reminded himself that he had worked for the Murder Squad and the Flying Squad and that he was a detective. Surely to Christ he could find a cleaner. He'd start with the local paper. Later. No, not later. Now.

It wasn't much past eight-thirty, but a woman took his call. Macrae told her what he wanted and between them they put together a short advertisement. There was an instant problem. He wanted the advertisement to go under the 'Home Help' heading and had suggested it start with the words: 'Woman wanted to—'

'I'm afraid we can't do that,' the woman said. 'Can't be discriminatory.'

'What's that supposed to mean?' he said.

'I'm sorry, sir, but you can't say "woman".'

'All right, "girl" or "lady" or just "female",' Macrae said.

'No, sir, you can't particularize. You can only say "person".'

'But what if a man appears? I don't want a man!'

'That doesn't happen very often.'

'How do you know? Do you check up?'

'Well . . . no, sir, I don't.'

'OK then, you don't know. What about "female preferred"?'

'I don't—'

'Listen, I don't want to make problems for you, but I need someone to help me in the house and I don't want some damn – hey, wait a minute! Let's see. Put in, "experience of breast-feeding a plus".'

42

'Experience of . . .?'

'Don't tell me breast-feeding's banned, too.'

'Oh, no, sir. That'll be fine. It'll run three days from this evening.'

He thought he had handled that rather well and had just replaced the phone when it rang, startling him.

'Who the hell are you ringing this early in the morning, George?' Les Wilson's voice was loud and clear. 'I've been trying to get through to you for ten minutes.'

'Domestic business, Les. And you're up bright and early.'

'It's this Underdown thing. We've had a report that he was seen last night in London.'

'Where?'

'Waterloo. I'm concerned about the woman.'

'Silver found her. She's married a doctor and lives up in Hampstead.'

'OK. She should be all right then.'

'You've no experience of breast-feeding, have you, Les?'

'Experience of . . . don't be bloody silly. Why?'

'Just checking. Not many men have, I should think.'

'Bread . . . butter . . . loo paper . . . oil . . . what's this?' Zoe was looking at the shopping list as she hurriedly ate a slice of toast. 'Oafs . . .? Munhooms . . .? Hottock . . .?'

'For Christ's sake, let me see.' Leo was also having breakfast on the run. 'Oats, mushrooms, haddock. It's perfectly plain. You should get your eyes tested.'

'My eyes are fine, but calligraphy ain't your strong point, old buddy. I thought it was some strange Jewish incantation. What do you want oats for anyway? You get your oats, if you don't mind my saying so.' She kissed him hurriedly. 'I'm off, see you tonight.'

He heard doors bang, then he was banging some himself. He got into his VW Golf and cut through the one-way systems in Pimlico making for the Embankment. He was into Exeter Square before he knew it. Two things happened at once. He realized where he was and saw a parking space. He parked, sat in the car for a few moments, thinking, then said out loud: 'Sixty-one.' Les Wilson, the memory man, would have been proud of him, he thought, until he remembered that he must have seen the number in the files the day before. But he might have remembered anyway. You didn't easily forget places where really awful things happened. He sat looking at the house. It was much as it had been, a tall house, four storeys high and part of a terrace that surrounded the square. It was a sunny morning and the whole area looked good, especially the square gardens with the well-cared for lawns and shrubs. Everything looked much the same as it had four years before.

Incredible to think of the blood and gore there had been inside number sixty-one.

He crossed the road and looked at the door-bells on the wall. Like all the other houses in the square this one had been converted into flats. There it was. Ground floor: Mrs B. Spencer.

He pressed and heard the bell ring. Then he thought he heard another sound but couldn't quite make it out. He pressed again. This time he only heard the bell.

'Looking for somebody?' He turned. An elderly man was standing on the pavement below him. He was tall and very thin and carried a full shopping-bag in one hand. He came up the steps and Leo saw he had a door-key in his other hand.

'Mrs Spencer,' Leo said.

'She's away.' He put down the basket and unlocked the door. 'She goes away a lot. I live a few floors up. Too much at my time of life, but what can you do?'

He picked up the bag and entered the communal hall. Leo heard the same unfamiliar sound he had heard before. Now it was more familiar. He began to think it might be . . .

'That's Hamish,' the elderly man said. 'She must be back. Good. I've got a parcel for her. Nearly killed me taking it up the stairs. I knew she was going into the country because she told me so. But that's Hamish all right. She never leaves him in the house alone in case he barks. When my wife was ill, in the months before she died, Barbara, that's Mrs Spencer, was marvellous, really. Never let Hamish bark at all. Shall I try?'

'Go ahead,' Leo said.

He went to the door and knocked. 'Barbara?' he called. 'Are you there?' He put his ear to the door. 'That's odd.'

Leo's gut began to contract into a hard lump. He took out his warrant card and identified himself. 'I wanted to give her some information,' he said.

'Oh, right. I'm Mr Warrender, by the way. Third floor.'

'Can I go round the back?'

'The yard's through there.' He pointed to a door at the end of the passage. 'It's not much, just a small terrace really. I'll open it for you.'

It was concrete with flowerpots on a stand containing the brown skeletons of last year's pelargoniums. There was a door into Mrs Spencer's flat from the terrace but the only window was frosted. In the background they could hear the occasional sound which Mr Warrender had identified as being Hamish, but which Leo thought sounded more like a cat than a dog.

'May I use your phone?' he said.

'You don't think something's happened, do you?'

Leo had been desperately trying not to think of what might have happened. The old man spoke again but Leo missed it.

'Sorry?'

'I said, I've got the keys if you need them. Barbara gave me a spare set a long time ago in case there was a flood or a fire when she was away. I'll get them if you like.'

Leo waited while the old man went up to this own flat to fetch the keys. It was only a matter of a few yards to his phone in the car and a single call could whistle up support, but what would Macrae say to him if he started something only to find Mrs Spencer fast asleep in bed with her dog at her feet? No, better go in first, then, if necessary, phone.

'I've only used them once,' said Mr Warrender, unlocking the door. 'It was when she was in Edinburgh for the Festival and she phoned and said would I go and see if she'd left her stove on. She hadn't.'

There were three locks and he finally got them open. 'There,' he said. 'Pray that all is well.'

But all was not well.

The flat was in semi-darkness. The passage was empty, so was the bedroom on the right of the front door. The bed had not been slept in and there was a small suitcase on the floor. On the bed was a coat and a dog's lead. The moment they had entered the flat the noise which Mr Warrender thought had come from Hamish, had stopped abruptly. Now it came again.

'He's in there.' Mr Warrender indicated a door in the corridor. Leo opened it.

'Oh, Christ,' he said.

'Oh, good God!' Mr Warrender said.

It was an airing cupboard containing the hot-water cylinder, the vacuum cleaner and the broom. Into this had been stuffed the body of Mrs Spencer. She had been thrust between the domestic cleaning tools so that she was held almost upright between the hot-water cylinder and a wall. At her feet, in among the fallen tools, was Hamish. His face was a mass of blood and for a moment Leo was convulsed with the thought that the dog might have been eating his mistress. Then he saw the inside of the door. Hamish had been trying to chew his way out.

Chapter Five

'For Christ's sake, shut your mouth and get on with it!'

The police photographer, who had been joking with one of the forensic team, turned angrily, saw he was being addressed by Macrae – a Macrae who had that characteristic look of a threatening weather system when he was angry – and hurriedly got on with his job of photographing the big cupboard where Mrs Spencer had been found.

Leo, feeling sick as he went about his own business, had never seen Macrae so dour. The big man moved through the flat as though he was personally involved.

The flat itself was now brightly lit by police lamps. The curtains had not been touched, nor had anything else. Outside, in the square, the police tapes fluttered in the morning breeze and a small crowd of people tried to gain the attention of the uniformed officer guarding the door of number sixty-one. TV trucks were slowly edging along the crowded road and a news photographer with a telephoto lens was being ordered out of one of the plane trees in the gardens opposite.

A pathologist had come and gone and now they knew that Mrs Spencer had been stabbed several times – at least six – in the chest and neck.

How many times had Edward Craig been stabbed?

Leo couldn't remember, but more than six. They'd found his body in the living-room. He'd fallen behind the sofa and, like Hamish in the present case, had tried desperately to get out. There were blood streaks all down the chintz at the back of the sofa and threads were found under his fingernails.

The room had been a shambles. Coffee-tables overturned, a book-case broken, two vases smashed and flowers and water over the carpet. That – the noise of things breaking – was what had brought the first copper. The neighbours had been paralysed with fear, but not too paralysed to phone emergency services. As Leo recalled, these had been two elderly women living above the murder scene. They had long since gone. According to Mr Warrender, everyone had moved out after the first murder.

What, Leo wondered, would they do after the second? There would come a time, probably now, when flats in this house would be difficult if not impossible to sell. A home developed an aura and this would be one not many people would like to live with. One murder was quite bad enough. Two . . .?

Leo went back to the passage. This was where they'd found Underdown. Jane Harrison had fled from the living-room to the bedroom and locked the door. Underdown had attacked the panels with his knife but these doors came from a different age and knives were not going to destroy them. So when the first coppers arrived, Underdown had been sitting in the passage, crying. Jane Harrison had been in the bedroom, screaming.

Underdown might have stayed that way if they hadn't let Jane out of the bedroom. When she saw what had happened to her lover she knelt beside him and cradled his head. He was dying. His breathing was ragged and with blood seeping into his lungs he sounded as though he was suffering from asthma.

That was when the anger returned to Underdown and he went mad. Leo thought quite literally mad.

He had been holding one arm, and another detective, Armstrong, the other, and Underdown had thrown them off like children. He'd grabbed a bottle, smashed it and stabbed Armstrong with the broken end, and would have done the same to Leo had he not been caught from behind by a couple of uniformed officers and flung to the ground. Leo remembered him there, his face on the carpet, his hands locked behind his back and a large copper sitting on him. He had looked at Jane Harrison and forced his head around and up so that his mouth was clear of the floor and said: '*I'll come back*'.

Ordinary words, but they chilled Leo now, just thinking of them.

Macrae came out of the kitchen where the knife drawer had been left open by whoever had stabbed Mrs Spencer.

Whoever?

'Come on, laddie, let's get the hell out of here,' Macrae said. Leo followed him into the square. The crowd of reporters pushed forward but Macrae elbowed his way through to his car and Leo got in beside him.

They went back to the station and circulated the information that Underdown was suspected of murder. Then Macrae said, 'I could do with a dram. But not round here.'

Leo knew what he meant. It was early, too early if he was seen. But after what *they* had seen he wanted one himself. He said, 'Let's go to my place. I've got some Glenmorangie. And some beer.'

Macrae had been to Leo's flat several times during their working relationship and now, as he followed him upstairs, he looked about. When they reached the top floor Leo went to the kitchen to get the glasses. Macrae followed him and said, 'Who cleans for you?'

'Cleans for us?'

'It looks clean,' Macrae said grudgingly. 'And neat.'

'No one cleans for us, guv'nor. We do it ourselves. Zoe does most of it, I suppose, but I help.'

'You?'

'When I can.'

Macrae grunted, took the Glenmorangie – kept by Leo for just such occasions – and drank it down. 'That's better.'

Leo gave himself a glass of beer but his stomach heaved when he brought it to his lips and he said, 'Don't think I can.'

'Make you feel better, but I know what you mean.'

'I should have bloody thought!' Leo said. 'In fact I did, that's why I stopped there this morning.'

'So should I.' Macrae's mouth turned down in anger and shame. 'I thought of the woman, Jane, but I should have thought of whoever was in the old flat. It's the first place he'd have come to.'

'We're sure it was Underdown?'

'Who else? Christ Almighty, it's got to be!'

'I suppose so.'

''Course it has. He comes back to London looking for Jane so he goes to the only place he knows and gets in – I'm not sure how, yet.'

'Old man Warrender said he'd taken in a big parcel for her. She was probably expecting it, so when Underdown comes to the door, she opens it.'

Macrae nodded. 'Aye, that'll do. Whose flat was it originally, by the way? When the first killing happened?'

'It belonged to Edward Craig's parents. They let

him use it after he'd left university and was working in London.'

'Right, so after their son was killed they sold it to Mrs Spencer. She wouldn't have a clue where Jane Harrison was living, would she?'

'And Underdown wouldn't believe her. Is that the scenario?'

'Something like that. Makes sense, doesn't it. So he threatens her with a knife unless she tells him. She can't, and of course, Underdown being Underdown, everything goes haywire and he kills her and stuffs her and her dog into the cupboard.'

'So where is he now?'

'We'll find him. I'm going back to the flat then I'm going to get those desk sods to work like they've never worked before and we'll get every bit of paper on him. But I want you to get up to Hampstead and check on the doctor's wife. I want you to make sure she gets that panic button in today.'

'I've been on to the security company that put in their house-alarm system. Told them to get on with it. But I'll go and check anyway. Another?'

Macrae shook his head. 'Glad to see you keep a decent drink. When you get there have a good look around. There are parts of Hampstead that are bloody difficult to guard, with all those trees and the big gardens. See if they've got security lights, that sort of thing. I don't want anything to happen to that girl.'

*

In all the years Jane had known Tamara Weston –
more than she cared to count now – she had never
known her to be on time. She had known her at
school and at university. Had held her hand when
she had married, dried her tears during that short
and unhappy contract, and had gone on holiday with
her when Michael couldn't make it. Tamara had
been late for her wedding, late for her divorce hearing and late to the point of missing a plane to Austria
for the skiing. Being late had also possibly saved her
life: she had been due to have a drink with Jane
and Edward on the evening Underdown had murdered Edward.

Who was to say being on time was a plus?

These thoughts went through Jane's mind as she
watched Tammy come through the gate and up past
the shrubbery to the front door. She had said, 'I'll be
with you in an hour.' It was more like two, but Jane
had not expected anything different so that after
Michael had left for the Old Bailey she had gone
round the house checking on the locks. In a high-
risk area like this part of Hampstead insurance companies made checks and suggestions before they
issued a policy and if you didn't meet their 'suggestions' they didn't pay. So the house was pretty
secure. There were deadlocks on the doors, there
were bolts, window locks and there was also an
alarm system. Even so, when Michael had gone Jane
felt as frightened as she had ever been. She had
expected that, but what she hadn't expected was that

the house in which she had lived relatively happily for the past four years, no longer felt like her territory. As she went restlessly from one room to the next, it seemed different from the home she knew. There was an air of menace in the grey winter rooms. Doors which had always just been doors, now hid parts of rooms or passage-ways. At the end of one downstairs passage was the door that opened into the garage where her own car lived. Nothing on earth would have made her go into the garage.

She unlocked the front door.

Tammy put down her basket and enveloped her. She was a big woman in her early thirties with dark coppery hair and a boneless body with soft buttery skin. 'I'm sorry I'm late,' she said, as Jane knew she would. As she took off her coat she went on, 'There was this blind guy at Tottenham Court Road tube station and he was walking along, you know, just like anyone else, no tap-tapping or anything like that – I mean, I didn't even know he was blind – and suddenly he turns right and bang! Straight into a wall. I dusted him down and asked him where he was going and he said Lancaster Gate, and he said he must have miscounted the number of steps he'd taken because he came this way every day. So I took him to his platform and waited for a train and put him in it and then I had to get back to my platform on the Northern Line . . . for Christ's sake, why am I going on like this! Listen . . . tell me . . .'

Jane made them coffee and told her what she

knew. Just having Tammy there made things a lot better.

'Have you heard anything today?' Tammy said.

'Not really. I mean, I had a call this morning from someone in the police. He said he'd get in touch with our security company and they'd come and put in a special alarm.'

'A panic button?'

'I suppose so.'

'Listen, darling, there's nothing to worry about really. They know he's escaped and they'll get him. And he doesn't know you've got married or what your married name is or anything about you now.'

'I've heard all that. It's what Michael says. And so do the police.'

'Well, it's true, but OK, I won't say it any more.'

They were in the kitchen and both lit up cigarettes with their coffee.

'Michael would kill us.' Tammy held up her cigarette and looked at it. 'You know, there was a time when people did this all the time. Had coffee and a cigarette and didn't feel guilty about it.'

They sat in silence for a few moments then Jane said, 'Why does everyone think he won't find out my married name? He's only got to go to the newspapers. There's a whole newspaper library in north London somewhere. We were in *The Times* when we got married.'

'Yes, but does he know that? Does he know about that kind of research?'

'He was pretty bright.'

'Do you remember that time he put a snake in Charlie Broadbent's car?' Tammy said. 'Not your ordinary grass snake or adder but some poisonous thing from the tropics?'

'No one actually proved it was him.'

'Charlie was interested in you and Underdown was interested in animals and the two things seemed to go together. He was the only guy at university except for the zoology people who would have known a good snake from a bad one, and where to get the bad ones.'

'Do you mind if we don't talk about him?'

'Sorry, love.'

'How long can you stay?'

'How long do you need me?'

'Michael's in court all day and God knows when he'll get back.'

'You want me to stay the night?' She went to her heavy basket and pulled out a filmy night-dress. 'I brought it just in case.'

'You're marvellous.'

'And I brought this.' She delved into the basket again and produced a pistol.

Jane looked at it in amazement. 'Where did you get that?'

'Legacy. Paul left it in the house and when he called after the divorce and said had I seen it in the top of the wardrobe, I said, "No".'

'God, I couldn't . . .'

'Of course you could. Just think if you'd had it in Exeter Square. Edward would have been alive now and Underdown would have been dead.'

There was no answer to that. Jane said, 'But I don't know how to use it and I would be scared anyway.'

'You probably wouldn't need to use it. Just waving it at people makes them run. Don't you watch the movies?'

'It isn't loaded, is it?'

'Yes, it is. I decided if I was going to keep it I'd have to know about it so I went to a gun-shop and told them some rubbish about my father having died and having a pistol and how would I know if it was loaded because I was going to take it to the police and I didn't want it to go off by accident. The nice young man showed me everything. So I went home and looked and it was loaded all right. I'm going to show you how to hold it and then all you've got to do is pull the trigger.'

'No thanks, Tammy. Really. I'd feel too scared to use it and—'

The door-bell rang and the two women looked at each other in sudden apprehension.

Tammy said, 'He'd never ring the bloody bell, would he?'

'You could never tell what he'd do.' Jane went to a window. 'No, there's a van in the drive. It's the security people.'

'I'll put this away then.' Tammy returned the pistol to her shopping basket.

Jane let in the security engineer. He was dressed in white overalls with an identity badge on his lapel.

Tammy stood behind Jane, a pillar of moral support.

'Where do you want the PA buttons?' he asked. He was small, middle-aged, with a moustache and grey hair and had an air of serious endeavour.

'Panic buttons?' Jane said. 'I didn't realize there would be more than one.'

'We usually put in two, one in the bedroom and one by the front door. And we don't call them panic buttons.' His tone was patronizing.

'So what do we call them?' Tammy said.

'Their real name is personal attack buttons.'

They trooped upstairs to the bedroom.

'May I ask which side of the bed you sleep in, madam?'

'Left side.'

'About here then?' He pointed to a spot on the wall.

Tammy said, 'Lie down and try it.'

Jane lay down and was able to touch the spot on the wall without moving more than a few inches.

He made a small mark. 'May we do the front door now?'

They trooped downstairs. The front door opened on to a small porch and the gravel drive that led to the gate. He opened the door, went outside, had a look around, then said, 'I'm going to pretend to be a caller. Just answer my ring as you would anyone's.'

He rang the bell. Jane opened the door and he suddenly pushed it and she stumbled backwards. He instantly put a small mark on the wall where she had nearly over-balanced.

'Sorry about that.' A brief smile hovered around his thin lips. 'People always think the PA button goes right next to the door but when you really need it is when something like that happens. We've found that when whoever it is who comes . . .' He floundered. 'What I mean is, the person you're expecting but don't want, if you understand me, usually pushes the door and that sends you backwards into the house so there's not much point in having the button right at the door.'

He came in again, closed the door and said, 'What I'll do now is connect the two PA buttons to your alarm system. And—'

'What's the point of that?' Jane said. 'I don't want our alarm to go off.'

'If I may just finish, madam. What I was going to say was that I'll connect the PA buttons to your alarm system and the telephone. If you press one of the buttons a signal goes down the telephone to our office where someone is monitoring twenty-four hours a day. If something comes in on your line it's a Code Two. We have a direct line to the police and a Code Two takes precedence even over a Code One, which is fire. And you get two police cars.' He paused. 'We always say we hope you never have to use it.'

'That's what we always say too,' Tammy said.

The door-bell rang and as the women stood, transfixed, the security man said, 'Should I?'

'Please,' Jane said.

On the doorstep stood a man of medium height in a black leather jacket, black polo, black corduroys and black brogues. 'Remember me?' he said.

Jane would never forget his face. It was the first she had seen after the violence of that night. 'You're Detective Silver.'

He smiled. 'You've got a good memory. I've come to see how you are and if the alarm system is going in . . . and I see it is.'

Jane invited him inside and left him with Tammy as she went back to the bedroom with the security engineer.

Tammy took Leo into the kitchen and gave him a cup of coffee. She said, 'Have you heard anything?'

'Not much. Nothing really. Have you known Mrs Stone long?'

'Years and years. And I was nearly part of that terrible evening in Exeter Square. I was supposed to be there but I was held up.'

'Do you know Underdown?'

'Oh, yes. I was at university with Jane and we both knew him there.'

'Could I come and talk to you?'

'You can talk to me right here, if you like.'

'I can't stay now. But later.'

'I'm going to be here, possibly for the night. I'll give you my home number and if I'm not here I'll be there. She's terrified, you know.'

'I'd be surprised if she wasn't.'

The phone rang and Jane answered it upstairs. After a few minutes she came into the kitchen. 'That was Michael,' she said. 'He's finished giving evidence and he's on his way home.'

Report 3/MSU/SVA 813/MS. (Ltr. Enc.)

BARROW, BURGESS & FREEMAN SOLICITORS

5 Percy Street Winchester Hampshire

Dr M Lomax
Senior Medical Officer
HM Prison Stockwell
London   14 February 1990

Dear Dr Lomax,

re: Malcolm Stephen Underdown

I act for the above named who is Defendant in the criminal proceedings that have been brought against him following his arrest for murder.

While Mr Underdown was on remand in Stockwell Prison he was seen by you and you prepared a report. As you will now know Mr Underdown has been sent for trial at the Old Bailey. He has pleaded not guilty to murder.

In your report you state that you think he was suffering from a borderline personality disorder which you suggest is treatable and that a custodial sentence would not be appropriate.

We would like our own psychiatrist to report on Mr Underdown and if he comes to the same conclusion as you, this would form part of our defence.

Since Mr Underdown is in the prison hospital I would be grateful if you could let me know when a psychiatric visit is possible.

I am,
Yours faithfully,

G T LAMPORT

Chapter Six

'Oh God,' Macrae said as their car ground to a halt again in the traffic. 'Where the hell are they all coming from?'

Leo pointed to a sign which said that Arsenal were playing at home that evening. Then he said, 'I wish we had a blue light we could stick on the roof like they do in the States.'

'We'd look like the bloody water company,' Macrae said.

Leo had no siren on his little car and no one paid him any attention. 'Now what?' he said.

Macrae looked around him. The traffic was solid. He switched on the inner light and looked at the A–Z book of London maps. It wasn't a very good light but he could make out that where they wanted to go was on the other side of the park. It wasn't Finsbury Park but one that ran parallel to it which Macrae didn't know and which he'd never, in all his Metropolitan career, been to. Indeed he knew very little about this part of London.

He said to Silver, 'Laddie, drive up on the

pavement and when you get to an opening on the right side, go into the park. Let's see if we can cross it.'

Leo drove up on the pavement. The Volkswagen Golf could fit there quite comfortably.

Macrae said, 'Slow down or you'll halve the local populace.'

'I'm only doing five miles an hour, guv'nor.'

'Eddie would never have got us into a bloody mess like this.'

The late Eddie Twyford had been Macrae's driver for many years when officers of Macrae's rank still had their own drivers. What he meant was that Eddie would have known that Arsenal football club was playing at home on their Highbury ground.

'There's an opening,' Leo said.

'Take it.'

It was early evening, dark and overcast, and the park was empty. Leo drove the Golf through the opening in the fence, across a stretch of bumpy grass, weaved in and out of several beech trees, then found a concrete path that ended at a duck pond.

'Keep going,' Macrae said.

He drove around the pond and found himself among swings, see-saws and a roundabout.

'Look where you're going!' Macrae said.

Leo backed into a sand-pit. He revved, spun the wheels and managed to get out.

Macrae said nothing.

He made for a second path and was getting along

just fine until he came to a low wire fence and another road.

He stopped. They were on grass. The wire fence was rusty and old. 'What do you say, guv'nor?'

'I say that wee fence needs replacing. I say the Finsbury Park town council or whatever they're called who run this place, should be ashamed of leaving a fence like that.'

Leo eased the car forward. There was a slight scraping noise and the fence collapsed and they found themselves facing a pleasant tree-lined street without any traffic or pedestrians and with few parked cars.

'Looks like they've got the plague here. You'd hardly believe there was a big match on only a few streets away,' Leo said.

'We want the next street.' Macrae looked at the map again. 'Go right and right again.'

Leo drove out of the park, across the pavement, weaved his way between the parked cars and drove down the road. Almost immediately he was stopped by a steel barrier. It was a single boom set in uprights on both sides of the pavement and sat across the road at windscreen height.

'What the hell's this supposed to be?' Macrae got out of the car. 'The bloody thing's locked into place,' he said. 'Turn and go back.'

They went back but there was another steel barrier at the next intersection, forcing them to go in the direction they didn't want.

'All right, let's walk,' Macrae said. 'It's not far.'

They walked round the block and in the distance they could hear the roar of the Highbury crowd.

'This is it.' Macrae pointed to a pleasant three-storey detached house. 'What did you say her surname was?'

'Weston.'

He rang the second-floor bell. A woman's voice coming out of the wall said, 'Yes?'

'Police.'

The door swung open and they were met by a smell of cooking that grew stronger and more delicious as they mounted the stairs.

Tamara met them at the door. The flat had a big living-room, a bedroom and a kitchen, from which the smells were coming.

'Sorry about the cooking. I'll close the kitchen door.'

'Not on our account,' Macrae said. 'It smells good.'

He watched her as she moved. She was dressed in a pink sweatshirt and jeans and her skin had a faint sheen on it from the kitchen heat. In Macrae's eyes this was a plus and he decided she was the best-looking woman he had seen since Frenchy had gone.

'*Coq au vin*. It's for a dinner party,' she said.

She caught his glance at a small table in the living-room. 'Oh, not here. It's what I do. I cook for people. Can I give you a glass of wine? Or don't you drink on duty?'

'That's just what they say in the pictures. I'll have a wee glass with pleasure.' She gave them both glasses of white wine – a drink Macrae did not rate as alcoholic – and he said, 'What are the barriers on the roads for?'

'They've recently been put up,' she said. 'Sorry, I should have warned you. I'm still trying to find my way through the labyrinth myself. It was because of prostitutes and kerb-crawlers. Now we don't have any. The kerb-crawlers are too scared of getting trapped in these streets by the vice squad so the girls have moved away.'

'How's Mrs Stone?' Leo said.

'Still frightened but that's only to be expected. She'll go on being frightened until he's caught.'

'Her husband's back with her now, isn't he?' Macrae said.

'I stayed until he arrived.'

'And the panic buttons work?'

'They work perfectly. But I'm not sure they'll be much good if Underdown ever got into the house. It'll take five or ten minutes for a police car to get there.'

'Everything possible has been done to protect her,' Macrae said.

'She could go and live somewhere else, I suppose. In some other country.'

'You can go to Tierra del Fuego. But if someone wants you badly enough, he'll find you.'

'What a chilling thing to say!'

She had swung round to look at Macrae, this big, hard man who was dominating her sitting-room.

Leo said, 'That's why we've come to see you. The more we know about him the more we can try to second-guess his movements. You said you knew him at university. Tell us about that.'

'I actually knew him before Jane. He was doing sociology and so was I at that time, before I switched to English.' She paused. 'I suppose the two things one remembers best about Malcolm are his size, he was very big and strong, and his gentleness.'

'Gentleness?' Macrae was surprised.

'Like Lenny?' Leo said.

She smiled. 'Yes. Maybe.'

Macrae, too, had read *Of Mice and Men* and said, 'Lenny was mentally deficient or whatever they call it now. Underdown was a student at a university and you don't get into a university unless you're reasonably bright.' He looked at Leo. 'With some exceptions.'

'He *was* quite bright. He also knew a lot about animals. That's another thing I remember. He used to have a ferret and he would take it to lectures and it would sleep in his pocket or he'd let it run up his sleeve. It never seemed to bite him. And he talked to horses. They'd come across a field as horses do because they like company and he would talk to them and they'd let him stroke them and scratch them.'

Macrae broke through these reminiscences. 'Being nice to horses doesn't tell us much.'

'Once he put a snake in someone's car. It was a poisonous snake. The man who owned the car was Jane's boyfriend.'

'If he did that he should have been prosecuted.'

'No one could prove it was him. But we all thought so.'

'You'd known her before university, hadn't you?'

'I was at school with her and if you've ever heard the phrase "golden girl", she was one. I mean she seemed to get on with her parents when most of us didn't, she was pretty and the boys flocked, but she was also bright and had a sense of humour.'

'Sounds too good to be true,' Macrae said.

'It was. What happened in the flat that night changed her.'

Leo said, 'Didn't she suffer that post-traumatic thing?'

'Post-traumatic stress syndrome. Yes, she did. She was pretty bad. She wasn't eating or sleeping and wouldn't leave her parents' house. By that time her real father had died and her mother had remarried. They had this big house in the country and that's where she went afterwards. The sad thing was she'd had a good relationship with her step-father up till then but Malcolm's attack on Edward changed all that. It was as if she didn't trust any man.'

'She seemed all right today,' Leo said. 'She dealt with the security man and me.'

'Michael achieved that. He took her over. Remade her if you like. He spent time with her and looked after her. He was really smitten.'

'Was he her psychiatrist?' Macrae asked.

'No, no, he was Malcolm's.'

'Underdown's?' Leo's voice had risen. 'My God, I'd forgotten that, if I ever knew it.'

Macrae said, 'So he's a forensic psychiatrist?'

'One of the best in the country. And one of the highest-paid. Malcolm's lawyers hired him to examine Malcolm and I know he talked to him in the prison. Then he went to see Jane and—'

Leo's mobile phone rang. He took it from his pocket, turned away and spoke softly into it. Macrae had also acquired one recently but loathed it and tended to sneer at people who used them in public.

Leo put the phone back. He was smiling, and said, 'They think they've found him!'

'Underdown?'

'That was the chief super, guv'nor. He heard it on his car radio from the Information Room. Wanted to let you know.'

'Where?'

'Sloane Square. They're still there.'

'Oh, thank God,' Tammy said. 'That's marvellous! Can I phone Jane and tell her?'

'No,' Macrae said bleakly. 'Let's make sure first.'

*

Jane sat in the drawing-room, feet up on the sofa, and debated whether or not to have another whisky. She was not a heavy drinker but she had had one with Tammy before Michael had arrived, then she'd had one with Michael. So better not. The room was bright, all the lights were on throughout the house, as she had always kept them since Edward was killed. Sometimes when she and Michael came home late at night they would drive into their street and there would be the house, all lit up. It reminded her of when she was a child, seeing a liner sail into Southampton Water at dusk. It was as though the house was sailing out over Hampstead.

She hardly thought of Edward now. Soon after it had happened, she had thought of him all the time. It was guilt, Michael had said, guilt because she thought she had been partially to blame for his death. And she supposed that however you sliced it, that was true. If Malcolm hadn't wanted her – no, you had to go back further than that, to their first meeting. If she hadn't met Malcolm he wouldn't have wanted her because he wouldn't have known her and if he hadn't known her he wouldn't have wanted her and if he hadn't wanted her he wouldn't have killed Edward. That was the thought process that Michael had demolished and it was only once he'd demolished it that she had begun to feel like some remote relation to a human being again.

She heard him now, clack-clacking away on the keyboard of the word processor as he did every night. God knows what he was writing. Reports, he always said, but he might have been writing a book for all she knew. He didn't often discuss his work with her, but then he was a doctor and bound by the rules of his profession. Still, it would have been nice to hear about some of his cases once in a while, and not have to read them in *The Times* or one of the tabloids.

Was Underdown out there somewhere, looking at the lights of the house? Was he moving?

She fought the thoughts as she had fought them all day. Concentrate on something else. Right. What was she thinking about? Oh, yes, Michael and his work.

He had never worked like this when they had first started going out. Then he had time and they used to do things that were fun. They'd make up their minds on a Friday afternoon, for instance, to go to Rome or Paris for the weekend and just do it.

Once he'd said, 'Let's go to Munich'. She'd never been there so they flew over on a Friday evening. It was her birthday the following day. He took her to dinner at Krottenbach's in Nymphenburg and the next day to the Bayerische Motoren Werke, just outside Munich, and gave her her first car, a black BMW cabriolet.

God, she was lucky! She thought of her friends. Their marriages had lasted three or four years. Tammy's had lasted a little over two and all that time she had been dominated by Paul. She remembered how Tammy would put off dates at the last moment because he wanted her to wash and iron his squash kit or prepare a meal for half a dozen of his friends at an hour's notice. Once she was married she was not the same person Jane had known at university. The point about Paul was that he had wanted a mother, not a wife. He had wanted someone to come back to when he'd finished screwing whoever it was he was screwing at the time, and he had wanted Tammy to kiss and make up and feed him and generally look after him as his mother had done.

She had spent her time being humiliated and now she was a woman no longer in the first flush of youth who had never held down a proper job and who was cooking like mad to try and make a living. Poor Tammy. She lived by herself once more, a little overweight, a little sad, a little suspicious – and always broke. When she had left today, Jane had given her a tenner for a taxi. Once Tammy would have objected. Now she took it. That's what Paul had done to her. He'd created a new Tammy.

Jane wondered, as she often did, whether Michael was having an affair with anyone. He'd been having it off with Jane herself when he was married to Jennifer, so why wouldn't he be doing the same with someone else when he was married to Jane? But she didn't believe he was.

Would their marriage last? Or would it eventually

go down the tube like the others? And if it did could she exist without him?

He had come to her when she was *in extremis.*

She had been staying down in Hampshire with her mother and step-father. Michael had telephoned, describing who he was and saying he wanted to see Jane. Her mother had said no, Jane wasn't up to seeing anyone about the case. He had said that he was an officer of the court and that he was coming anyway.

Julian, her step-father, had asked if she would like him to tell Michael that in no circumstances would she be willing to talk to him. It was the first time Julian had spoken to her for weeks. He had been reacting to what he thought was her need to be left alone. She had not answered him and had seen the hurt in his eyes and yet been unable to do anything about her own feelings or her behaviour. What made it worse was that he had died a few months later.

Michael had just turned up. Julian was away and her mother told him he wasn't welcome and he had said he could imagine how Jane must be feeling after what had happened because he had come across cases like hers before but that he had something to discuss with her that would make her feel a great deal better. Her mother had argued and threatened to call the police and Michael had given her his number in Winchester. Finally Jane had come out of the room where she had been listening and had said, all right, here she was, what did he want to say?

Sometimes when she thought about their meeting she tried to see herself as she was then. It was difficult. Michael was much the same now but when she saw photographs he had taken of her in those early weeks of their relationship she realized how much weight she had lost. The word 'waif' came into her mind. Yet she knew that in another way she had been looking at her most appealing. Tammy had always said that in those months after Edward's death she had been even prettier than before. She must have had *something* because of the effect she had had on Michael.

It had been a lovely summer's day. He had asked if they could talk outside. There was a rose arbour with a table and chairs and the view stretched out across the Meon Valley to the South Downs.

'First of all I want to apologize for exaggerating somewhat,' he had said. 'I'm not an officer of the court. But I needed to see you very badly about the case. I'm the forensic psychiatrist for the defence and—'

'I don't want to talk about it,' she had said. 'I never talk about it.'

'We won't discuss it now, not if you don't want to, but I think you'll want to talk when you hear what I have to say in regard to the benefits for yourself.'

'I don't want to talk to you about anything.'

'Fine. But I hope you don't mind me being here.

I promise I won't talk about it. Would you mind if I had one of your cigarettes?'

She had been smoking continuously since his arrival and her fingers had been fretting with the pack and her lighter on the garden table.

'I didn't think doctors smoked.'

'Occasionally. Like when they're having a cup of coffee with a beautiful woman.'

Watching him take a cigarette and light it made her feel slightly less tense.

Gradually, and with the experience of much practice, he began to bring her into a frame where, if they were not actually talking with much verve, she was at least answering simple questions about her family and the house and the fact that her real father had died some years ago and that she had been to school in Winchester, then to university there and had then moved to London and got a job in television. Finally he had said, 'It's such a lovely day, is there any place we could walk?'

She had taken him through fields and down to the river and they had walked along its banks and watched the occasional trout break the surface as it came up after a fly.

'It's very beautiful here,' he had said. 'You must love it.'

She realized that she had not come down to the river since that terrible night. He seemed to guess this for he said, 'You don't walk down here by yourself, do you?'

'Not now.'

'Do you go anywhere by yourself? Winchester or London?'

'No.'

'Look, isn't that a woodpecker?'

A green and black bird flew from the branch of a nearby beech tree and disappeared.

'We sometimes see kingfishers here,' she said.

'Did you come here much?'

'I used to come with my step-father. He had the fishing. He didn't care if he caught anything. Often he used to put the trout back. But I quite enjoyed coming and I sometimes carried his net.'

She stopped suddenly and realized that something unfamiliar had happened.

He smiled. 'Those were whole sentences.'

They walked on and he said, 'Wouldn't it be nice to have lunch somewhere outside?'

'I can't.'

'Why can't you?'

'I just can't.'

'All we'll do is have a drink and something to eat.'

'I've got to go home.'

'OK, I'll come with you.'

She had kept expecting him to ask about Malcolm but it seemed far away from his thoughts. She realized that this was how a professional would handle such a situation yet she was grateful for his forbearance.

They were at a stile. He held out his hand to help her over it but she jerked away.

'Sorry,' he said, and he followed her up the path by the river and then walked with her across the fields and back to the house.

'That was really very enjoyable,' he said. 'Could we do it again some time?'

She hadn't replied and he had got into his car – she remembered that it was a Porsche in those days too.

He came again two days later. The spell of fine weather was holding and he said, 'I found a pub on the river and I booked a table. You're not going to say no, are you?'

Her mother was with her. She said, 'Oh, Jane, it'll do you so much good.'

She had gone with him to the pub. They'd had a table in the window looking out over a weir and because it was early they were almost the only ones there. He had talked about the river and the pub and the beauty of the countryside. He accepted another of her cigarettes and then he said, 'I saw him this morning.'

'Malcolm?'

'Yes, Malcolm. It's odd to hear you use his Christian name. Everyone just calls him Underdown.'

She didn't comment and he said, 'How are you feeling today?'

'The same as yesterday and the day before and the day before that.'

He ordered drinks. She had orange juice and said

she didn't want anything to eat. He said he hoped
she didn't mind if he had something because he was
hungry. He looked at the menu and said, 'I'm going
to give myself a treat . . . a real fry-up. Sausages,
bacon, eggs and chips.' It came with the chips in a
basket and when he saw her eyes on it, he pushed
it towards her. Then he cut off a piece of a sausage
and offered it to her. After a moment's hesitation,
she took the titbit and a chip and it was the first
food she could remember tasting or liking or wanting
since Edward had been killed.

He fed her with pieces of sausage and chips as
if he was feeding a baby and then he ordered ice-
creams. She finished hers and he ordered another
and she finished that.

'You're like me, an ice-cream junkie,' he said.

She had been expecting him to start talking
seriously about Malcolm then and had gathered herself to rebuff him, but all he said was that he'd had
a lovely lunch and it was a lovely place and now
he'd take her home.

He came the next day. The weather had changed.
There was a gale blowing up from the south-west and
she took him into the study, where she lit the fire.

In answer to a question about her father she said,
'He was a travel writer. Then he founded his own
rather recherché travel company. He was one of the
first to offer safaris in Africa and India.'

They sat in front of the fire in silence for a few
minutes, then he said, 'Right. You ate most of my

lunch yesterday and two ice-creams so my prognosis for you is excellent. But only if you talk to me. I know you've had a medical because your mother told me, so really what we've got to deal with is up here.' He tapped his head.

'Why "we"?' she said. 'You're not my psychiatrist.'

'That's true. At the moment I'm Malcolm's.'

'I don't think I've got anything to say then.'

'What I'm doing is, I suppose, in one way unethical. I mean, coming to you to talk about my client. And he is my client and I want you to remember that. But there's one thing I think you should consider. At the moment the Crown Prosecution Service is charging him with murder. But I think they will agree to him pleading guilty to manslaughter, in which case it is almost certain he will go to Loxton which, like Broadmoor, is for the secure detainment of the mentally disordered offender, or what the media might call the "criminally insane". '

'For how long?' Her fingers fretted at her cigarette packet.

'That's my point.' He was a different man now from the one who had walked by the stream and had taken her to the pub. 'I'm sure of one thing: if he goes to Loxton it will be for very much longer than it would be if he went to prison. It might be for the remainder of his life.'

'How long would he be in prison?'

'It's only guesswork because no one really knows. Let's say he pleaded guilty to manslaughter.'

'Why not murder? That's what he did!'

'A fight over a woman. Love. Jealousy. Violence. That's how it'll come out. For murder there has to be intent. I don't think the prosecution could make a good enough case for that to stick.'

'How long for manslaughter?' she said.

'Six years. Maybe a year more, maybe a year less. With good behaviour he could be out in three or four.'

'Oh, God!'

'But if we get him into Loxton he would have to prove to a mental health tribunal that he was making such good progress he could begin the process of being returned to society as no threat to anyone. And that could take for ever.'

So it became a simple equation: help us and you help yourself.

Remembering what Malcolm had said – '*I'll come back*' – she had little option.

So she agreed to talk about him, and what she didn't realize at the time was that she was agreeing to her own rehabilitation as well. Because that's what happened.

The phone rang and gave her a fright. She no longer answered it when Michael was at home. She heard the keyboard clatter stop and then his voice. Then he called out that Tammy wanted to talk to her.

She picked up the phone in the drawing-room

and Tammy said, 'Hi, darling. Listen, I was told not to phone you about this, but the police have got Malcolm.'

'What!'

'Those two officers, Macrae and Silver, were at my flat questioning me when they got a call. Isn't it wonderful?'

'Oh, Tammy!'

'Don't cry, darling. It's over. It's finished.'

They talked for a few moments longer and then Jane went into Michael's study. He had his back to the door and the only light was over the screen. It was a mass of figures. He turned as he heard her and she thought how lucky she had been that he had come to Hampshire and persuaded her to talk to him.

'They've got him,' she said and told him what Tammy had reported. The expression on his face changed from concentration to doubt. 'Hadn't we better wait till the police call us before we take that as a fact? You know what Tammy is like.'

'For God's sake, Michael, can't you be happy for me!'

He stood up and took her face between his hands and kissed her on the forehead. 'I'm always happy for you, my love. And happy for me that I found you. I'm sure Tammy's right and when we know for sure, we'll celebrate.'

Chapter Seven

'No, not that way, go left then right.'

'I've done that, guv'nor.'

'Well, do it again. Jesus, Eddie would never have got us into this mess.'

'I don't think even Eddie could cope with the anti-tart measures of the Finsbury lot. Everywhere I've turned there seem to be bloody barriers.'

'Isn't that the park?' Macrae said.

'Doesn't look like the same park.'

'Never mind what bloody park it is, go across it.'

They negotiated a reservoir, a sports field, more children's play areas and a skate-board ramp before coming out on the Seven Sisters Road. By that time Leo was sweating and Macrae was swearing loudly.

As they turned left and shot down towards the Caledonian Road and the West End, Leo was feeling aggrieved. Eddie had been dead for many months yet whenever Leo had to drive Macrae somewhere difficult he always started invoking Eddie's perfection. To take the big man's mind off transport, he said, 'D'you think she will?'

'Do I think who will what?'

'Tammy whatsit. Do you think she'll call Mrs Stone?'

'I hope not but it'll be your bloody fault if she does. You should have kept your mouth shut when that call came through. Go right here.'

Leo felt even more aggrieved.

There were three police cars in Sloane Square.

'Who's in charge?' Macrae said.

A uniformed sergeant pushed forward. 'I am and there's not a sausage. Nobody here.'

'What! We come all the way here from the other side of London for damn all?'

The sergeant, who was nearly Macrae's age and looked to Leo as tough as old boots, said, 'Can't help that, sir. All we can do is act on orders and those were our orders. Tube station Sloane Square. Waiting for us here would be the gentleman who phoned, a Mr . . .' He held his notebook under the car lights. 'A Mr Redmond. No Mr Redmond. No suspicious character called Underdown.'

'Oh, Christ, I'm sorry, Sergeant, but if I had a quid for every time I've come to a job like this and it's a cock-up – I'd be a rich man. Give me what you've got.'

'I've got nothing, sir, not a bloody—'

The phone in Leo's pocket rang again and he handed it to Macrae. 'It's for you, guv'nor.'

Macrae listened for a moment, then he signalled for a pen and pad. 'When, Les? Aye. All right.' He handed the phone back to Leo. 'Sergeant, your Mr Redmond's phoned again. The suspect was in the pub over there but he only bought a sandwich and then starting walking along the King's Road. Redmond followed him and he's now given a second location. Drake Square, just before World's End.'

The uniformed men returned to their cars and Leo led them at speed west along the King's Road. Drake Square lay past Sydney Street. It was a small complex of houses and shops and Leo knew it well because sometimes he took Zoe to the cinema there to see a film that wasn't on the *schlock* circuit.

'He said he'd be opposite the cinema and the library,' Macrae said. 'There he is.'

A man of middle height with stringy black hair, whom Leo would have placed in his mid-thirties, came to the car window.

Macrae leaned over Leo and said, 'You Mr Redmond?'

'Are you the police?'

'What's it look like?' Leo said.

The three white patrol cars turned into the square and the man said, 'Christ, you lot have taken your time. I've been here more than an hour.'

'Get in,' Macrae said.

Redmond opened his mouth, then closed it. Macrae had the same effect on him as he had had on the barman of the pub in Battersea.

'Where is he?' Macrae said.

'In the cinema I think.'

'You think? For God's sake, you called us, you—'
He broke off and said to Leo, 'Go and find out when
the picture ends.'

'Right, guv'nor.'

Macrae said to Redmond, 'How did you know
Underdown? Who the hell are you, anyway?'

'Didn't they tell you?'

'Laddie, I wouldn't be asking if they had.'

Redmond seemed to recognize danger signals.
'Oh, right. Sorry, chief. No, I'm a mental health
nurse, you see. I work at Loxton, the secure—'

'I know what Loxton is.'

'Right, fine. Well, I knew Underdown from there.
And I knew he'd gone to Rakesbury and—'

'What's Rakesbury?'

'Medium secure psychiatric unit outside Southampton. And I knew he shouldn't be in London. No
way. So I phoned Dr Michaelson at Loxton because
I didn't know anyone at Rakesbury, and he told me
what had happened and he said to phone the police
and I did and the rest—'

'Is history,' Macrae said dryly. 'You sure it's
Underdown?'

'You don't make mistakes about people like him,
chief.'

'No, I don't suppose you do. And for God's sake
stop calling me chief.'

Leo came back. 'The picture ends in seven
minutes, guv'nor.'

'You speak to the manager?'

'No, just the usherette. I asked her what it's like and she says it's only just opened. It's a Portuguese—'

'I don't care what it is,' Macrae said.

'I'm just telling you because she went on to say there are only four people inside.'

'Ah, that's something. Where's the sergeant?'

'Here,' the sergeant said.

'Right. I'd call in for more troops but we haven't got the time and anyway there should be enough of us to stop him. I want you to send a couple round the back in case there's a lavatory window or a rear door. Leave four out front here. Sergeant Silver and I will go inside now.'

It took them less than three minutes to deploy, which meant there were only a couple of minutes left before the film ended.

'All right, laddie,' Macrae said, 'let's get inside where it's dark and maybe we can grab him before he gets into the foyer.'

Leo felt his stomach tighten. 'This is where I'd like a gun.'

'You'd only shoot yourself in the foot.'

They showed their warrant cards to the doorman and stepped quietly into the rear of the small auditorium. It took Leo a moment to accustom his eyes to the light. The film was coming to an end and the closing credits were beginning to roll. If there was a moment to take him it was now.

The four people stood up. There was an old lady

who began searching for her coat, a middle-aged man and what appeared to be a pair of Japanese tourists. Of Underdown there was no sign.

'I thought so,' Macrae said. 'Bloody cock-up as usual.'

The two detectives went out and Macrae told the uniformed men to stand down. 'I'll just have a wee word with Mr Redmond,' he said.

Redmond had got out of the car and was standing in a semi-crouched position as though about to take off. But he stayed his ground and Macrae said, 'He's not there, Mr Redmond.'

'Call me Gary, chief.'

'And you call me Mr Macrae.'

'Oh, right. Fine.'

'Well?'

'I saw him. That's all I can say, chi— Mr Macrae. I saw him.'

'Where were you standing?'

'Over there.' He pointed to the far side of the square.

'Show us.'

They walked across and stood in front of a row of houses. The cinema and library complex was on the corner of the square and abutted the King's Road.

'You stood here and you saw him go up the cinema steps, buy his ticket and go in, is that right?'

'Well, not actually buy his ticket, you can't see that from here.'

'All right. You saw him go into the foyer where the ticket desk is.'

'Well . . . now that I come to think of it . . . I didn't actually see him go in.'

That great weather system which the meteorologists call a low-pressure area but which Leo knew as 'Hurricane Macrae', began to form and Leo hastily said, 'Explain.'

'Look, it wasn't my bloody fault,' Redmond said. 'I mean, I phoned from Sloane Square and then I walked all this way and I was standing here and just as he was going up the steps of the cinema a huge great lorry came in front of me, just a few seconds, no more. Well, what am I expected to think? That he's taken off in a helicopter?'

Macrae seemed to be contemplating throwing Redmond through the nearest window, but instead said, 'Oh, Christ. What's the bloody point?'

'What's the bloody point of what?' Zoe said when Leo reached this part of his story.

'What d'you think it is?'

They were in the little kitchen which was part of the top floor of their Pimlico maisonette. They each held a glass of wine.

'Life? Creation?'

'Macrae doesn't think in those terms. Anyway he was bloody tired and so was I and I think it was just a phrase.'

'Like for "bloody tired" you say, "what's the point of it all?" '

'Exactly.'

'You want pesto in this? It's got dried tomatoes.'

'Yes, please. Anything. I'll eat anything. My God, you should have smelled that *coq au vin*.'

She loaded the pasta on to his plate, took only a little herself because she had eaten earlier, and then said, 'So what happened then? You tell stories so badly, Leo.'

'I took Macrae home. And you're lucky to see me at all tonight. I thought it was going to be one of those evenings when he locks the door and takes out a bottle of whisky and says, "No one moves till it's finished." But we hadn't been there for more than a few minutes when there was a ring at the bell and someone arrived about a job he's advertised.'

'A job?'

'A home help. This woman came in and you've never seen such knockers in your life. They stuck out a yard. And you know what she said? She said – and so help me this is true – she said she'd had experience of breast-feeding.'

'Experience of *what*?'

'Breast-feeding.'

'My God, you don't think Macrae's been reading *The Grapes of Wrath*, do you?'

'Could be. He was on to Steinbeck earlier. Anyway, he choked on his whisky when she said that and I got up and fled.'

'Leo, you've got to find out!'

'How? Just ask?'

'No, I don't suppose so.'

'You want to leave the dishes?' Leo said.

'What's on your mind?'

'It's all this talk of breasts.'

'Mine don't stick out a yard.'

'Prove it.'

'Come on then, tiger.'

They heard a taxi draw up in the street downstairs.

'That's Macrae,' Leo said. 'I told him to bring the big-breasted woman over to join us in bed.'

'Very funny.'

The door-bell rang.

Leo went to the window and looked out. He saw an elderly couple standing on the pavement outside his front door while the taxi that had dropped them went off towards Buckingham Palace Road.

'Oh, Christ,' he said. 'It's my parents.'

'Your what?'

'Mother and father. Everyone has them.'

'Switch the lights out!'

'Don't be bloody silly, they'll have seen them by now.'

The bell rang again.

'I'll have to go down.'

Zoe tidied as best she could, and when Manfred and Lotte came into the sitting-room, still in their heavy coats, she went forward dutifully to kiss her presumptive parents-in-law. Lotte was red of face and even more untidy than usual. But she enveloped Zoe and said, although a trifle vaguely, 'Hello, my darling.' Then Zoe went to Manfred. His face was chalky white and the skin above his Vandyke beard was cold.

'Let me have your coats,' Zoe said. Lotte wriggled out of hers but Manfred, who had not spoken yet, kept his tightly around himself.

Leo said, 'Let me get you a glass of something.'

Lotte said, 'Arsenic, maybe?'

Leo and Zoe glanced at each other.

'What about a nice glass of white wine instead?' Zoe said.

Manfred refused and Lotte held her glass without drinking.

'The string quartet!' Leo said. 'I'd forgotten it was tonight.'

'Yes,' his mother said. 'The Graben string quartet.'

'But aren't you out a bit early?'

Lotte said, 'Manfy, we've got to tell them.'

Manfred still did not speak and Leo thought he looked to be in shock.

'They are flesh and blood,' Lotte said. 'If you won't, I will.' She turned to Leo. 'Your father has had an accident.'

'Oh, Lord,' Leo said. 'What happened? Sit down, Dad. You want me to get a doctor?'

'Not that sort of accident,' Lotte said. 'Manfy, sit.'

But Manfred went on standing.

'He can't sit properly,' Lotte said. 'Even in the taxi he couldn't sit properly. That is why we came here.'

Various ailments flicked through Leo's mind. He knew his father had suffered from piles from time to time, although they had never spoken of it. Just to mention such a thing would have been anathema to Manfred.

'I'm waiting,' Leo said.

'All right . . . all right . . . so we come to the Graben. The last time I heard them my father took me to—'

'Yes, you told me.'

'Don't rush . . . don't rush . . . well, you know it's a long journey in the tube train and we get there with only a few minutes to spare. Good seats. I booked them. Right down near the front row. I won't tell you how much they cost. When we get there we hear the bells are ringing in the foyer but your father says he must go and wash his hands . . .'

The washing of the hands, Leo knew, was an integral part of his father's music teacher's life. Had he been with him he would have accepted the washing of the hands as something quite natural. But – and it surprised him to hear this from his mother – she had decided he would have to wait.

'For what I paid for the seats I wanted to hear every note,' she said. 'You know they don't let you in once the piece has started. And they were starting with the Haydn. How many times didn't I go to

Eisenstadt with your grandfather? We used to go
there when we went down to the Neusiedler See for
lunch in that restaurant over the lake and—'

'What happened?'

'Oh . . . yes . . . well, I said, Manfy, not now. You
can go in the interval. So we go down to the expensive seats near the front. We are in the middle. Just
where I vant to be. I like to see what is happening
while I listen. Once at the Musikverein with Klemp-
erer conducting the Beethoven A major, the strings
of the first violinist broke and—'

'Mother, for God's sake!'

'Oh, yes, so I go into the row first and your
father follows me and we listen to the Haydn and
the Mozart C major. I can't tell you . . . fantastic . . .
that is the word. I mean . . . the Melos . . . the
Amadeus . . . nothing . . . nothing to the Graben. So
then there is interval and your father says now he
is going to wash his hands and he starts to go out.
I say, Manfy, buy ice-creams. He doesn't hear, or
pretends he doesn't hear. But the woman sitting next
to him tells him what I have said. She just touches
his jacket to get his attention but you know what
your father is like. Big deal as they say. And so he
glares at her and goes on and I say so sorry my dear
and the woman glares at *me*. She is one of those
middle-aged women that dress too expensively. You
know the sort. Don't know flats from naturals so
they go to impress. Such is what I thought.'

Manfred reacted for the first time. A guttural noise came from his throat.

'What, Manfy?'

He shook his head but whether it was in refusal to repeat the noise or just a mark of deep philosophical incomprehension Leo did not know.

'Who was she?' Leo said.

'The Austrian ambassador's wife,' Lotte said.

Leo began to breathe more easily. His father being rude to a diplomat, while not nice, was not an indictable offence.

With a mother's understanding, Lotte knew what he was thinking and said, 'Vait, that is not the crox.'

'Crox?' Zoe said.

'Climax?' Leo said.

'So your father goes to the place. And there are hundreds of men. Isn't it, Manfy? Hundreds all going to wash their hands and so your father has to wait and . . .' She lowered her voice. '. . . it is not easy in crowds you know. It takes time. Too much time. For the Graben are already beginning to tune their instruments when he comes back. The moment he comes into the row I know something is not right. Here . . .' She pointed vaguely at the lower part of her abdomen. 'It is open, yes? From the washing the hands. He has forgotten the zip. And so I said, "*Manfy . . .!*". The word came out as a hiss. And when he looked at me I pointed.' She paused.

'Hey, wait a sec!' Leo said. 'You're having us on!'

'*Having you on?*' Lotte used the phrase in quotation marks. 'That is not a nice way to talk to your mother.'

'Oh, come on. That story's got cobwebs.'

'Shut up, Leo,' Zoe said. 'Don't be so rude.'

'That's very nice, my darling.' Then to Leo. 'It's a free country? You let me finish? Zank you so much.'

Leo shrugged, said nothing.

'Your father looked down and saw what had happened and he . . . oh, *lieber Gott* . . . he zips himself up and just as he does this the woman, the Austrian ambassador's wife, she starts to stand up to let him past, and her thing . . . the strap of her handbag . . . is caught in the zip.'

Leo's eyes widened. They were moving into unfamiliar territory now. 'And?'

'Oh, so, now you vish to know. Well, I tell you. She . . . this stupid woman . . . she thinks your father is stealing her bag. She gives a little pull. He thinks, your poor father, she is maybe interfering, you know, with him. And so . . . and so he gives a strong pull. And she screams and gives a stronger pull and there is a tearing sound and . . . and I can't tell no more . . .'

'You mean the zip . . .?'

She nodded. 'An old suit. From the 1950s maybe. And the stitching . . . show your son, Manfy.'

Manfred didn't move.

Zoe turned away with delicacy and Lotte briefly parted Manfred's navy blue overcoat. Around his thighs was Lotte's shawl. She raised it. The front of his trousers had torn away and Leo could see his striped underpants.

'It is not your father's fault,' Lotte said.

'Oh, God.' Manfred spoke for the first time.

'What happened?' Leo whispered.

'The woman screamed again,' Lotte said. 'That is what happened.'

'But . . .

'Well . . .' Lotte was careful how she phrased the next few sentences. 'Well, she is screaming and your father is tugging at his trousers and it looks, I mustn't speak such things, but it looks like . . . rape. So I put my shawl over him and we have to go out. The ambassador, and your father and the ambassador's wife and me. You ask what happened? That is what happened.'

'But what about the ambassador? I mean . . .'

'In the foyer the ambassador says he is going to call the police, he is going to have us arrested, he is going to sue. I say go ahead, Mr Ambassador, call the police . . . sue. It will be so nice for the newspapers. That is what I say.'

'And so you came here.'

'Where must we go? We cannot go in the train. We cannot afford the taxi to north London.'

Manfred spoke. 'Get a pair of trousers for me.' His voice was almost unrecognizable. 'And then take us home.' He turned to Lotte. 'You make me cross the river. That is what happens in south London.'

*

Macrae couldn't sleep. This had been happening more frequently since Frenchy had disappeared. That's how he thought of it. Not 'left him', but 'disappeared'. As she might have done in Amazonia.

He was lying awake in his big double bed and in his mind's eye was the picture of the breast-feeding woman who had come to apply for the job of cleaning his house. He had thought, when he put the advertisement in the paper, that it was a simple matter: either you wanted this kind of work or you didn't. If you did, you came at a convenient time to your employer, cleaned the house, took your money and left. But not a bit of it. She could come only at the weekend because she had another job and she would have to bring her two tiny children. Macrae had given the matter one second's thought and wished her luck and said goodbye.

How had life become so complicated, he wondered? When Frenchy was around he never had to worry about the house. And that also applied to his second wife, Mandy. Even she had eventually cleaned the place. But best of all was his first wife, Linda. Often he thought of her with deep longing, and not only her, but that whole period. Life had been simpler then, more innocent. He remembered after their daughter Susan had been born, the three of them, Susan in her pram, would go to a park at the weekend and walk through it. That's all. Nothing more. That was their entertainment for the day.

And he'd enjoyed it.

They had rarely eaten in restaurants in those days, hardly even gone to the cinema. Money had been tight as hell. But they'd been happy. Then, their entertainment had come from sex, the TV, and reading. He'd always read a lot, he'd got that from his mother. She had been a great reader and he realized only much later that the reading had been her defence against his brutal and drunken father. Reading had given her a separate world into which she could escape. But her unhappiness did have one positive result: it caused Macrae to read. By the time he was in his teens he was reading Poe and Dickens, even Scott, for these were three of the authors on his mother's shelves. She had inherited the books from her parents but never read them herself. Her choice was cheap romances but Macrae had not been able to stomach those.

He and Linda had wheeled Susan down to the library on summer and winter evenings and they had—

He sat up in bed.

'Oh, Christ!' he said out loud. 'Oh, bloody hell!'

Chapter 8

Report 4 MSU/SVA 813/MS (Encl.)

The enclosed photocopy of the Underdown trial verdict is taken from the *National Chronicle* which contained the most complete coverage.

'I'll-come-back' man guilty of killing former student
'Murder scene like abattoir' – says officer

A killer who threatened to return and repeat his crime on a young woman was sent to a secure mental hospital by a judge at the Old Bailey in London today.

Malcolm Steven Underdown, 25, of no fixed address, was told by Mr Justice Shaw that society must be protected from him until he was restored to mental health.

He had pleaded guilty to manslaughter on the grounds of diminished responsibility.

He was arrested in August last year for the murder of Edward Craig, also 25, with whom he had been at the University of Winchester in Hampshire.

The court was told that Underdown had become jealous of Mr Craig's friendship with another graduate, Jane Harrison, 24, and that he had killed Craig in a fit of ungovernable rage.

Miss Harrison said she and Mr Craig had planned to marry in December. They had known each other for several years, first becoming friendly at university.

She said that Underdown had also been a friend of hers at Winchester. She had gone out with him for a short time but he had become too possessive and she had decided that the friendship should end.

She had then become friendly with another student who was attacked by Underdown, who was arrested and cautioned for this attack and was sent down by the university authorities.

Miss Harrison then formed a relationship with Mr Craig.

Underdown was now living some miles away in Hampshire and would often return to the campus. Miss Harrison said she and Mr Craig were always aware that they must be wary of him.

After leaving the university neither Mr Craig nor Miss Harrison saw Underdown for nearly two years and then, one day, she saw him standing outside her office block in the Euston Road, near the main doors.

Although he saw her he did not speak to her. She was frightened but managed to avoid him following her back to the flat she was sharing with friends in Camden Town. She saw him several times after that in the same place.

When she and Mr Craig became engaged she moved with him to his parents' flat. She did not think that Underdown knew of the Exeter Square flat because she had changed her place of work.

Then, on 8 August, when Miss Harrison and Mr Craig were expecting friends, the bell rang and they found Underdown outside the door. He forced his way in and stabbed Mr Craig eleven times in the neck and chest. Miss Harrison had locked herself into the bedroom and her screams alerted neighbours who phoned for the police.

Detective Superintendent George Macrae, who led the investigation, had earlier told the court that the flat was 'like an abattoir' when he arrived. The living-room, where Mr Craig had died, had a pool of blood on the floor, and there was blood on the furniture. Underdown was found in the passage outside the bedroom in which Miss Harrison had locked herself.

Superintendent Macrae said the police found several knife marks in the panelling of the door where he had been trying to force an entrance.

When the police arrested Underdown he

attacked an officer with a broken bottle, and threatened another.

After Miss Harrison's release, Underdown was heard calling to her, 'I'll be back.' Superintendent Macrae said he had taken this to mean that Underdown would try to return and harm her.

For the Defence, Dr Michael Stone, a forensic psychiatrist, said that Underdown was suffering from a borderline personality disorder. He had been an only child and much of his childhood had been lonely.

He had developed an obsessive need for Miss Harrison because he had convinced himself that she was deeply in love with him.

The killing had taken place after a long period during which Underdown had been living by himself. It came at a time when he felt his mother had rejected him.

Dr Stone said there was a chance that Underdown could be successfully treated in hospital but that it would take a long time. In view of this he had decided to recommend that Underdown plead guilty to manslaughter on the grounds of diminished responsibility.

The court was told that Underdown's mother, a former airline stewardess, said she had done everything she could to help her son, but had reached a point in her life when she no longer wished to have anything to do with him and would not have him in her house. Underdown had been living rough for some time before the murder.

In his summing-up, Mr Justice Shaw said,
'In some ways one cannot blame this woman
but it is a sad commentary on modern life.'

'Ten o'clock,' Macrae said to Silver. 'What would
happen to the world if *we* started at ten o'clock?'

They were standing outside the Drake Square
library at a little before ten o'clock on a freezing
morning. A wind was bringing in sleet from Russia.

'They work late,' Leo said.

'So do I.'

They were sharing the portico of the library with
a motley assortment of tramps and dossers, some of
whom still had their newspaper blankets wrapped
round their bodies to keep out the wind. One old
man with an orange-coloured beard and a face like
a schnauzer was shuffling his feet to warm them. He
had watched Macrae and Silver arrive with obvious
interest.

'Morning, squire,' he said to Macrae. 'You selling?'

'Selling what?' Macrae said testily.

'Books o'course. It's a library. What'd you think,
squire? Nutmeg?'

Macrae turned his back on the old man and tried
to stand upwind of him. The others tittered at this
exchange. One was counting the books in the
window. He counted them twice in a low voice and
had begun again when the big glass doors were
opened and the homeless pressed forward into the

reading room. One, a tall thin man dressed in an ancient shooting suit, took off a battered trilby, gave a slight bow and said to Macrae, 'You don't want to pay heed to the riff-raff.' Then he too pushed forward into the warmth.

Macrae said to one of the women behind the desk, 'Is the librarian in?'

'Are you thinking of joining, sir?' The woman, in her thirties, was small and bright, like a little robin, with a rounded chest and piercing dark-brown eyes.

Macrae identified himself and held out his warrant card. 'Can you tell me where his office is?'

The woman's eyes flashed and her face changed to bird-like inquisitiveness. 'What'd Miss Fellowes do?' she said. 'Lose a book?'

'No. Not that I know of.'

She pointed to a door on the far side of the book-lined room.

Macrae and Silver crossed and knocked and Macrae pushed the door open before being invited in. A woman in her late forties with thin grey hair and heavy glasses was sitting at her desk. She had a thermos next to her and had bitten deeply into a cheese roll. She hastily cleared her mouth with coffee, swallowed convulsively, and said, 'Yes?'

As Macrae identified himself and held out his warrant card again, a crimson stain of embarrassment spread over her neck.

'Sorry to barge in,' Macrae said, 'but it's necessary.'

Miss Fellowes, thin and bony, began to recover herself. She put the remains of the cheese roll into her top drawer and brushed the crumbs into the wastepaper basket. 'The police, is it? Well, what can I do for you?'

'What time do you close in the evening?'

'Eight o'clock.'

'Did you close at eight o'clock last night?'

'That's what it says on the door.' Her embarrassment at being caught with a mouthful of cheese roll was beginning to fade and he could see annoyance replace it.

'Aye, well, I'll question the door later, if that's what you want me to do. But in the meantime it's got to be what *you* say. I take it that you closed at eight then. Just before you closed, say between seven and eight, we think a man came into the library. He was a very big man. And if you'd seen him you'd remember.'

'It was my afternoon off.'

'Well, someone must have been here.'

Miss Fellowes rose. 'Please follow me.' She led them back to the desk, past the watchful eyes of the roomful of tramps.

'Janet was here.' She indicated the first woman Macrae had spoken to then turned on her heel and walked back to her office and her cheese roll.

He repeated his question to Janet.

'How big was he?' she said.

'Big enough for you to remember.'

She shook her head. 'I don't remember anyone like that, but I wasn't on the desk all the time. Anyway, I left early. I had to go to my classes.'

'Classes?' Leo said.

'Yoga,' she said. 'It calms me down when police ask me questions.'

Macrae opened his mouth to comment when a voice said, 'You lookin' for a big man, squire?'

Macrae turned and found Ginger Whiskers behind him. He moved away a few feet. 'Were you here yesterday?'

'That I was, squire. That I was. And I seen him. The big fella. I seen him and I heard him. Kept on asking for a machine.'

'A machine? What sort of machine?'

'You got me there, squire. You come to a library you get books, not machines. Anyway the blonde woman dealt with him.'

'Lady,' Janet said. 'Blonde lady. That'll be Deirdre.'

'Lady!' Ginger Whiskers said. 'Woman! What's the bleedin' difference?'

They ignored him as the door was flung open and a middle-aged woman with severely blonded hair came bursting in. Her coat was awry and seemed to be falling off her body. She was clutching two shopping bags full of groceries.

She looked with fear towards Miss Fellowes'

office but the door was closed. 'Oh, God, Jan, I'm sorry I'm late. But if I don't do the shopping now it never gets done.'

'You're not late, you're just in time. These gentlemen are from the police.'

There was a sudden movement and Ginger Whiskers darted into the reading room, said something, and in a moment the group of dossers was making for the street.

'Well, that's one way of clearing them out,' Janet said.

Macrae said to Deirdre, 'Do you remember last evening, some time before you closed, a very big man coming into the library?'

She stood there like a scarecrow in her badly adjusted coat and the bags hanging on the end of each arm. Then she smiled and said, 'Yes I do. A nice man. Gentle. He wanted the *Times Index* and a reading machine and I said we didn't have the *Index*. So he said could I let him see all the telephone directories we had. And I said we didn't have many, just some of the counties in the south, and he said that was fine and I gave them to him. He sat at that table over there and looked at them for about ten minutes and then he left.'

'Out the front door?' Macrae said.

'Of course.'

'But did you see him leave that way?'

'No, I didn't.'

Janet said, 'We don't watch every movement.'

'Is there a back way?'

'Oh, yes. It's for the staff.'

'Let's have a look at it.'

Janet took him past the lavatories to a door that led into a small alley.

'Where does that go to?'

'The King's Road.'

'That explains that, then,' Leo said.

'Oh, it's you.'

Tammy was standing in her doorway, Macrae in the passage outside. It was nearly lunchtime and Tammy was still in a kimono. She had that soft, buttery look that had attracted Macrae the previous evening. It had taken him some moments of argument with himself before he had decided to come. Now he was glad.

'Come in. Excuse me for a moment.' She went to the phone and said, 'Someone just called. I'll have to ring you later. No. You phone me. Tonight? OK.' She put the receiver down and Macrae noticed that her face was flushed and her eyes watery.

'You all right?' he said.

'Oh, yes. It's just my ex. He always makes me feel guilty.'

The room was as they had left it the previous night. Macrae's glass was still where he had put it.

'Haven't had a chance to clean up yet, I've been cooking.'

The flat smelled of last night's *coq au vin*, but nothing else.

'I was passing,' Macrae said.

She frowned and he realized how silly it must have sounded. He had never met anyone before who 'passed' this area of London. It simply didn't lead anywhere.

'That's nice,' she said. 'Would you like a coffee?'

'If you're having one.'

He found a chair and watched her as she made fresh coffee. She was wearing only a nightdress under the kimono and her breasts and buttocks moved in the fleshy way Macrae liked. Again he congratulated himself for coming.

She gave him coffee and said, 'Where did you put him?'

'Who?'

'Malcolm Underdown.'

'That's partly the reason I dropped in. I wanted to tell you about it because we got the call here and I knew you were friendly with Mrs Stone.'

'Go on.' Her voice had grown cold.

Macrae told her briefly what had happened and she said, 'Oh, Christ!'

The way she said it and the expression on her face gave Macrae the clue he was looking for.

'You told her, didn't you?'

'Yes. I rang her. I couldn't not. You don't know what this is doing to her!'

'I asked you not to.'

'I know you did. But what if she'd been your wife or daughter? Wouldn't you have wanted her to know as fast as possible?'

The face of his daughter, Susan, came briefly into his mind. He said, 'Only if it was true.'

'Of course you're right. But it might have been true. I mean, you didn't know, did you? It might have been.' She lit a cigarette and threw the pack on the table and then said, 'Oh, sorry,' and pushed it towards Macrae.

'I'll smoke one of these if you don't mind?' He lit a short panatella.

She said, 'I smoke them too sometimes. They're supposed to be better for you than fags. Look, I'm sorry, that's all I can say. Bloody sorry, but mainly for her.'

Macrae thought of pointing out that Jane Stone was the one he was sorry for too, but decided he'd said enough.

Tammy said, 'She's like a child, you know. She never was, but she is now. That's what it's done to her. My God, I know I was wrong, but wrong for the right reasons.'

Macrae finished his coffee and was about to stub out his half-smoked cheroot.

She said suddenly, 'I've had an idea. Why don't we have lunch?'

In case he was about to make an excuse she went on rapidly, 'You know I was cooking last night for a customer. I was supposed to deliver tonight. Well, the fucking . . . sorry, the nice customer phoned this morning and said they didn't want it. So it's all here and . . . and if you don't eat it I'm going to throw the whole mess away. I'll go and get dressed and tidy up this bloody place and you go and get a bottle of wine and we'll have lunch.'

There was an urgency in her voice which Macrae recognized. He'd heard it before and guessed it came from loneliness.

'All right,' he said, 'let's do that.'

'There's a supermarket two streets down and they do a very nice line in Australian chardonnays.' As he pushed himself out of his chair she said, 'Don't often have the fuzz to lunch.'

She had a way of saying things that changed them. The word fuzz lost its American pejorativeness and made it acceptable, even to him.

The supermarket was further than he had thought and didn't stock his cigars so he had to find a pub and he was away for nearly half an hour. When he got back she said, 'I thought you'd gone for good.'

'When you've been in the Force as long as I have you never give up the chance of a free meal.'

She was at the stove in the kitchen area and swung round, frowning. But he was smiling at her.

'I got what you suggested,' he said, holding up two bottles of chardonnay. 'They were in the fridge. You want me to open one?'

'You'll find the glasses over there.'

He opened the bottle and poured two glasses. She had put on a pair of jeans and a loose-fitting white cotton polo-neck and had done her face and hair. Macrae thought she looked a lot better than she had. She had also tidied the flat.

'Cook's drink.' He handed her a glass.

'Oooh, that's good. Specially as I haven't had any breakfast. What do you say we go the whole hog and have some *rösti*? You're not on a diet, are you?'

'What's *rösti*?'

'A kind of potato pancake. But better.'

She drank again and said, 'Can you find my cigarettes?'

He lit one for her and she said, 'It's disgusting to smoke while you cook but occasionally disgusting things are nice, don't you think?'

'The only disgusting thing I can think of at the moment is called Underdown.'

'Oh, yes, poor old Malcolm. And poor old Jane.'

'And poor old Edward Craig,' he said, finding himself slightly irritated.

She tested the potatoes in the boiling water. 'And poor old Michael.'

'Who's Michael?'

'Dr Stone. Jane's husband.'

'Why "poor" Michael?'

'I don't think he knew what he was getting into.'

'What was he getting into?'

'Well, you know, with Jane.'

'You were telling us about Jane,' he said. 'You said you knew her at school.'

'I was in her class for four years and then with her at Winchester.'

'Had she any problems with boyfriends before that?'

'What do you mean, problems?'

'Did any of them try to beat her up or beat up the boy she was with? That sort of thing.'

'Oh, no. Actually when she was at school she was very pious. Not religiously, but morally. I think it was a father problem. She was her father's girl. I don't mean that in any nasty way,' she said hurriedly. 'You've got to be bloody careful how you say that sort of thing these days or else the social services and the police . . . well, not the police . . .'

'I know what you mean.'

'So we were all pleased when she began to relax at university and actually went to bed with someone.' She tested the potatoes again, drained them and began to rub them on a grater.

'Did she ever go to bed with Underdown?'

She mixed in salt and pepper and began to shape the grated and sticky potato into one thick pancake.

'Odd you should ask that. It's something she never talked about and I've never been able to ask her, but she probably did. They had quite a thing going at one time but I think as far as she was concerned it was less important than it was for him.'

'How long did it last?'

'Less than a year. I have a feeling she knew she had to get on with her own life and not always look to her father, and old Malcolm was an experiment.'

She put some oil in a large frying pan and slid in the potato pancake. 'Now it gets fried until it's crisp on both sides.'

'You say she never discussed Underdown with you. I thought girls always discussed their lovers.'

'She didn't talk about any of her boyfriends much. There were quite a few and this got Malcolm down. When they were still having their affair he was around at her flat every night. And they would always have lunch together in the cafeteria on campus. He would wait for her outside her lectures and tutorials even if it meant missing his own. It was really hot – for him, anyway.'

'You said something about him putting a snake in someone's car.'

'Hey, wait a minute. I've got to remember you're from the police. I don't want to get run in for slander. I don't *know* it was him, but it must have been. I mean, he was an expert on small animals. There wasn't anyone else who wanted to harm the person he did it to.'

'This was after Jane and Malcolm had broken up?'

'A few weeks after. Pass me that big plate, would you. I've got to turn this thing.' Expertly she slid the *rösti* on to the plate and turned it upside down in the pan. The side that showed was a golden brown

117

and Macrae began to feel hungry. There were also wonderful smells coming from the oven where the *coq au vin* was heating up.

'You said it was not just an adder or anything ordinary.'

'I've never been able to remember the name. I try to forget everything about snakes. Can't stand the bloody things. But the word adder comes in. Rough adder. Something like that.'

'I think there's a snake called a puff adder. Comes from somewhere in Africa.'

'That'd be it then. I saw it before they killed it. Nasty thick thing with teeth like a crocodile.'

She took a casserole dish out of the oven and carried the food to the table. 'You sit there. How's the wine?'

He filled their glasses and said, 'I'll open the other bottle.'

She served the *coq* and the *rösti*. The chicken came on to the plates in several brown pieces surrounded by shallots. Even though he had been drinking Macrae could still smell the winey aroma in the steam.

'That's the secret,' she said, tasting the sauce. 'The best burgundy you can afford.'

They began to eat. Macrae hadn't tasted anything like it for a long time if, indeed, ever. The chicken was succulent and contained in its flavour the dark rich taste of the wine mixed with the shallots and little pieces of smoked bacon. This was all sopped up with the *rösti* with its crisp skin and its soft interior.

They did not talk for some time and then both of them finished at much the same moment and leaned back, glasses in hand.

Tammy said, 'Well, that'll serve the buggers right.'

'How many were there going to be?' Macrae said.

'Four.'

'You mean we've eaten four portions between us?'

'Not quite. There are a couple of teaspoons left. How about a brandy?'

He gave her a small cigar and they sipped a Hines.

'I want to go back to Jane and her husband.'

'I thought you would.'

'He's older than she is, isn't he?'

'Years. I think he's in his mid-forties and she's my age. Twenty-nine.'

He glanced at her and she said, 'All right, thirty-one. I'm a bit older than she is.'

'What made her marry him?'

'He took her over. He used to go down to Hampshire and be with her and talk to her and slowly he pulled her out of the post-trauma thing. And she was grateful and started to live again. He was incredibly generous. He gave her cars – expensive ones – and whenever he had to go to a conference he made it up to her by giving her a holiday

somewhere. If he couldn't go he would pay for me
to go.'

'That sort of money?'

'Oh, Lord, yes. Heaps. There was a time when
he used to go racing. He took her to Ascot and
the Derby, the Cheltenham Gold Cup, that sort of
meeting and he always had a box. He took her to
Wimbledon and Henley. The big social occasions.
But all that stopped a few years ago because of his
work. That's all he seems to do now. Work.'

'So from her point of view he was her saviour
but from his point of view he just fancied her?'

'Well, he had a wife who did something with
computers. I only saw her once at their divorce
hearing and she looked cold.'

'Don't women always look cold then? Mine certainly did.'

'You too? Join the club. I was too drunk to look
cold. I remember going round to the loos and throwing up, do you want to go to bed with me?'

Macrae wasn't quite sure whether he had heard
aright, since the question had been dropped in at
the end of a sentence as though it was part of it.

'Wouldn't it be nice on a dreary winter's afternoon?' she said.

Macrae had originated in a Scottish community
in which the Free Presbyterian Church dominated.
The 'Wee Frees' were very strict and adultery or
sexual liaison of any kind outside marriage was
unthinkable. He had taken a long time to shake off

this part of his upbringing. But shake it off he did. In spades. Yet no one had ever propositioned him as bluntly as Tammy, certainly not on such slender acquaintanceship.

On the one hand he was in the middle of a murder inquiry, on the other he was full of good food and good cheer and as randy as a billy-goat.

'I think that would be a grand thing to do,' he said.

They fell on each other like Turkish wrestlers. Clothes were flung aside. A chair was knocked over. They landed on the bed in a single interlocked lump and it slid across the floor and crashed into the wall. She turned her back to him and he gripped her under the belly and mounted her as a stallion mounts a mare and she cried out with delight.

It was over for both of them quickly and they lay sweating and breathing heavily for a few moments before she patted him on the chest and said, 'My God, that was better than a smack in the face with a wet herring.'

He laughed, which was rare for Macrae, and she said, 'You know, you look just like a Minotaur. All you need is a pair of horns.'

He finished his brandy and said, 'I've got to go.'

'How many times haven't I heard that phrase over the years.'

There was a sadness which touched him for a moment but then he sat up and said, 'Don't forget, Underdown is moving.'

Chapter Nine

Report 5/MSU/SM

First interview: This has been conducted, with informed consent.

Following is a tape-recorded interview between Dr Sidney Michaelson, Consultant Psychiatrist, Loxton Special Hospital, and Malcolm Stephen Underdown. The interview was held ten days after Underdown's admission.

The tape begins:

Dr Michaelson: Hello, Malcolm. I would like to put this interview on tape so my colleagues and I will know how best to treat you. It is purely for our use and I will not let it be the subject of a medical or an undergraduate study. You have a right to say no and then, of course, I won't tape it. Are you happy about that?

Underdown: Yeah, all right.

Dr M: Sorry if that sounded a bit formal but we have to get your permission. How are you feeling, Malcolm?

U: I'm OK.

Dr M: That's good. You know you only have to tell us if you're not. Some of the questions I'm going to ask, you may not have an answer to or you may not wish to answer them for reasons of your own. I will quite understand. What I would say to you is that everything we do today is designed to try to help you. The first thing I think we should deal with, Malcolm, is why you're here. You know what Loxton is, of course.

U: A mad-house.

Dr M: We don't use those terms any longer. Haven't for years. We're first and foremost a hospital. We're here to help you get better.

U: At Stockwell they said no one came out of here.

Dr M: Who said so?

U: One of the prison warders, I think. May have been a prisoner. Can't remember.

Dr M: If it was a prison officer he had no right to say anything of the kind. People do leave here. They go back into the community and become useful citizens. Don't you believe me?

(*A noise like a laugh. Blurring on tape.*)

Dr M: Malcolm? Don't you believe me? (*Blurring noise again.*) All right we'll leave that for the moment. But you're an intelligent man. You went to university. You should know that the days of the mad-house are long gone.

U: OK, insane asylum.

Dr M: We don't use that either nowadays. But never mind, you're more important than semantics. Our job is to get you well again, and get you out of here. So let's make a start. I've got your prison papers here, the interviews you had with the prison doctor, the

Crown psychiatrist and the Defence psychiatrist. And
I've also got a copy of the letter your mother sent to
your lawyers – I must say I was very sorry to read
that, Malcolm – and one or two other reports. So let's
start at the beginning. Your mother was an airline
stewardess . . . that's a rather glamorous occupation,
isn't it? Or it was years ago when she was one. Did
you know that?

U: Yeah. She kept on about it. And about where she
was travelling and things like that.

Dr M: And your father was in the Royal Navy. What
rank did he hold?

U: Lieutenant Commander.

Dr M: How old were you when your parents
divorced?

U: Eight.

Dr M: And who looked after you then?

U: My grandmother.

Dr M: Did she look after you when your mother was
working and your father was away in his ship? There
must have been times when they were both away.

U: Yeah.

Dr M: Did you love her?

U: Yeah, I suppose so.

Dr M: And then after the divorce your mother
married, let's see, yes, here it is – Harold Stokes. He
became your step-father.

U: Yeah.

Dr M: How old were you then?

U: Nine.

Dr M: So she didn't have too long a gap. Was she
worried about you? About how you would react to a
step-father?

U: I dunno.

Dr M: She didn't talk to you about it beforehand?

U: Don't think so. Can't remember.

Dr M: How did you get on with your step-father, Malcolm?

U: He was a drunk and a shit.

Dr M: Aaah. I see. So you didn't like him very much?

U: I hated the bastard and he hated me. All he wanted was to be with my mother. He didn't want me anywhere near her. If I was there he'd send me out of the house. Tell me to go and play; that sort of thing.

Dr M: And did you?

U: What?

Dr M: Go out to play.

U: I went into the woods, if you can call that playing.

Dr M: Wasn't there anyone to play with, you know, farm workers' children?

U: There were a couple but they were much older than me and anyway my mother would never have let me.

Dr M: Why not, Malcolm?

U: Workers' kids? You must be joking. I might have picked up a bad accent or something.

Dr M: So what did you do? I mean when you played. What games?

U: You know, you ask bloody silly questions. What games can you play by yourself? Hopscotch is about all. I played with animals, that's what I played with.

Dr M: Live animals?

U: What's that supposed to mean?

Dr M: It doesn't mean anything, it's just a question.

U: Oh, yes it bloody does. This is what you ask serial killers, isn't it? Well, I didn't cut them up, if that's what you're trying to get at. Some were dead and some weren't. Some were injured like a pheasant I found with a broken wing. Some were shot by me.

Dr M: You had a gun?

U: Christ, I was nine years old. 'Course I didn't have a gun. I made a bow and arrow and I had a catapult.

Dr M: OK, Malcolm, don't take offence. What sort of animals did you shoot?

U: I can't remember.

Dr M: Let's try the other way. What sort of animals did you play with. The live ones?

U: I dunno. Frogs . . . toads . . . lizards . . .

Dr M: Right. So when you weren't playing with animals what about school? Didn't you have any friends at school?

U: When my mother married again I went to a different school. I didn't want to know anyone and they didn't want to know me.

Dr M: Do you think they didn't want to know you because you didn't want to know them?

U: I don't want to go on with this.

Dr M: Why not?

U: This is what the other psychiatrists used to ask me. Who did I play with? What animals did I play with? Where did I play with them? Didn't I have any friends? I'm sick of it! Why don't you get their reports? It's all there.

Dr M: I've got their reports, Malcolm. What I'm trying to do is make my own report. You see, I'm on your side.

(*Heavy noise and blurring on the tape.*)

Dr M: All right, Malcolm, fine. Don't worry. Just

relax. If you don't want to go on with this, that's fine.
I think you've done very well and—
U: I don't want any of that stuff.
Dr M: What stuff?
U: It makes me numb and dizzy and out of focus.
Dr M: What we've prescribed for you are drugs that
will help to stabilize your condition and allow you to
improve. That's the only way you're going to get better
and rejoin society. (*Noise of chair being moved.*) OK,
Malcolm, if you'd rather not go on that's fine. Just hang
on a second and I'll get someone to take you back to
your ward. (*Noise of door opening.*) Oh, Freddy, will
you take Malcolm back now? Thanks, Malcolm. That
was a good start. I'll see you again soon. (*Noise of door
closing.*) I'm switching off the tape now.

Tape session ends.

Note by SM
*Previous obsessive infatuation suggests possibility of
frank mental disorder, query De Clerambault
Syndrome, but on interview today no suggestion of
psychotic thinking. Projects hatred of his step-father on
to me: male nursing staff to be advised. Key nurse at
present should perhaps be female. Already a bit
psychiatrically sophisticated following remand
interviews and reports x3*

Ticking . . . There had never been so much ticking,
Jane thought. Clocks and watches and timers and
God knows what else all over the house.

Perhaps it had always been like this and she had

never heard it. Now she heard everything. She would lie awake at night and hear the central-heating pipes expand and contract against the wood, as though the whole house was moving. In the daytime she would hear the ticking.

Before – before his escape, that is – she had hardly been aware of the house as a source of noise. It had just been a house, Michael's house. Now everything was different. The house seemed to have come to life, to have developed a personality, a will of its own. Short of throwing the clocks into the street and unplugging half the sockets it would go on ticking.

Click! There went the fridge.

She went to the sitting-room windows and stared out into the garden. Bulbs were pressing up through the earth. Soon, in a matter of weeks, the lawn would be spotted by daffodils. It was time to get out into the garden and begin to clean up some of the worst of the winter mess, but she knew she wouldn't. She didn't like being outside now.

That was just bloody silly! Tammy had phoned. Malcolm had been found. Why couldn't she accept that? Be happy. Be free.

She knew what was happening to her. She was reverting to the condition she had been in soon after the initial trauma, soon after Edward had been murdered; when she had been afraid to leave her mother's house and had been unable to talk to her step-father. She knew it, and that frightened her almost as much as Malcolm did, yet she could do nothing about it. There was a world outside which she feared, and now she was becoming afraid of the world inside – the house itself. The house, she knew, could become her enemy.

The afternoon began to grow dark and she went round switching on lights. It wasn't four o'clock yet but on grey days the interior was already shadowy by this time. Normally she would have been out shopping. Not now.

She went into Michael's study and switched on the light. Tick . . . tick . . . tick . . . That was the clock on his wall. She touched the dead screen of his word processor and there was dust on the tip of her finger. He hated dust and she didn't blame him but the static always attracted it. She fetched a cloth and cleaned it.

She really must pull herself together. After the trial Michael had said, 'Don't let your imagination take over. Let the facts speak for themselves. Don't exaggerate anything or minimize anything. Don't lie to yourself. The best thing you can ever do is face reality. Don't try to put it out of your mind, because you can't. It'll just go deeper and stay there and fester.' That was part of his therapy at the time, the therapy that had made her well again.

She went through to the kitchen and made herself a cup of coffee. This was the seventh or eighth she'd had that day. She lit a cigarette. She did not know what number that was.

Michael wanted truth. What she wanted, she supposed, was lies. She wanted what had happened not to have happened. Since it had she didn't want to think about it. Tammy used to say to her: 'You want it to go away and it won't.' That was just Michael again.

She turned away from the kitchen back into the living-room and heard something. It seemed to come from the garage. She stood quite still. The house ticked and her heart raced in her chest.

Michael?

But she would have heard the Porsche.

It came again. It was as though it was a footstep on gravel or a hard concrete floor. Well, they didn't have gravel but the garage floor was concrete, so were the steps coming up out of the garage into the house. That door was locked. She always checked it. But had she checked in the past hour? Once she had gone back to it six times, one after another, checking the checking.

She was so afraid that the coffee began to shake in the mug and she had to put it down. She did it so softly that the action did not make a sound.

What was she going to do?

There was a panic button by the front door. There was another by her bed. But that meant going upstairs.

Go upstairs, then. Lock yourself into the bathroom. Then you've got the panic button, a telephone and a locked door.

But no escape.

She couldn't jump down from the windows, they were too high.

The noise came again. This time more of a thud, as though something had softly hit a wooden door.

It wasn't at the garage now, but at the side of the house.

Suddenly a security light in the garden came on.

Sometimes, she knew, the lights were activated by dogs or cats. But dogs or cats didn't make scraping noises or sound like something thudding into wood.

It had to be someone out there.

Then she panicked and ran upstairs and locked herself into the bedroom. She wanted to go under the bedclothes, fought it and went to the window. The light shone on to the lawn and the flower-beds, but she could see nothing.

There was a sudden violent noise. It took her a shocked moment to realize it was her front door-bell. She strained at the window but could see nothing, for the roof of the porch blocked her view. There was no point from which she could easily see the front doorstep.

She threw herself over the bed and pressed the panic button. Nothing happened. She looked down. She had pressed the telephone jack by mistake. She was moving her hand to the button when a voice called from outside her windows: 'Mrs Stone! Mrs Stone, are you there?'

She ran to the window and saw a big man in an

overcoat standing in the porch light. Her heart gave a massive leap but it was one of gratitude. She knew this man. She banged on the window and when Macrae looked up she shouted, 'I'm coming down.'

'Oh, thank God it's you!' she said when she let him in. 'I've been hearing noises and I thought – well, you know what I thought.'

'Sorry, that's my fault. I had a little walk around to see that everything was all right. You know the lock on your garage door is sticking? Have you any oil?'

'There's some in the kitchen.'

She gave him the oil and watched as he went down into the garage. Her BMW stood, dark and handsome in the bright light. She loved to drive it but had no desire to take it out at the moment.

Macrae came back. 'That's better. I've oiled the lock but the garage door creaks when you open it. The creak is good to have so I've left it.'

They went back into the house and Macrae said, 'Mrs Weston phoned you last night.'

'She wanted to give me the good news.'

'I'd asked her not to.'

'Yes, I know, she told me.'

'I had a reason. And I'm sorry to say the report wasn't true. Someone who recognized Underdown in Chelsea, or says he recognized him, phoned the police, but that's as far as it got. If it was him, he's long since gone.'

She felt a surge of terror. And yet, there had been

no feeling of safety even after Tammy's call. She fought the terror and the tears and after a moment she said, 'I don't think I really believed it. I never believe things that seem to go too well, that are solved too easily. I'm a pessimist. Tammy's an optimist.'

Macrae accepted a cup of coffee and they stood in the kitchen. It was now dark.

'Michael didn't believe it either.'

'What's he, optimist or pessimist?'

'I don't know. One thing one day, another the next.'

'I've just come from Mrs Weston. She told me he works very hard. Is that where he is today?'

'He's with a client, I suppose. He doesn't like talking about his work. I think he feels it might depress me, especially now.'

'Why's that?'

'Because of the people he works with.'

'Aye, I can understand that.'

'Mr Macrae, can I ask you something?'

'Of course.'

'What can I do?'

'Do?'

'What do other people do? There must be other people like me. People who are – I suppose you'd call us targets. What do they do in circumstances like this?'

'Just what you're doing, protecting yourself as far as possible. That's all you *can* do.'

Michael came back then and Macrae left soon afterwards.

She said, 'Michael, can't we get the police to put a guard on the house?'

'I've checked that. They won't. It's too expensive. It takes between ten and twenty officers to put a serious guard on someone if you take into account days off and weekends and shifts.'

'What about private guards?' she said.

'I checked that too. Darling, we can't afford it.'

It was then that she broke down. She had managed to control herself when Macrae was there. She had been almost calm. Now something snapped.

'You bastard!' she yelled. 'You penny-pinching bastard!'

Chapter Ten

Clack-clack . . . clack-clack . . .

The windscreen wipers kept up a continuous pattern that drilled into Jane's head. The snow was coming in sloppy wet flakes and melting the moment it hit the road. She was on a motorway, the M25, but exactly where, she wasn't certain. The only thing she was certain about was that here, in the car, on the snowy motorway, she was safe from Malcolm and safe from the terrors of the house in London.

Clack-clack . . . clack-clack . . .

She felt as wound up as a violin string. She hated having rows and hated herself for what she had said to Michael. She had gone to her study to sleep and he had said, 'That won't help,' but she had gone anyway. And then, of course, she had not been able to sleep and lying there in the narrow divan she had felt caged, almost claustrophobic. So she had reacted. If she had thought clearly she would have stayed but she was not thinking clearly and she had gone to the one thing that was her own: her car. She had braved the passage-ways and the garage stairs, she was so wound up she had hardly even noticed them.

She was reacting to the thought of closing her eyes. What she was terrified of, so deep down she hardly ever faced it, was going to sleep and opening her eyes and seeing Malcolm's face. Not the face that everyone knew, but the face she had seen when she had come out of the bedroom after Edward had been killed and the policemen were pinning him to the floor. That was the face she feared: red and contorted and murderous.

Seeing that face again had been her waking nightmare when she had gone to stay with her mother and step-father after the murder. And now it was back.

The driver of a huge truck behind her flashed its lights and blew on a hooter loud enough to be a foghorn and she realized she was travelling at thirty miles an hour in the inside lane on one of the most dangerous motorways in Britain.

She put her foot down and the BMW responded and soon the lights were lost in the snowflakes.

Clack-clack . . . clack-clack . . .

Malcolm's ordinary face, the face that everyone who knew him had seen, had conveyed nothing very much. It was just a big and sometimes gaunt face that matched his large body though that hadn't been gaunt. It was bulky and heavy. Not well shaped, but angular and bony, all the bones large and hard like cast-iron.

Clack-clack . . . clack-clack . . .

She had met him at one of the many student parties the first year she had been at Winchester. He had been living in the same flat as the host and someone, she thought now it had been Charlie Broadbent, had said, 'Where's Underdown? Isn't he coming?' A few of them had gone to his bedroom. She had heard them arguing with him and finally he had allowed himself to be brought into the room. 'Allowed', she thought, was the right word because he was so big he might have made his decision to stay away and no one would have been able to do anything about it.

For the first few minutes his size and unfamiliarity had made him a figure of some interest but when he did not return the interest, attention on him dropped and he sat by himself on one side of the room holding a glass of cheap wine. She had gone over and talked to him. It had been hard going. He had little small-talk, so she channelled the conversation to what they were studying and what they hoped for the future. He had no real idea what he wanted to do after leaving university and she got the impression that he was only there because he could not think of anything else to do.

'I wanted to be a vet,' he had said. 'Something to do with animals, but I never got the grades.'

Clack-clack . . . clack-clack . . .

The snow seemed heavier than before. She must watch for an exit sign.

That first meeting with Malcolm might have been the last. She had almost no memory of him the following day. It had been Charlie who had caught her eye, but Charlie already had a girlfriend.

So it was with some surprise that when she got back to her own flat the following evening there was a note from Malcolm asking her to have a drink and saying he would come round about eight-thirty.

He had no car and nor had she, so they could not go to any of the student pubs in the outlying villages. Instead they went to the Wykeham Arms and sat in one of the old school desks with which the pub was partly furnished. Talking was just as difficult as it had been at the party. But, as though anticipating this, he had bought a chameleon which he called Speedy and he let it walk slowly up and down his hands and arms. Jane had taken it for a moment, and felt its sharp little feet dig into her skin.

He would stroke it with his finger and talk to it and it would roll its big round eyes. He had bought it, he said, at a pet shop. It came from Africa. He obviously loved it and its presence helped to break up the longish silences.

The next time they met was two days later. Again he wrote a formal note asking her to go out and he took her for a meal at an Italian restaurant. They talked books. He was reading Salinger's *Catcher in the Rye* for the third time.

She asked about Speedy, the chameleon. He said it was dead. She waited for him to express some note of loss or sadness, but he seemed to be indifferent.

Clack-clack . . . clack-clack . . .

She saw an exit sign come up indicating Guildford, and took it. The car clock was showing 4.40 a.m. and the snow was still drifting down. Tiredness was creeping over her. The road was deserted, her speed dropped and she coasted along in the warm and dimly lit world of her own.

But memories of her past association with Malcolm kept intruding. She remembered how, after the Italian meal, she had seen him two or three more times, just for a drink in a pub. Then he had taken her to a rock concert on campus and walked her home afterwards. He had been tense, almost as though he had been wound up by the music.

Her flatmates were away for the weekend and she invited him in for coffee. Even when she did so she knew what might happen but she told herself that she cared for him, that in a way he was like some great lost sheep and that going to bed with her might help him.

That was the rationalization but there was also the plain and simple fact of her new-found sexuality. There was a kind of possessiveness about Malcolm that was a little frightening as well as exciting. So when he had asked her – and there was a faint

Victorian echo in the question – whether he could kiss her, she had let him take her in his arms. She would never forget the sweaty, fumbling act that followed. What she did not know until later, though she might have guessed, was that it was his first time.

It was the beginning of a nightmare. The following day he was waiting outside her lecture theatre wanting to lunch with her in the cafeteria. And then, at the end of the day, he came to her flat. After that the same thing happened every day. There were no notes now. An assumption had been made by him that the time for such formality was over. That she was his.

Possession had become obsession.

Clack-clack . . . clack-clack . . .

The road began to rise steeply and she realized she was on the Guildford by-pass. She kept going.

The months that had followed her first sexual encounter with Malcolm were, she thought, the strangest in her life. Although she lived with three other girls in a flat near the campus, she hardly saw them. Malcolm occupied all her time. In a way it was flattering, in another it was scary.

He had moved out of his shared flat and taken a large room on the hill overlooking the town and wanted her to share it with him. It contained a bed, a table, a chair, a wardrobe, a chest of drawers and a wash-basin. That was all. It was like a monk's cell in one of the more austere orders and she knew that nothing on God's earth would cause her to give up a pleasant, sunny flat and go and live there.

At the beginning there had been, she thought, a certain style in their relationship: Malcolm so big, Jane so small and slender. And there had been the challenge of his introversion and loneliness.

But all this began to get her down. His size and strength became less of an artistic juxtaposition and more of a danger; his introversion did not diminish, for often he would take her to a pub and sit for half an hour or more without speaking. It was only after he had drunk several pints of beer that he seemed to find the words. As for his loneliness – well, he wasn't lonely any longer because he was always with her.

Her friends began to avoid her. If they made arrangements for her to go anywhere it meant they had to accept Malcolm as well, and they didn't much care for that.

She tried to go out without him, but it didn't take her long to realize that he would not allow this. Once she put him off when she and her flatmates were going up to London for the day. He arrived at the station five minutes before the train left and walked with them along the King's Road and Oxford Street as they shopped. He hardly spoke but stayed by Jane's side until she could have screamed.

That was the last time she was invited to go anywhere by her friends and it was also the moment she knew that she had to end the affair.

There was another reason. Charlie Broadbent had broken up with his girl and was showing unmistakable signs of wanting Jane.

She had been conscious that breaking with Malcolm was not going to be easy, and planned it carefully. Fortunately it was in the summer term with exams on the horizon. She told him she could not see him for a time because she had to work. He said they would work together. She said she couldn't do that.

He said they had to.

Had to?

How were they going to live together for the rest of their lives, he said, if they couldn't do a little work together now?

There it was, a threat that grew in intensity until it expanded in her head like a balloon. He was a judge and this was his sentence: you are to have me for the rest of your life.

She began a rearguard action, helped by her flatmates. When Malcolm came to the door they said she was out. No, they didn't know where. Studying in the library, or shopping, or in London... anywhere...

During this time she was mostly at Charlie Broadbent's flat. Sometimes she spent two or three days at a time there, never going to a pub in case she met Malcolm.

'We can't got on like this,' Charlie had said.

'I'm scared of him.'

'What the hell can he do?'

What he'd done was put a snake in Charlie's car, a short, fat, poisonous snake. No one could prove it, but they were all pretty sure he was responsible. Luckily it had been on the back seat, curled up in a ball when Charlie had opened the car door and it had hissed at him like air coming out of a tyre. He'd managed to pull it out with a golf club and beat it to death.

It was then that Malcolm started following them. Wherever they went, to a pub, to a disco, to London, they would find him somewhere near.

Jane became more nervous and Charlie angry. After a few weeks he told Malcolm that if he didn't stop he would call the police. Malcolm attacked him.

She wasn't there at the time but was told that the attack had been violent. Charlie had suffered concussion and a broken collar-bone and was away from college for nearly a month.

Jane had been called to the Dean's office. She had told him what she knew and there had been witnesses to the assault. By the time Charlie returned, Malcolm had been sent down.

Soon after that, Malcolm had come to her flat and told her he had to leave the university and wanted her to come with him, they would live at his place. Fortunately her flatmates had been there at the time. She had said she wouldn't speak to him after what had happened to Charlie and had gone to her room. One of the other girls had told him she was ill from worry and he didn't want to be responsible for that, did he?

He had gone away and she hadn't seen him again for a long time. She had left college and was working in London. She and Charlie Broadbent had split up and she had met Edward Craig when she had seen Malcolm one day, waiting outside her office.

Now, as she drove past Guildford at five o'clock in the morning, she thought that if he could find her once, why could he not find her again?

Here on the high ground the snow was worse and she began to drive erratically. There were few other cars on the road but each time one came into view to pass her going the other way she braked and felt the tyres skid on the wet snow. She knew she had to stop. A lay-by came up on her right and she pulled across the road and parked. She wasn't sure where she was but she knew she could not go on. There was a rug on the back seat and she pulled it round her. She was overwhelmed by tiredness and put her head back against the head restraint. In a moment she was asleep.

She slept for three hours, a restless, dream-filled sleep that had her twisting and turning, her hands gripping the rug as though it was a lifeline.

In the grey, snowy dawn, she woke. She had turned partly on her side and her face was only inches from the window. A split second before she opened her eyes, something in her brain seemed to warn her what was about to happen.

And there it was. At the window.

She screamed and held up her hands as though to guard herself from the red, twisted face which stared in at her. It was split by a rictus grin, a great bush of grey hair, and its eyes were shadowed and far back.

She screamed again.

Hands came up against the window as though feeling for entry, the palms pressed against the glass becoming bloodless. She thought she heard manic laughter coming from the widely smiling mouth.

The hands were out of proportion to the face and at last she saw them for what they were: a child's hands. The face was a mask. She heard the kid laugh in delight at her fright, then run to a second car in the lay-by. In a few moments it was driven off down the snowy road.

She was left shivering and shattered. The snow had stopped and she could look out over the surrounding countryside which was brilliantly covered in white.

She knew she was near Guildford. Charlie Broadbent lived there. He would understand how she was feeling, in fact he was the only person she could think of who might understand. She turned the car and drove back along the road. The car clock was showing 7.45 and the light was strengthening. She felt dreadful. She saw the sign which said 'Town

Centre' and took it. But it was the beginning of the rush hour and the streets were choked.

She turned off the major traffic artery and found herself in a maze of tree-lined streets. This was the side of town where Charlie lived. He was married now and she had been to his house several times over the past few years, first to his wedding reception, and later she and Michael had been there several times to dinner. She drove slowly through the streets until she reached the house.

It was double-storeyed, built in the thirties, with a small garden and white-painted walls. She stopped the car outside it, recognizing a magnolia tree in the garden.

She went to the door. After a few minutes a woman came. She was in her dressing-gown and had a small child in her arms. The child seemed to be balancing on the heavy bulge of its mother's pregnant belly.

'Yes?'

'Deborah, it's me. Jane Stone.'

'Jane Stone? Oh, my God. Jane! What's wrong? What is it?'

'Can I come in for a moment?'

Deborah paused and then said, 'Charlie's getting dressed.'

The child, whose name Jane could not remember but to whose christening she had sent a present, was holding a spoon in its hand.

'Please,' she said.

'Oh, of course. You'll have to excuse us and—'

A male voice called, 'Who is it?'

Deborah turned to the staircase and called, 'It's Jane Stone, Charlie.'

'Jane Stone?' He came down the stairs, knotting a tie. 'Jane, hi! What's happened?'

He clattered down the remaining stairs and kissed her on the cheek. 'My God, what a morning.'

Deborah was watching her with enquiring and, she thought, cold eyes. At any other time Jane would have sympathized with her but now she was too bound up in her own fears and unhappiness.

'Charlie, Malcolm's out.'

'I read that.'

'He's trying to find me.'

'Let's go into the sitting-room. What about some coffee?'

'Oh, yes, please. I've been driving half the night.'

'I'll get it,' Deborah said. She handed the child to Charlie.

Jane told him what had been happening. She sat on the edge of a chair and nervous tremors ran up and down her body.

He listened with growing concern. 'A woman in your old flat? Killed her?'

'He must have gone there looking for me and when I wasn't there he asked her where I was and when she didn't know he killed her.'

'Jesus! Listen, does Michael know you're here? Why don't you phone him? He must be worried stiff.'

She thought of the questions Michael would ask and the explanations she would not be able to give and said, 'Charlie, could you?'

'Sure. Give me the number.'

He was back in a few moments. 'There's no reply but I left a message on the answering machine.'

Deborah came in with the coffee. Charlie looked at his watch and said, 'I'll eat and talk.'

He fetched a plate of cereal and came back. Haltingly, Jane filled him in on everything she knew. As she talked, she began to feel less tense and absorbed her surroundings. The house was untidy in the way that houses containing tiny children whose fathers are in a hurry to leave for work, are untidy. Deborah had been without make-up when she came to the door. Now there was a slash of red across her lips. Jane felt for her.

When Jane had finished her story, Charlie said, 'My God, you were lucky not to have had a crash last night. Look, you're here now and you can catch your breath. My problem is that I've got to get to work and—'

'Of course,' Jane said. 'I'm all right now.'

Charlie said, 'The roads should be all right in a little while. The sun's coming up.'

Deborah said, 'Let me get you something to eat.'

'No, no, I'm fine.' She went to the window and looked out at the road. 'The snow's not as thick as it was.'

Then she screamed.

'What? What?' Charlie said, put down his plate and joined her.

She pointed towards the road. 'There he is! Oh, God, look, there he is!'

'There's who?'

'It's him. Can't you see?'

There was a figure out in the street. A big man in a heavy raincoat. It was an old coat and small for him, hanging only half way down his thighs.

'Malcolm Underdown?' Charlie said.

'Yes. Malcolm.' She said it as softly as though the man in the street might hear her.

'You sure?'

'Of course I am! Don't you see, Charlie, he's come to your house just like he went to the flat in London.'

'A bit coincidental, isn't it?' Deborah said, shifting Mark to her other thigh.

'These things happen! What's he doing now?'

The man was walking slowly along the road and disappeared behind the magnolia tree.

'Can't see,' Charlie said.

'There he is again! Charlie, phone the police.'

'Hang on, hang on. Look, he's . . . oh, Christ, I know what he's doing.' Charlie went to the front door and opened it. 'Leave it alone,' he shouted.

The tramp, who had opened the rubbish-bin which was waiting on the pavement to be emptied, looked up. He was certainly a big man, but also a very hairy man and his hair was grey. He raised a hand in acknowledgement and went to the rubbish-bin of the next house.

Jane had watched the scene unfold with fear and foreboding and then embarrassment.

'I'm sorry, Charlie,' she said when he came back. 'But it could have been.'

'Sure. It could have been.' He looked at his watch again. 'I've got to be getting on, Jane.'

'Of course. Sorry. Yes, you go. I'll be on my way.'

'Stay as long as you like. Deborah will be here.'

She sensed hostility in the very way Deborah was standing and said, 'No, no, I'll be getting back.'

Chapter Eleven

The sign at the gate said 'Donna's Place'. Leo drove in and stopped. Macrae said, 'Christ, what a bloody name to call a house.'

'Better than "Mon Repos",' Leo said.

It was the first time they had spoken for nearly an hour. They had come down from London that morning and Macrae had spent most of the drive reading the *Daily Telegraph*. It was just past eleven o'clock and they were in the Meon Valley, on the northern side of the South Downs in Hampshire.

'What did you say her name was?' Macrae said.

'Stokes. That's from her second husband. The farmer.'

'Her first was in the navy, wasn't he? What's happened to him?'

'They're both dead. The first of a heart-attack on a squash court, the second of drink.'

'That's what my mother used to call it in Scotland. Not alcoholism. "The drink".'

The two detectives went to the front door. The house had once been a barn and was now decked out with white walls and fake black beams to give it a sixteenth-century-with-television look, for the thatched roof sprouted a TV aerial and a satellite dish. Outside was parked a pink and gold Ford Capri dating from the 1960s. The car and the house were making statements which Macrae did not much care for. And Leo expected worse to come, for when he had telephoned Mrs Stokes she had sounded less than willing to see them and he had threatened to bring her to London with a police escort. He had not been certain whether this was a legal threat. But he had been working long enough with Macrae so that legality was beginning to shade into something amorphous which might instead be called opportunism or pragmatism or just plain cunning.

The woman who opened the door was wearing leggings, a bright red top, a mass of bangles and heavy necklaces and hair that was streaked with henna. She was lamp-tanned and heavily made-up, with what must once have been an attractive broad face. She was bare-footed and Leo thought her feet were really not bad for a woman of sixty-four.

'Hello, boys,' she said. 'Welcome to Donna's Place.'

She led them into a room which had a thick gold carpet and steel and glass furniture. In one corner was a small bar. There were several wooden panels with pokerwork lettering, one which read, 'If you can't be good – great!'

She stubbed out her cigarette in a large brass

ashtray and said, 'Sun's over the yard-arm, what's your fancy?'

Leo waited for Macrae but the big man shook his head and, to Leo's surprise, said, 'Nothing, thank you.'

'You're not going to give me that I-don't-drink-on-duty-stuff, are you?'

'Mrs Donna Stokes?' Macrae's voice came straight out of the Cairngorm Mountains in winter.

She ignored him, which gave Leo pause. He had seen other people try this ploy only to end up wishing they hadn't. Hastily he said, 'I'll have juice of some kind if you have any.'

'Gin juice? Vodka juice? I've—'

'Just anything soft.'

'Jesus,' she said. 'The police have changed. Well, I mean, haven't they?'

She picked up a glass already full of some sort of alcoholic juice and drank. Then she put tomato juice in a glass, mixed in Worcestershire sauce and tabasco and gave it to Leo.

Macrae watched with mounting impatience. 'You know why we've come?'

'Of course I know why you've come. Someone told me on the phone.'

'That was me,' Leo said.

'But I'd have known anyway. Half of my life has been made up of people coming to me about Malcolm. They came when he was a child. Teachers came from school because of his behaviour.

153

Parents came because he was threatening their kids or they said he was. They came from university, they came from the police, from the social services, from God knows who else.'

'And what did you say when they came to see you?' Macrae said.

'What do you mean, what did I say? I said whatever I had to say. Like go and take a running jump at yourself. That's what I said.'

'What I mean is, did you take advice from anyone?'

She splashed more vodka into her drink and said, 'Listen, what have you come to ask? I said to him . . .' She pointed at Leo. '. . . that I didn't want to see anyone and he threatened to have me brought to London by force.'

'No, I never said force,' Leo said quickly.

She waved a beringed hand. 'So I said to myself, don't mix it with the cops. Calm it. So I calmed it. Now you ask what isn't your business, but still I say, Donna, calm it. OK?'

'Have you seen him?'

'No, I haven't. I never went to see him at Loxton and I never went to that Rakesbury place in South-ampton and I never went near the hostel. No, I have not seen him. I do not want to see him. He's made a complete botch of my life if you must know.'

'Can we just touch on that for a second?' Leo said. 'You were an air stewardess, weren't you?'

'I was an *air hostess*. That's what we were called

then. Not like today. These are just waitresses. We were models and we looked like models. My God, it wasn't like it is now. Then we carried a few gracious people. Now it's bloody great jumbos with hundreds of lager louts. In my day there were no crowds fighting for luggage or queueing up at the loos. I flew in Comets from London to Johannesburg, London to Singapore, London to Sydney. Now the waitresses think they're great if they go to bloody Glasgow.'

'Could we . . .?'

But she was not to be deterred. 'We'd get into Jo'burg on a Friday morning and wouldn't have to come back until the Tuesday and we'd go to the Kruger game park or down to the beach at Durban and mostly we'd go with the flight crew but if not there were enough men to fill in any gaps. Now you talk to the crew and they've all got mortgages and are insomniacs and worried stiff about losing their jobs and—'

'What was your son doing when you were on the beach with the flight captain?' Macrae said.

'What was that?'

'You were in Singapore or Sydney and Malcolm was in England and your first husband was at sea a lot of the time.'

'Well?'

'So who was looking after Malcolm? He wasn't old enough to look after himself, was he?'

'My mother, who's now dead, if it's got anything to do with you.'

'Oh, yes, Mrs Stokes, it's got a lot to do with us. You see, he's moving again and killing again – at least, we think he is and—'

'Yes, but you don't know, do you? I mean he—' She pointed at Leo. 'He told me you weren't positive.'

'That's only our way of saying we're sure,' Macrae said. 'So tell us about him when he was little. He went to stay with his grandmother. Where did she live?'

'In Winchester, near her church.'

'You mean the cathedral?'

'No, not the cathedral, the Church of the Citadel. She was a religious nut. She was translating the Bible into Amharic and —'

'But that's an Ethiopian language,' Leo said.

'I wouldn't know.'

'So when he was a little boy he stayed with her most of the time. What about when he was older?'

'By then I'd been divorced . . . you sure you're allowed to ask me questions like this?'

'Quite sure,' Macrae said.

'Well, I'm going to have another drink. Might as well be pissed as not.' She looked at the staircase and shouted, 'Kev!'

A voice said, 'What?'

'You awake?'

'Yeah.' It came out thick and slow.

'You want a drinkie-pooh?'

'No.'

'You sure?'

'Yeah.'

She turned to the two detectives. 'Kevin's my . . . lodger,' she said.

'Can we get back to your son?' Macrae emphasized the word 'son'. He was looking dark and angry.

'Go on then.' She had drunk enough to be impervious to gibes.

'You were still an air stewardess when—'

'Hostess, you bastard. *Hostess.*'

'Aye, all right, Mrs Stokes. Hostess. You were still a hostess when you married Mr Stokes, and Underdown was still a little lad, so who looked after him then?'

'He had a step-father, didn't he?'

'Did he get on with him?'

There was a pause and Leo saw for the first time some confused emotion on her face. 'Well . . .'

'Did he?' Macrae pressed.

'No, not really.'

'What's that supposed to mean?'

'Harold was the kind of person who had lived alone a lot of his life and he wasn't used to sprogs. He never had any. So it wasn't easy for him.'

'It wasn't easy for your son either, was it?' Leo said.

When she didn't answer immediately Macrae said, 'Was it?'

'How do I know?' She put one hand on her hip and said defiantly, 'You don't always have things your own way, you know.'

Macrae ignored that and said, 'What happened between them?'

The defiance evaporated as quickly as it had come. 'Well, he used to hit him. Not hard, no, no, never hard but . . . but I didn't like that. Not hitting him. My parents never hit me. I said don't hit the boy and he used to say you have to teach them now. He said they were like sheep-dogs. You had to teach them who was boss or they gave trouble later.'

'Where did he hit him?' Macrae said.

'He made him take down his trousers and his underpants and he'd give it to him on his bare bottom. I said I didn't like it but he'd get angry, so what was I to do?' She lit another cigarette and drew heavily on it.

Macrae said, 'Did he cry?'

'I never saw him cry. I don't think Harold liked that. I think he wanted to be the boss like he said and he wanted to punish Malcolm and if you punish a child for doing something wrong and he doesn't cry or look like he's been punished, then it aggravates you.'

'And Malcolm didn't look like he was being punished?' Leo said.

'I'm sure Harold didn't think so and Malcolm used to have his bottom smacked quite often.'

'Smacked?' Macrae said. 'With his hand?'

'Oh, yes, always with his hand. Harold said he didn't want to use a stick. He said the hand was better.'

'So what did your son do?' Leo said.

'He'd go out into the fields.'

'And?'

'Play with the animals.'

'What sort of animals?'

'Christ, I dunno. Any sort.'

'We believe he knew about snakes,' Macrae said.

'Oh, yeah, about snakes all right. He brought one into the house once. Kept it in his bed. Said it wasn't a snake but a slow-worm and I said it's a snake and get it out of here and Harold got very cross and smacked him in the mouth.'

'Tell me,' Leo said, 'didn't he have any companions? Other children to play with?'

'I didn't like him playing with the farm workers' kids.'

'Weren't there any others?'

'You mean school kids? Who'd want to play with Malcolm?'

'No one?' Macrae said.

'They were all scared of him.'

'We've heard he was a gentle person most of the time,' Leo said.

She laughed grimly. 'But not all the time.'

There was a noise above them, then a man showed himself at the top of the stairs. He was only half-dressed in a shirt and socks. He had short black hair cut *en brosse* and a small ring in one side of his nose.

'You seen my trousers?' he said in a thick Hampshire accent.

'In the bathroom. Where you left them.' She turned back to Macrae and Silver. 'I have to go.' She rose and teetered on her bare feet and then said, 'You think you can find Malcolm?'

'We'll find him,' Macrae said.

'Well, for Christ's sake put him away somewhere safe this time.'

Jane heard the Porsche and waited for Michael to come up the stairs from the garage. 'Oh, God, Michael, I'm sorry. I was so stupid! So selfish!'

He held her in his arms. 'I'm sorry, too. It's just that—' He raised his hands in mute explanation.

'Going off like that in the car! It was unforgivable of me. And I made such a bloody nuisance of myself to the Broadbents!'

'Listen, it's natural! You're worried sick – and so am I. Not so much about Underdown because he doesn't know where we live and—'

'Yes, but he can find out.'

'I know, darling, but it takes time and time is on our side. Every policeman in London is looking for him and they all have contacts in the underworld and those contacts have contacts, so you see, hundreds of people – if not thousands – are all looking for Underdown.'

She turned away from him and caught sight of

her face in one of the mirrors in the hall. It was ravaged by worry and tears and she knew she looked years older.

There had not been snow in London, but it had started to rain and the house had been empty when she reached home. Michael had been out scouring the streets for her. But now he was back and for that she thanked God.

He touched her face and said, 'You OK now?'

'Yes, I'm OK now.'

'Because I have to get moving.'

'I'll be fine.'

And she was fine most of the day. But then the dark had come and with it her fear.

Michael was home early. 'They don't want me until tomorrow,' he said. 'You still OK?'

'I'm always OK when you're here. I'll get you a glass of fizz.' She wanted to be doing something for him.

'Any post?'

'Just bills. They're on your desk.'

He went into his study and closed the door. She got a bottle of Krug from the fridge and struggled with the cork but could not get it out and took it to him. He was bending down, putting papers away. She held his head against her stomach and said, 'I love you, Michael.'

'And I adore you.' He rose and took the bottle from her. 'That looks pretty good. Did Tammy come today?'

'She had to go and see her mother. She's ill.'

'Darling, it won't be for much longer.' They sipped the champagne and then he said, 'I'll go for a shower.'

She went back to the drawing-room. This was where he had hung the two Schiele drawings. They weren't there any longer. Not that she minded. She didn't like Schiele. But they'd disappeared one day and when she had mentioned it to him he'd said he'd got bored with them.

That was what made him so fascinating – the unpredictability.

There had been the racing, for instance. She'd never known he was a keen follower of the turf. And then suddenly he was and they were going to the races all the time.

Then suddenly he wasn't.

There were the business deals when there were often men in the house having drinks and dinner and then moving into his study and talking for hours.

Then they didn't come any more.

And they had gone to Europe for weekends.

And then they hadn't.

So even the unpredictability had become unpredictable.

She heard him coming down the stairs and handed him the glass of champagne. He was looking tired, she thought. Well, he had every right to be, the way he worked.

"There's something I have to tell you which you

won't like,' he said. 'And I know it's a bloody awful time for you, but I'm going to have to go away for a few days.'

'Oh, Michael!'

He saw the fear come back into her eyes.

'I know . . . I know . . .' He took her hand. 'I have a case at the Crown Court in Portsmouth. I'd give anything not to have to go but a man's future may depend on it.'

'Oh, God!'

'You know how I feel. But anyway, they might have caught Underdown by now.'

'They'd have told us if they had. You'll get back in the evening, won't you? It's only a couple of hours in the car.'

'The problem is, it's a complicated case and there's bound to be night work involved. I'd be an absolute wreck giving expert evidence if I was racing back and forth morning and night. You see that, don't you?'

'I could come and stay in a hotel in Portsmouth.'

'That way lie problems. What if they take ages to find Underdown? Would you want to go to a hotel whenever I was away?'

'There must be some other way. I know! I could stay with Tammy.'

'Why not give her a call?'

'I'll call her now.'

She came back a few minutes later and said, 'Only the bloody answering machine. What if she can't have me, Michael? What if she has to go and stay with her mother?'

'Well, I won't be away for long. They don't think the case will last for more than a week. Two weeks at the most.'

'But you just said a few days!'

'I'm giving you the worst scenario.'

'God, two weeks!'

'It won't be. You can bet on that.'

'I don't know . . . wait . . . I've got an idea. What about me going down to Highlands? That's near Portsmouth. You could come home every night and I could cook a proper meal for you, not just smoked salmon and brown bread. That'd be terrific! You see, it would be all right if I knew you were coming home. It's the thought of spending the nights by myself I don't like. Even at Tammy's I might have to do that and who knows, Malcolm might have found out where she lives. Don't forget he knew her.'

'Are you sure he doesn't know about your mother's house?'

'Absolutely. I never invited him there. Never mentioned it as far as I know. The phone was in my step-father's name so my name wouldn't even be in the book for him to discover.'

'Let's think about it. Let me make some calls in the morning and see what this bloody case really involves.'

She put her arms around his neck. 'Please, Michael, please!'

Chapter Twelve

REPORT 6/MSU/SM

Second interview. With consent.

Following is a tape-recorded interview between Dr
Sidney Michaelson, Consultant Psychiatrist, Loxton
Special Hospital, and Malcolm Stephen Underdown.

The tape begins:

Dr Michaelson: Hello, Malcolm, nice to see you, are
you over your sinusitis? Good, good, it can be very
painful. I believe you had a letter from your solicitors?
Malcolm?
Underdown: Yeah.
Dr M: You feeling all right?
U: I told you last time I didn't want that stuff any
more. It's like walking in mud. I mean, I'm out of
focus.
Dr M: Yes, well, we'll reduce the dose as you get a
little better. You saw that letter from your solicitors?
U: Yeah.
Dr M: You see, Malcolm, in the circumstances of your
trial . . . you pleaded guilty to manslaughter, don't

forget, and in those circumstances there is no appeal.
(*Noise on tape.*) What? Listen, get it out of your
system. Say anything you like. OK? When you're ready
I'd like to ask you a few more questions about your
life, but if you don't want to answer them now we can
make it another time. We've got lots of time and you
know what they say about time?

U: What?

Dr M: It's a great healer.

U: I don't want to stay here.

Dr M: I don't think anyone wants to stay here but
you'll soon get used to Loxton and I hope you'll begin
to realize that what we do here we do for you. Being
here isn't a punishment, if that's what's worrying you.
You're not being punished for anything at all. You were
sick at the time. Technically, mentally disordered.
What we're trying to do is heal those wounds in your
brain which caused this in the first place. OK? So let's
get going. Ready?

U: Yeah, I suppose so.

Dr M: Right. The last time we spoke we talked about
your school days. How did you get on in sport at
school, Malcolm?

U: Didn't play any.

Dr M: Nothing? Didn't they make you play?

U: They made us do aerobics. They said we didn't
have to play games.

Dr M: Didn't you want to play games?

U: No.

Dr M: I would have thought that someone with your
physique would have done well in almost anything.

U: They didn't want me.

Dr M: Who didn't want you?

U: The other boys. They said I was too big.

Dr M: I can understand that, I suppose. You were pretty big even as a young lad, weren't you?

U: Yeah.

Dr M: OK, we'll leave sport. Academically you were quite bright but the reports I've seen said you were . . . they usually say lazy, but yours didn't. They used words like 'not motivated' and 'uninterested'. Didn't you like any of your school work?

U: I quite liked history.

Dr M: What history?

U: We learned about the French Revolution.

Dr M: Yes, that's fascinating. What did you like?

U: Not the blood and guillotine, if that's what you thought.

Dr M: What then?

U: I liked the idea of the aristos getting (*Blurring on tape.*)

Dr M: Sorry, I didn't catch that. Are you feeling OK?

U: It's that fucking stuff.

Dr M: Oh. OK, don't worry about it. What was it about the aristocrats?

U: What do you think? They got their heads taken off. That was good, wasn't it?

Dr M: Depends if you were an aristocrat, I suppose. Anything else?

U: A bit of English. I liked some of the books.

Dr M: Any in particular?

U: *The Catcher in the Rye.*

Dr M: I liked that too. Any others?

U: Can't remember.

Dr M: Try.

U: Well . . . later on I liked *Gormenghast* and the other *Titus* books.

Dr M: The Mervyn Peake gothic stories. How would you describe them, Malcolm?

U: Don't know. Strange.

Dr M: So would I. Did you have any friends at school?

U: You asked me that last time.

Dr M: Yes, I know. You see, I read a report from the educational psychologist who says he thought you were a loner. He says, and I've got it here, that you were, and I quote, 'hard hit by adolescence'. He was a bit worried about you.

U: He was right then, wasn't he?

Dr M: He says you made no efforts to make friends.

U: Christ, I'm sick of this.

Dr M: All right, let's go on to something else. Your step-father.

U: Oh, Jesus.

Dr M: I think I know how you feel but I've got to ask you about him. First, do you remember your real father?

U: He was at sea most of the time.

Dr M: He must have come home on leave sometimes.

U: He and my mother used to go on holidays. I think her working for BOAC meant they got cheap tickets.

Dr M: And they didn't take you?

U: I suppose they wanted to be together.

Dr M: After the divorce, did you see much of him?

U: Not much. Then he dropped dead playing squash.

Dr M: The last time we spoke you told me much the same things about your step-father. You said he always

just wanted to be with your mother and would send
you out. You remember that?

U: Vaguely.

Dr M: You never really got on with him, did you?

U: No.

Dr M: And I see from one of the reports that you
were the only one in the house with him when he
died. How was that?

U: My mother was away in some bloody place.

Dr M: So what happened?

U: He got pissed as usual.

Dr M: When was this?

U: I dunno, evening I think.

Dr M: And?

U: I told you. He got pissed. And then he went to
sleep in his chair and then he started choking. And then
he died.

Dr M: What did you do?

(*Indecipherable sounds on tape.*)

Dr M: Don't you like to talk about it?

U: No.

Dr M: I'd very much like to, you know. I'd like to
spend a bit more time on this. I'd like us just to talk
through it. What do you say, Malcolm?

(*Indecipherable sounds on tape.*)

Dr M: Poor old chap. Let them come. I've been rather
hoping you would. Crying's normal and that's a big
word here. I'll tell you what . . . Let's call a halt now
but what I would really like you to do if you can is
write it down. Everything that you can remember about
his death. I know you're not crying for him, Malcolm,
so I don't think that'll be a problem, but it is pretty
nasty for a young lad to be present at something like

that. It'll get it off your chest anyway and allow you to
vent any feelings you may have. What do you say?
Will you do it for me? Is that a nod? Well, that's great,
so let's end it now for the time being.

Tape session ends.

Note by SM
This man is now less well defended. I think it would be
therapeutic for him to write rather than talk.

Macrae closed Wilson's door and said, 'I got him!'

Wilson looked up from the folder he was reading.
'Got who, George?'

'That bastard Scales.'

Wilson looked past Macrae to make sure the door
was closed and said, 'How was that?'

'He called me in, wanted to talk about the Underdown thing.'

'The shit's landing on him.'

'Aye, that's what I'm on about. And when the shit
lands on him he always comes to us, isn't that the
case?'

Wilson nodded and Macrae said, 'Well, I was
ready for him. I knew what he wanted to see me
about, bloody obvious, isn't it? So when I went in I
said, "I've been thinking, sir," – really gave the "sir"
a bit of a push – and he looked up and started
scratching his bloody bald head and I said, "About
being a beat copper again." I said I thought it was

an excellent idea and when did I start? I was ready
any time, the sooner the better.'

'Oh, Christ, you didn't!'

'And he looked as though I'd taken his sandwiches away from him – you know his mother
makes him peanut butter and jam? Well, she does –
and he said, "Hang on a minute, George" – and I
always know when he calls me George he wants
something. So we started on the Underdown case
and I said I didn't think we'd lay a finger on him
because he was too bloody smart and I thought he
had a bloody good chance of getting the woman in
north London, Jane Stone. He went quite pale and
you could see the brass had been on to him asking
what the hell he thought he was playing at not getting Underdown.'

'So?'

'So there's going to be no beat for me, that's for
sure. Practically begged on his knees for me to go
out and bring Underdown in and I said I would if
there were no more bloody balls-ups like the Chelsea
library.'

Macrae was smiling as he finished speaking.

Wilson said, 'I wouldn't feel too pleased with
myself if I were you, George.'

'What's that?'

'Several things. While you're having your fun and
getting your political end off with Scales, this bugger
Underdown is running about and nobody knows

where. And I hope you didn't mean that about Jane Stone.'

'What do you think . . .' And then Macrae caught himself. A picture of his daughter's face formed in his mind. 'Aaah, Les, I didn't mean it that way. I'm not tempting fate. No, no.'

'Well, what way did you mean it?'

'Och, it was only a wee pin to prick Scales with. So dinna fash yersel', as my mother would have said.'

But it wasn't said with his usual abrasiveness and they both knew it. To cover their embarrassment Wilson said, 'What's new?'

'On Underdown? Nothing that I know of. He might have been in the library and he might not. Nobody knows. He might not even have been in London. He might not even have killed that woman and stuffed her into the cupboard.'

'Hard to think of a big sod like that going missing, but they do.'

There was a knock on Wilson's door and the desk sergeant put his head round. 'Call for you, George.'

'Right. I'll take it in my office. See you later, Les.'

A woman's voice said, 'Is that Inspector Macrae?'

'No, it is not Inspector Macrae, it is Superintendent Macrae.'

'Oh, I'm sorry. It's Tamara.'

'Who?'

'Tammy'

'Oh, yes, sorry. Of course. How are you?'

'Listen, I'm in town and I wondered if we might have a drink?'

'A drink?'

'You sound as if it's an unfamiliar concept.'

He heard her laugh. It was a throaty, loose laugh which spoke of whisky and cigarettes. Macrae's head was still filled with images of Scales, and Jane Stone, and Les Wilson, and pictures he had been looking at of Underdown and reports of sightings that hadn't been sightings. For a second he thought she was making fun of him and his voice was a growl. 'Look, I'm—'

'If you'd rather not, I understand. It was just that I thought we'd had a nice time and a drink was a nice thing to do when you'd had a nice time.'

'I'm up to my eyebrows—' Then the images of his colleagues were replaced by a naked image of Tammy and he thought: why not? 'What about a meal instead of a drink?'

'When?'

'Tonight? Tell me where you are and I'll pick you up and—'

'I'm like Malcolm. I'm a mover. Why don't I come down to the station? I know where it is.'

'Fine. In an hour? Do you like curry?'

'Yes, I do.'

'OK, I'll see you here.'

She was nearly three-quarters of an hour late. Macrae had decided to go home and was on his way out of Cannon Row when he saw her.

She was wearing a white mackintosh over black trousers and a white polo-neck and the desk sergeant was drooling over her.

Macrae was a punctual man. His job made him so. But he had always been, for his father had beaten punctuality into him. Non-punctuality was something of a crime to Macrae, like petty larceny: people were stealing time.

He waited, as he had often waited with Mandy or Frenchy, for Tammy to come up with a bromidic phrase. But she just said, 'Good evening, Superintendent. It is Superintendent, isn't it? That's what you said?'

Macrae glared at the desk sergeant and shepherded her out of the building to the car-park. He waited for the phrase but still it didn't come.

'Where are we going for the curry?'

'Battersea,' he said.

'That'll make a change.'

'I was just about to go home,' he said as they drove along the Embankment.

'Oh, was I late?'

He didn't reply.

'There's a phrase for what you've got,' she said. 'It's called the hump. Except we drop the "h". You've got the 'ump. Isn't that what the criminal classes say when they're about to do someone in? "You give me the 'ump, bang, bang!" '

Macrae pushed the old Rover along.

'What d'you want me to say? Sorry? All right. Sorry.'

They went to an old stamping ground of Macrae's, the Pukka Sahib, and Ganesh met them at the door.

'Good evening . . . good evening, Mr Macrae . . . good evening, madam . . . you like your usual table?'

There were several other tables full or booked, but Ganesh moved some reserved notices about and Macrae and Tammy were seated in the window.

'You're getting the treatment,' she said.

'I've known Ganesh for years.'

The menus and the wine list came and Macrae said, 'I usually have lager. What about you?'

'If I drink lager I have to keep going to have a pee. What about wine?'

'Liebfraumilch?'

She stared at him. 'Are you serious?'

'What then?'

She glanced at the wine list and said, 'You're not supposed to drink wine with curry, so they say, but if you don't drink lager, what the hell do you drink? What about a white rioja?'

The wine came and then Macrae ordered their food. She listened with interest.

'And Ganesh,' he said. 'Don't forget—'

'—the chilli sauce,' Ganesh finished for him.

Macrae said to Tammy, 'Ganesh says I'm in the curry cycle. Sooner or later I'm going to explode.'

He had ordered Madras lamb with stuffed

175

parathas and onion bajees. Ganesh also brought a little dish of chilli sauce which Macrae ladled on to his rice and meat. Tammy watched him and shook her head when he offered it to her.

She tasted hers and he said, 'All right?'

'Very good. But I'd like to make one for you one day. There are other ways of doing it with other flavours and spices which don't blow the top of your head off.'

'I like to sweat under the eyes.'

'So did Paul, my ex.'

'Has he been in touch again?'

'Who? Paul? Oh, yes, I told you he'd phoned, didn't I? No. Not again.'

She ate for a while in silence and then said, 'I assume that if you had any news of Malcolm you would have told me by now.'

'I might've. Depends what it was. But no, there's nothing. Except sightings, of course.'

'Where? When?'

'Don't get yourself excited. They've been as far apart as Yorkshire and Scotland. And a dozen in London itself. This always happens. Takes us a hell of a long time to sort out the totally impossible from the improbable and then look into those. You want some more lamb?'

'This is fine. So none of these sightings have been real?'

'Not as far as I know.'

'God, I wish they had been. I wish ... well, I

wish it was all over or had never happened in the first place. And that goes right back to university. I wish he'd never come.'

Macrae went on eating. He drank the white wine as though it was beer, in large mouthfuls, and then ordered another bottle.

'Don't you?' she said when he didn't comment.

'Don't I what?'

'Wish it had never happened.'

'I don't go in for the might-have-been routines.'

'No, I suppose the police don't. It's just that I feel so bloody sorry for Jane. And for Michael too, for that matter. It's so unfair. I mean, she had to put up with so much. Now I'm worried about her and he's worried about her. I had a call from him.'

'About Underdown?'

'About Jane. She's slipping back into what she was when he first met her. He says she's become depressed. And I can vouch for that.'

'The poor wee kid. I remember how it was the first time.'

'He calls it "spousal dependency".'

'Would you like some lychees to take the taste of the curry away?'

'Fine.'

He ordered and sat back. 'What's it supposed to mean?'

'He's asked me not to go round there. He says she's becoming too dependent on us all. Me in particular. You've heard of stories about people who won't go out of doors by themselves or cross roads or go into strange buildings . . . well, he's afraid she's getting into that. It means she won't do things without her spouse and a spouse doesn't have to be her husband. It can be a great friend who is always available.'

'You?'

'That's right, me. So he wants me to stay away for a bit and, my God, that takes some doing. She phones me and phones me and I have to make excuses. I've said my mother is ill. And I've told her I've got cooking orders to fill – that's a bloody lie as well. I hear her crying at the other end though she always denies it. It must be bloody awful for her.'

Macrae said, 'My mother was a bit like that.'

It seemed that he might stop there and she said, 'Oh?'

'We lived in Scotland. My father was a keeper on an estate. Towards the end of her life my mother didn't go out of the house much at all. We used to shop in Inverness on a Wednesday and that's the only time she went out. She went with my father because he expected her to and she was too bloody scared not to. The only time after that she went out by herself was the day she went down to the Findhorn River and threw herself in.'

'What a terrible story! I had no idea. I wouldn't have brought it up if I had.'

'I was minded of it when you spoke about Mrs Stone. Another drop?' He gave her the last of the wine then said, 'My house is just round the corner, would you like some coffee there? It's the one thing they can't make here.'

His house was dark and cold and smelly. He collected some of his clothes from the sitting-room floor, drew the curtains and switched on the lights and the gas fire. 'I'll get the coffee.'

He went into the kitchen and she followed him. 'Don't look at the mess,' he said.

She went out. He made two cups of instant coffee. In the doorway he said, 'Here, or in the bedroom?'

Her face had changed. It no longer wore the amused, slightly cynical expression he had seen earlier. Now the corners of her mouth were down. She said, 'Here, please.'

He raised his eyebrows and handed her the mug.

She said, 'I know what you're thinking, but there's another reason I phoned you tonight. Have you got a cleaner yet?'

'No.'

'I've been wanting to ask you—'

'What? About cleaning my place? You?'

She nodded.

He said, 'Bullshit. You've only just thought of it. I'm sorry about the place but that's how I live and you can put up with it or leave, as you like.'

She saw the anger in his eyes and said, 'George, I'm not lying to you. I rang you because I'm desperate. My ex has disappeared and doesn't pay me any maintenance and my cooking business is kaput. I'm drawing income support as it is and I just don't bloody know where to turn. When you said you were looking for a cleaner I thought . . . well, why not?' Her voice rose. 'Listen I'll get this place looking really good and I'll keep it clean and if you want me to I'll cook something and leave it for you before I go. What do you think?'

'I don't know what the hell to think. I thought—'

'I know what you thought.' She indicated the room. 'You can't go on living like this. I'm not the neatest person in the world but I couldn't stand this, no way.'

'Women are all the same, always wanting to tidy things. I've got an assistant whose mother does it all the time.'

'You deserve better than this, George. And so do I. I can tell you one thing. I'd never go to bed with you in this house. Not as it is.'

'Oh, Jesus, don't give me that crap.'

'It's true. You've got used to it. You don't see it or smell it as I do. Now you can tell me to go and jump in the lake, but think about it.' She looked at her watch. 'I must get going. Can I ring for a mini-cab?'

He was about to say he would take her back, but instead said, 'I'll ring them.'

She smiled then, a somewhat sad smile and said, 'Thanks, George.'

Chapter Thirteen

'There it is,' Macrae said.

'Christ, what a place!' Leo said.

'You've never seen it before?'

'No, guv'nor, never.'

They were on the high ground in east Hampshire, the escarpment that runs from the West Sussex border almost to Winchester. At around eight hundred feet its winds were well-known as roof raisers and it had a temperature at least five degrees lower than the valleys. They had come from the eastern side and now, as they wound up the escarpment, the tall Scottish-style baronial turrets of Loxton Secure Hospital rose out of the beech hangers.

It was a day of racing black clouds coming in over the South Downs bringing with them cats' paws of rain and rocking the car from side to side.

They were allowed through the outer security gate and drove up the wide, gravelled drive to the hospital buildings.

'There's only one name for it,' Macrae said, indicating the Victorian red brick turrets, the black slate roofs and the long barred windows, 'and that's a lunatic asylum.'

'They don't call them that any more, guv'nor. And you can't blame them.'

'Bloody political correctness.'

'I looked it up. It was built in the 1860s. It was called the Hampshire Asylum for the Criminally Insane. I think Loxton Secure Hospital sounds better.'

'Aye, well, maybe you're right. It's a hell of a place though, isn't it?'

As they drove up to the administration building they saw little groups of men and women walking in the grounds. Apart from the fact that they walked slowly, many with their heads bowed as though to keep out the wind, they could have been any ordinary people. Until, that is, you registered the walls and the spikes and the guards on the gate who were watching them.

The interior of the building smelled of stale cigarette smoke and food, and all the lights were on, giving it a garish brightness. The floors were vinyl and the walls were cream. Efforts had been made to cheer the place up by hanging framed posters.

Dr Michaelson was waiting for them in his office, which was large and had a view over the hospital grounds. The central heating was on full-blast, and it needed to be.

'Good day, gentlemen, sorry about the weather up here.' He rubbed his hands together. 'I've just got back from skiing in the Guaderramas and we had more sun there than here.'

He was a plump man in his forties with a prematurely bald head. He wore a Zapata moustache but he had large, blue, friendly eyes. He showed them to chairs and asked his secretary to bring coffee. Then he said, 'I know it's Malcolm Underdown you've come to talk about. The moment something like this happens we expect the worst and we get it.'

'You mean from the media?' Macrae said.

'The media and the Home Office and anyone else you can think of.'

'Unfairly?' Leo said.

'Ha!' It was an explosive sound. 'That question is so big we could spend the next few days discussing it, because we come at it from diametrically opposed points of view. Our job here is to deal as humanely as possible with our charges. Your job is to keep the peace in society. We spend our lives dealing with the problem of dangerousness. We have symposia on dangerousness. We have papers and discussions and committees and tribunals, all on dangerousness. We live with it on the inside. You live with it on the outside. Theoretically we could keep everyone inside for the rest of their lives. That would be the safe way, the way our ancestors did it. But our ancestors also used to live in trees.' He rubbed his hand over his bald head. 'Sorry about that. Let's just say it was a cathartic moment.' He laughed. 'You wouldn't want to bet on me being given a clearance from this place if the tribunal had been listening.'

Macrae said, 'I think we'd better leave that aspect of it, Doctor, don't you?'

'That would suit me fine.'

He had the habit of fiddling with his watch. Leo noticed that his hands were large and soft, like his own father's, and he wondered if Michaelson was a pianist.

Macrae said, 'What we've come to try and get is a profile of Underdown, or at least the part of it you know about. You treated him, of course.'

'That's right. And didn't you . . . weren't you on the case before?'

'We talked in London, Doctor.'

'Of course. At Cannon Row. Right. I've got you now. And I'll help as much as I can.'

'The problem is we can't find him,' Macrae said. 'What we need are clues to where he could be.'

'It's been a long time, you know. But I'll tell you something. When we let Underdown go to Rakesbury, the medium secure psychiatric hospital in Southampton, we did so because of his response to his treatment. He has good periods, and they've got longer. There are some reports that describe him as a gentle man.'

'Except for lapses,' Leo said.

'Yes, except for lapses. Well, we all lapse once in a while.'

Leo was suddenly irritated. The doctor seemed

to be seeing Underdown through spectacles that were just too rose-tinted. 'We don't put a poisonous snake in someone's car though. That's quite a lapse.'

Dr Michaelson frowned. 'You're not telling me he did that?' He looked for confirmation to Macrae.

'That's what we're told,' Macrae said.

'It's the first I've heard of it. And I agree. Most of us don't lapse like that.'

He stirred his coffee and there was a pause. A discussion that had been getting off to a promising start seemed to have got bogged down, Leo thought.

'I'll tell you what I'll do,' Dr Michaelson said. 'I'll let you see the texts of the interviews I had with Underdown, if you like. You didn't see them before, did you?'

Macrae shook his head. 'There was no need to. He pleaded guilty to the Craig murder.'

'Yes, of course. I should tell you that I'm not really allowed to show you the reports. They're confidential. But since he is thought to have killed again and might yet again, I think my responsibility to confidentiality is at an end.'

He pressed his buzzer and his secretary came in. He said, 'Lucy, I want you to find some of the "U" files.' He turned to the two detectives. 'We're putting everything on disc at the moment and a lot of the files have been stored in another part of the building.'

'If they're the Underdown files I have them on

my desk,' the secretary said. 'They've been photo-copied.'

'That's fine. Would you photocopy them again and give them to these two gentlemen.'

As she left, Macrae said, 'I suppose we're not the only ones who will want them.'

'I suppose not. And there's still no sign of him?'

'No. The closest we got was when you told that male nurse to phone us. He'd followed him into—'

'What male nurse?'

Macrae looked at Silver. 'What's his name?'

Leo consulted a notebook and said, 'Redmond.'

'Who?'

'He said he worked here.'

'Oh, Lord, you don't mean Gary Redmond? Smallish, thin face, long black hair?'

'That's him. He said he'd phoned you because he'd seen Underdown in London and knew he shouldn't be there. He said you'd told him to call us. He was very cooperative. He followed Underdown half way along the King's Road and kept him under surveillance.'

'I'm sure he did,' Dr Michaelson said. 'Excuse me for one second.' He picked up his phone and punched in a couple of digits. 'Mary? Sidney. Listen, you had Redmond, didn't you? Yes, Gary Redmond. He went to Rakesbury. Can you remember when? He and Underdown were pretty close here, weren't they? They left at almost the same time. Yes . . . I know Underdown went on to the hostel in

Winchester. What about . . . oh, there too. No . . . I've got a couple of detectives from the Metropolitan Police here and it transpires that Redmond has been up to his tricks again. OK . . . thanks, Mary.'

He put the phone down and said, 'So Gary was pretending to be a male nurse, was he? His ambitions are a bit lower than they were in the old days. Maybe that's all to the good.'

Macrae said, 'You mean he pretended to be a doctor?'

'A doctor wasn't good enough. It had to be the top, a consultant of some sort. I've known him to be a neurosurgeon, a vascular surgeon, an orthopaedic surgeon. There was nothing modest about Gary.'

Leo said, 'It sounded from what you said that he was an inmate at the same time as Underdown?'

'We call them "patients". Yes. They were friends. Left at the same time to go to the medium secure unit in Southampton and then Underdown went to the hostel in Winchester and my colleague thinks that Gary went too. I can check that.'

'Why would he report seeing Underdown if he was his friend?' Macrae said.

'Why would he pretend to be a consultant surgeon?' Michaelson said. ' "Why?" isn't a question we ask much around here. Our patients are in here because they don't know why and we only know the . . . I was going to say the cause of some of their problems, but even that's exaggerating.'

'So him reporting seeing Underdown is rubbish?' Macrae said.

'It may be and it may not be. That's the problem. Often there's a little truth mixed up in the fantasies.'

'But he seemed exactly right for a male nurse,' Leo said.

'When he spoke to you, he was. Gary's an actor of sorts. He used to have a stage show of his own.' The doctor rose. 'I'm sorry, but I've got to get on. Sometimes in my own neurotic way I think that when I'm away things just stop. Wasn't it Bishop Berkeley who said that when you're not in a place, the place doesn't exist? I think I should probably go into analysis.' He laughed loudly in case Macrae and Silver by some remote chance had taken him seriously.

His secretary came in with the photocopies and the two detectives found themselves back in the cold world of upper Hampshire.

'Let's find a pub and have lunch,' Macrae said. 'I need something to take the taste of madness out of my mouth.'

'You used to describe them as fruity things.'

Zoe was naked in their bedroom, standing in front of the wall mirror holding her breasts up with her hands. 'Lemony things makes them sound small.'

'They are small.' Leo was lying on the bed, also naked.

'You never said that before. You said they were perfect. Now you say they're like lemons and they're small.'

'Small but perfectly formed. Anyway, haven't you seen those big Cyprus lemons? They're more like those.'

'I like fruity things best.'

'You want to come to bed or are you going to continue with your anatomical survey?'

'Sex, sex, sex. OK, but I've got some arrangements to make.' She went to the window and looked out. She took the phone off the hook. She locked the door.

'For God's sake, what are you doing?' he said.

'Keeping your parents out.'

They twined about each other like mating boas and when they had regained their composure Leo said, 'I went to see them this afternoon after we came back from Hampshire.'

'Who?'

'The aged p's.'

'And?'

'They were strange.'

'Oh, so you're beginning to realize that?'

'Not strange the way you think. A different strange.'

'That's English, is it?'

He had gone to the big untidy flat after leaving Macrae. He'd had, at the back of his mind, the feeling that his father might never be the same again after what had happened in the Queen Elizabeth Hall.

'It's me!' he had shouted through the letter-box and his mother had come to the door.

'Leo, darling.' She had given him a hug and brought him into the kitchen. 'I'm making marmalade. Your father says he can never get it bitter enough but if you don't put in lots of sugar it won't set.'

She stirred the pot. 'I don't know why he wants marmalade. In Vienna we never ate marmalade.'

Leo said, 'How is he?'

'How should he be?' She did not seem to register the weight of the question.

Leo heard his father usher a pupil from the flat and come along the passage.

'Hello, Dad.'

Manfred smiled briefly. 'If some pupil says once more that is how Glenn Gould plays it, I am going to break their fingers.'

'Why not play like him if they can? I've got the Goldberg and—'

'Three times he recorded the Goldberg. Each time different. When he plays Forty-Eight, it's adagio for allegro, forte for piano. When I correct them they say but that is how Glenn Gould does it and I say, but that is not how Herr Peters wishes it played and I show them the Edition Peters and point to the instructions and I say, please just do it this way!'

'How are you feeling, Dad?'

'Who vants to know?'

Leo turned to his mother. 'Has he been watching American TV?'

'Don't be smart with your father,' Manfred said. He went to the sink and washed his hands with soft liquid soap and dried them on a special towel hanging behind the door. These were his soap and towel and no one else was allowed to use them.

'I just wondered about the other night,' Leo said.

'What other night?' his father said.

Leo saw his mother swiftly shake her head at him and said, 'You know . . . oh, nothing.'

'Your father's composing again,' Lotte said.

'That's good, Dad.' Leo was more confused than ever.

His father didn't reply but his mother said, 'A new symphony. Very big. It's called The Hemispheres.'

'Sounds impressive.'

Manfred finally stopped drying his hands and said, 'I must go to chess.'

After he had gone Lotte said, 'Don't speak of the other night. It never happened. You understand me? It didn't happen.'

Zoe turned in the bed and said, 'And so? Is that how things are going to be left? A man is interfered with in the Queen Elizabeth Hall and—'

'Not interfered with. An accident.'

'You go to a concert and you come home without your fly . . . that's being interfered with!'

'Anyway, he doesn't want to talk about it and Mother says he's never mentioned it again, so it didn't happen. Goodnight.'

Zoe lay on her back, her arms under her head. After a few minutes she said, 'I wonder who you take after, your mother or your father?'

Chapter Fourteen

London had been clear when Jane left, the night clouds had been high and the weather cold and still. When she reached the South Downs in Hampshire she might have been on a different planet. Here the clouds had descended to such a point that they lay on the Downs. Her father, coming as he had from the east coast, would have called this a *haar*, a raw sea-mist. She had come down on the motorway, with Michael somewhere behind her and had kept her speed up because she did not want to hold up the mettlesome Porsche. But now in this thick mist she was in twisting country lanes and her speed was down to twenty miles an hour. She hoped that Michael would be at Highlands before her.

Highlands House was named after the nearest village. She knew all the lanes to it like the veins in her hands. But not in mist where the visibility was fifty yards. They looked totally unfamiliar and the reduced visibility was reduced even further as the south-west wind sent eddies of mist tumbling and billowing around the car.

As she had left London she had, as on her earlier snowy drive, suddenly been less afraid. There was no way Malcolm could know where she was, she thought, as she weaved her way down through St John's Wood and Shepherd's Bush, making for the M3. No way at all. And she felt almost an intoxication. This feeling had lasted until she had come off the motorway at Odiham and begun to cut across country, and it was mirrored by the weather. Rain had begun to dot the windscreen. Then she had moved into the low mist which now surrounded the slow-moving car.

She began to feel afraid again. Now that she was near Winchester she was also relatively near the area where Malcolm had grown up. Had she ever described the whereabouts of her home to him? She was certain she hadn't. But he had found her in London, not once, but twice.

Look at it logically, she told her frightened self. She was a reasonable – no, more than that, she was a good – student. OK, she hadn't used her brain much since university, but she must use it now. Right. Logically, what would Malcolm do? No answer. What would she do if she were Malcolm? Hypothetical and simply not possible to answer since she would never be doing what Malcolm was doing.

So what if she were looking for someone she hadn't seen for a long time. How would she go about it?

The first thing she would do would be to find a few of that someone's friends and ask them.

But most of her friends had simply got lost after Edward's death. She hadn't meant to lose them but it had happened. She had made no effort and they, she supposed because of what had happened, had not tried to make contact either, possibly because of sensitivity or just because they didn't want to be touched by her ill-luck. It was the same feeling as medieval people had had about crows or ravens, those portentous symbols of ill luck and doom. Had she become a symbol of ill luck?

She had thought she was a lucky person. So had Tammy, who was always saying, 'Meet the golden girl.' And then her luck had run out. First she had met Malcolm. She had known he wasn't really for her, but she had felt sorry for him. He didn't seem to fit into the university ethos. There was a patent loneliness about him which was much more obvious than with other lonely people. It was his size, she imagined, that made it so obvious; this big hulking man who always seemed to be by himself.

She had thought of Malcolm as being her first piece of bad luck, but of course he wasn't. The death of her father was. Her father's death; then Malcolm; then the murder of Edward; then her mother's death ... they all added up to a lot of crows and a lot of ravens.

Her only piece of good luck was Michael.

The gateway of Highlands House came into misty view and she turned into the drive. The big flint house stood high above the surrounding countryside looking gaunt and cold in the headlights. The drive was empty. Michael wasn't there.

She sat in the car, keeping the engine running. The glow from the dashboard and the warmth of the heater had produced a cosy driving nest which she was loath to leave. Then she wondered if Michael was lost in the lanes and thought that it would be nice if she had the house ready and welcoming when he arrived.

She had brought smoked salmon and brown bread and their usual champagne but had decided that this was the last such meal he would have. She would cook for him in the evenings down here and, if she could, she would try and continue that when they went back to London. They had slipped into bad habits.

She switched off the engine and immediately the noise of the wind became worse. Well, it wasn't as if she did not know this countryside high up in the Downs. Tammy always quoted Ezra Pound when the weather was chilly and windy: 'Winter is icummen in, lhude sing Goddamm'. It was appropriate for the moment and Jane said it over to herself to take her mind off what she had immediately to do.

She took a small suitcase and one of the food boxes and went to the front door. It was a heavy door with big brass hinges, a brass knocker and brass handle. The brass was badly neglected and would need polishing up before the house was put on the market. The key was stiff but she managed to turn it. The smell inside hit her. It was a smell of damp, decay and mould, and was brought to her on ice-cold air.

She put down the food box and pressed the light switch, but nothing happened.

'Bugger,' she said, assuming that the bulb in the hall had gone.

What her mother had named 'the small sitting-room' lay on the left side of the front door and she reached in for the switch, but again nothing happened.

She stood for a moment, considering the proposition that the light bulbs in two sockets had gone at the same time, then rejected it. She was no expert in house management but had heard of fuses without ever having had to replace one.

She put down the parcels and decided she would have to find the fuse box. This meant going along the passage to the kitchen. It was an area of darkness just ahead of her. She felt her way along the wall and came to the kitchen. She tried the light, but it didn't work either.

She knew the fuse box was just inside the kitchen door. Here there was a glow from outside and she could see the cooker and the fridge – that would be a mess if the fuse had gone some time ago, for she had left it on.

She stared at the fuse box. Now she had found it, what was she going to do with it?

She found a box of matches in a drawer. Then she saw a series of buttons below the box and remembered how they worked. On several occasions when the electricity in the house had failed – once when her mother had used a knife to extract a piece of bread from the toaster – her step-father had pushed the green button and the lights had blazed. She pressed it, but nothing happened. She froze. Why weren't they working? Had someone been in the house and meddled with the fuse box?

Then she remembered that for emergencies her mother kept a supply of oil lamps in the cellar. If she could find them, at least there would be some light.

The cellar housed the boiler, a huge old wardrobe that her mother had never wanted to throw away, some shelving units holding, among other things, the oil lamps, a gas heater, and lots of spiders.

'Don't think about them,' she told herself as she lit a match to see her way down the stairs.

The cellar smelled of damp and its two windows, half below ground level, were rattling in their old and wormy frames.

It was very dark. She lit another match and saw that there were only four or five left in the box. By its light she could make out two lamps on a shelf.

When she was a child she had liked the tall glass chimneys and the soft light which came from them.

In the dark she began to unscrew the chimney of one to get at the wick. She lit another match and saw that the wick was black. She touched it. It was brittle and hard. Oh, hell, she thought, no fuel.

She looked around, searching for a tin or other receptacle which might hold kerosene, but there was nothing. As the match went out, she heard a noise upstairs. It was just above her and sounded like someone walking along the passage or in the big sitting-room. She stood very still and held her breath. It came again.

She went to the foot of the cellar stairs and listened but all she could hear was the thudding of her own heart.

She called shakily, 'Michael! Is that you?'

She thought she heard a door click.

'Michael!'

She didn't want to stay in the cellar, yet didn't want to go upstairs in the dark. Perhaps the fuel can was in the wardrobe. She lit one of the last two matches and turned the wardrobe key. The door was stiff. She pulled it and at the same time dropped the match as it burnt her fingers. In the last flicker of its light as the door opened, she saw a squat figure. It came at her, arms outstretched.

She screamed, turned, slipped on the vinyl floor. The figure fell on top of her, its coarse furry skin rubbing against her face. She screamed again.

'Jane!' a voice called from above. 'Jane, where the hell are you?'

'Michael! Michael!'

A torch beam pierced the darkness and she saw what had fallen on her. It was her giant panda which she had loved when she was a child. Like the wardrobe, it had never been thrown away.

Michael was by her side, helping her to her feet. 'Oh, God, I'm so glad you've come!' she said.

Then the lights came on as the power cut ended.

'What have we got?' Les Wilson said.

Macrae and Silver were in his office and his desk – much to that tidy man's irritation – was covered in photocopies and tearsheets.

'We've got a lot of paper,' Macrae said. 'And no bloody axe murderer.'

'Why axe murderer? He never took an axe to any one.'

'Some new poll says that most of us think that people who're let out of secure hospitals are mad axe murderers.'

'They're not too far wrong about Underdown, are they?'

'There've been ten more sightings,' Macrae said. 'And we've had to check out five. It's getting bloody ridiculous. All our strength is going out checking sightings that never took place, or else they're just leads that don't work.'

'You're in the police, old son,' Wilson said. 'You don't get free rides.'

'Aye. Well, we've been through this paperwork we got at Loxton and it doesn't tell us anything new. Underdown was part gentle, part violent. They stuffed him full of drugs which he didn't like, and then said he was getting better.'

'I've glanced at them, too,' Wilson said. 'And you can see what goes on. You could see it at his trial. There's too much of the old *crime passionel* in this case. It's overshadowed the state of his mind, if you ask me.'

'How's that?' Macrae said.

'We have a trendy psychiatric report saying Underdown has a personality disorder. Nothing very much. And then there's the whole business of him being in love with the girl and she dropping him for someone else. Underdown gets jealous and does him in. So it's not really his fault, you see. Poor boy was forced into it by circumstances.'

Macrae frowned; he was not what people would normally describe as a soft touch but he did not go all the way with Les Wilson. He'd seen many killers or would-be killers who were so affected at the time that they were powerless to stop themselves.

When he did not respond Wilson said, 'Don't tell me you buy all this psychological crap, George. I mean, look at these profile blokes. It's like they're trying to pull facts out of a magician's stocking. It's all the old Sherlock stuff. *The murderer is a left-*

handed Presbyterian with bad breath. That sort of
crap.' He flicked the paperwork on the desk and said,
'I want to see the handwritten stuff. It says in one
of those reports that this psychiatrist, Michaelson,
asked Underdown to write down his thoughts about
the death of his step-father. Where is it?'

'Aye, we want that too, Les.'

'Are we supposed to think that Underdown killed
him as well?'

'We're getting on to that. But we only finished
looking through the paperwork after we got back
from Hampshire and by that time when Silver
phoned the hospital Michaelson was in a meeting
and his secretary had gone home. Silver's going to
try again.'

'What about Redmond?'

'We're seeing him tomorrow in Southsea,' Silver
said.

'You didn't phone him, did you?'

'No, we thought he'd take off if I did.'

Wilson began gathering up the papers, something
he had been itching to do since the interview had
started, and said, 'All right then, George, keep me
posted.'

Macrae went back to his room and stared at his
telephone. He had been thinking about Tammy on
and off all day. And he had been thinking of his
house. At one point he had also thought of Frenchy
but since she had left him, there was no way he was
going to feel guilty about Tammy.

He dialled and heard her voice. 'Are you busy?' he said.

'It depends.'

'You're either busy or you're not. And if you're not, I thought I'd come round.'

'I'm busy.'

He paused, then said, 'If I said anything to hurt you when you were at my place, I'm sorry.'

The words dropped out like coins forced from a piggy-bank.

'If you don't know what you said, then don't apologize.'

'Look, I'm trying. That's all I can do.'

There was a moment of silence and then she said, 'I don't think so, George.'

Suddenly the empty, dirty house seemed like the last place on earth he wanted to go back to, and he said, 'I really am sorry.'

'I haven't got any food or drink – at least, not much. There's a little wine.'

'Why don't I bring something?'

'Why don't you?'

Half an hour later he was on her doorstep carrying a bottle of Glenmorangie.

She indicated the glasses and he poured a couple of shots. He sat on the sofa and she sat on a hard-backed chair opposite him. She sipped the malt whisky and he waited for it to work its wonders.

As though reading his mind she said, 'This isn't very subtle, you know, and I can drink this till the cows come home without getting tight, so let's talk about something else.'

'Tell me about Mrs Stone then.'

'First you tell me about Malcolm.'

'Nothing to tell.'

She was looking even more attractive than he remembered, wearing a yellow blouse without a bra, and white trousers. Her hair was caught back in a red scarf.

'Now you tell me,' he said.

'I do have news. She's gone out of town. She and Michael have gone down to her family home in Hampshire.'

Macrae frowned. 'She didn't tell us.'

'Why should she? She's not wanted for anything.'

'That's true, but it's as well to know where she is. If Underwood gets close to her, we'd want to know.'

'Hey, wait a sec! You sound like you're thinking of her as bait.'

'This isn't some cops-and-robbers film,' he said irritably. 'We don't use people as bait in real life. It's just that we can't look after her as we could in London. Where is this place? Is it in the country or a village or what?'

'It's remote, if that's what you mean. But you don't have to worry. She says Malcolm never went there, doesn't know where it is, and anyway Michael is with her, or at least he will be during the night. He has a case at the Portsmouth Crown Court.'

'I still don't like it.'

'Listen, she was sick with fear and the only person who makes her feel safe is Michael. He's got this case and wasn't going to be able to come back to London at night. What else was she to do?'

He poured himself another whisky and offered her the bottle. She shook her head. 'Nothing's going to happen tonight, George.'

He nodded, drained his glass and said, 'All right then. I won't disturb you any longer.'

She came downstairs and saw him to the front door. 'Goodnight, George.'

He took a few steps on to the pavement, stopped, half turned and said, 'You're right about the house. I mean my house. Would seven pounds an hour be all right?'

She thought for a moment. 'You want me to come and clean it?'

'And keep it clean.'

'And cooking? I could leave something for you.'

'Let's think about that.'

'All right, George. Seven pounds will do at the start.'

'Tomorrow?'

'Yes. I could do tomorrow.'

He fumbled in his pocket. 'Here's a key. I'm usually gone all day from about eight-thirty.'

'When do you get back?'

'Not till eight sometimes.'

'That gives me plenty of time. I'll be there in the morning.'

He walked into the barrier-encased street and put his coat collar up against the wind. Only then did he realize that he had left the almost full bottle of whisky at her flat.

Chapter Fifteen

'Redmond?' the man said. 'Gary Redmond?' He was standing beside a small table that served as a reception counter in the hotel.

That's if you could call it a hotel, Leo had thought when he and Macrae had stood outside it a few minutes earlier. The battered sign had read *S angri La R sidenti l Hote* . The inside was not much better. It was very cold and Macrae had thought on entering that Tammy would not have gone much on the cleanliness or the ripe smell of cabbage.

'Gary Redmond?' the man repeated. He was small and dark and in his forties. 'You from Social Services?' His eyes kept flicking above and beyond the two detectives as though to check that the furnishings in the small foyer were in reasonable nick.

It had taken Macrae and Silver some time to find the place in this back street of Southsea and Macrae was not in the best of humours.

'No, we're not from the Social Services.'

He held out his warrant card.

The man said, 'What's that?'

'That's my police identification. Why don't you look at it?'

'Police? Oh, Christ. Listen, it wasn't our fault. She was going to take a knife to him. She had to be restrained. That was all we did. Restrain. Nothing more. We've told all that to Social Services a hundred times and . . . hey, what's Gary Redmond got to do with it, anyway?'

'Can you just stop a moment?' Macrae said. 'No one said anything about a knife or restraint. We just want to see Mr Redmond.'

'Oh.' He was visibly relieved.

'Are you Mr . . .' Leo craned to see the name on the little sign on the table. 'Mr Kossuth? The owner?'

The man licked his lips. 'That's me.'

'Right, let's start again,' Macrae said. 'We want to see Mr Redmond . . .' He held his hand up. 'Don't say anything for a moment. We want to see Mr Redmond and it's got nothing to do with you or the palace you own. He's come to you from a hostel, hasn't he?'

'That's right.'

Leo said, 'Is this one of those hotels where you take in former mental patients?'

'What's wrong with that?' Kossuth said. 'Someone's got to do it.'

Macrae said, 'Just say yes or no.'

'Well, yes, I do.'

'Right, then tell us where Redmond is.'

'He's in the garage.'

For a moment Leo had a mental picture of Redmond bound and trussed, placed in a steel cage and locked behind garage doors. 'He's giving a show,' Kossuth said.

'What sort of show and who to?' Macrae said.

'To some of the other residents.'

'In the garage?' Leo said.

'Can't very well do it in the dining-room ... sorry, yes, in the garage.'

'Show us,' Macrae said.

Kossuth led them to the rear of the hotel. It was a red brick house that had once been pleasant. Now the garden was a mess and the rubbish-bins were overflowing.

The garage was separated from the house and the big doors were closed. Kossuth led them to the side of the building and opened a small door.

Leo was suddenly reminded of plays he and his sister had performed when they were kids in the garages of friends in London, where the parents sat on a few dining-room chairs and clapped loudly.

But these were not parents and the man who stood behind an old table was the man from Chelsea, Gary Redmond.

In the freezing cold three people, a thin young man and two middle-aged women, were listening to what sounded like a magician's spiel. Then Redmond bent slightly, raised his hand, took a gold-fish out of his mouth and put it in a bowl of water on the table where it swam about slowly.

There was a wooden sign behind him which was even more battered than the hotel sign. It showed a man in evening dress with a black mask on his face and a string of gold coins emerging from his mouth. Underneath was the lettering:

GARY REDMOND, THE PHANTOM REGURGITATOR

See him swallow living things and bring them up alive.
See him swallow coins.
See him count them in his stomach.
See the show of a lifetime.

Some of the lettering was so badly worn they could hardly make it out.

Their arrival caused the three-strong audience to look around apprehensively. The man rose, followed quickly by the two women, and pushed past them into the daylight.

Redmond looked at them with a sudden frightened expression and brought up from his stomach two more goldfish and put them in the water.

'Remember us?' Macrae said.

There was a moment when Leo thought Redmond was going to deny ever seeing them but then he shrugged and said, 'Yes, chief, I remember you.'

They went with him to a small greyish room smelling of damp with a window overlooking the unkempt garden. There was a single bed, a chair, a cheap wardrobe and chest of drawers and a wash-basin. Along one wall Redmond had made a book-case of planks and bricks which held half a dozen paperbacks.

Now he placed the bowl of goldfish on the chest of drawers and gave them a pinch of food. 'Eeeni, Meeni and Mini,' he said. 'I had a bit of an accident with Moh. I brought her up the wrong way and her fins caught in my throat so I had to put my finger down and squash her. Out of practice, I was.'

Macrae and Silver sat on the bed. Redmond stood by the dressing-table.

'You haven't been totally truthful with us, have you, Gary?' Macrae said. 'Not the whole hog.'

'How d'you mean, chief?'

'Nurse at a secure hospital. Isn't that what you said?'

Redmond had brought with him a black plastic bag and now he put his hand into it, took out a couple of coins and swallowed them.

He heaved and brought them up into the palm of his hand. 'Used to be able to swallow half a dozen and bring them up one or two at a time, depending on what the audience wanted.'

'And surgeon and neurosurgeon,' Macrae said.

He felt in the black plastic bag again and took out a little phial containing, Leo saw with astonishment, bees. He opened it and swallowed the lot, crossed his eyes, said, 'The audience used to love this at first then they thought it cruel. But the bees don't mind.'

In a moment they were up again and in their phial. He pointed to his stomach. 'Listen. Can you hear him? That's Billy. Always the last up. I seen Stevie Starr do it with bees. He's terrific.' He brought up Billy and put him in the phial too.

Macrae said, 'Mr Redmond—'

'Call me Gary.'

'We've been through that before.'

'Oh, right.'

'We know all about you. We know about the operation you performed on that woman in Basingstoke when you were at the hospital there pretending to be a vascular surgeon. And the appendix you didn't quite manage to take out in Portsmouth.'

Redmond took a piece of broken glass that looked like part of a milk bottle, and swallowed it.

'And we know you were a patient at Loxton and then Rakesbury in Southampton, so we know you knew Underdown and—'

The glass came up and Redmond said, 'See? Not a scratch. Yummy, yummy.'

'What we don't know is if you made the whole thing up about seeing Underdown in London.'

'They used to pay me good money to see this. Sometimes I used to go to universities, sometimes working men's clubs. They tried to stop me swallowing a couple of frogs once. Threatened to bring the police. Said it was cruel. Rubbish really. Frogs enjoyed it. Yes, of course I saw him. I told you. At the cinema.'

'Or maybe the library.'

'Yeah, or maybe the library.'

'Why did you ring the police?'

'Why not?'

'But wasn't he a friend of yours?'

'Who, Underdown? Underdown was never a friend of anybody's. I saw him near kill a man in Loxton. I dunno why. But you don't need to know the whys in a place like that and we didn't like the man he attacked so we never let on. But it wasn't very nice, if you know what I mean.' He held up a squash ball. 'Don't really like swallowing squash balls. Horrid taste. But what the hell.' He swallowed it and brought it up quite dry.

Macrae said, 'What did you talk about?'

'Where?'

'In places like Loxton and Rakesbury.'

'I talked about regurgitating. He talked about his farm.'

'What farm?'

'That's what he was, a farmer. Didn't you know that?'

Redmond smiled, then swallowed a padlock. He brought it up and held it out to them. 'It was open when it went down. Look at it now.' It was locked. 'I used to be able to take a ring from someone in the audience and lock it on to the padlock in my stomach. But not any more. A loony bin's no place to practise. You do this sort of thing and they think you've gone crazy.'

'What did he say about his farm?'

'You don't know old Mal, do you?'

'What do you mean by that?'

'He doesn't say much about anything. I wanted him to become a regurgitator like me. Would have taught him and we could have become a double act, but no. He never said anything. That was before I knew what he was really like, before he attacked that geezer. Only thing he ever talked about was his farm and the animals, except they didn't sound like farm animals to me. I mean rabbits and hares and mice and voles . . . I'm no countryman, but you don't farm those things.'

'Where was this farm?' Leo said.

'Hampshire. He only talked about it properly once and that was after we'd smoked some grass. Could hardly stop him then. Talked about his little house and his little farm and the woods and God knows what else. Thought he'd never stop.'

'Did he talk about women?'

'We all talked about women, or men, depends if we were ac or dc.'

'What was Underdown?' Macrae said.

'You could never tell with old Mal. He wasn't much of a talker.' Redmond took three glass marbles from the bag and dropped them into his mouth and swallowed. 'You listen now.' He began to swing his body in hula-hoop style. 'You hear them click?' He started a different rhythm. 'Rumba,' he said.

'Let's get back to these women,' Macrae said.

Redmond regurgitated the marbles and drank a glass of water. 'Always got to drink a lot of water,' he said. 'It dilutes the stomach acid, otherwise the fish would die. The women?'

'Or one in particular,' Leo said. 'Her name was Jane. Did he ever speak about her?'

He shook his head. 'Never mentioned her by name, but I know who you mean. I had read about Mal so I knew and he knew I knew what he'd done. But in a place like Loxton everyone was in for something . . . well, not quite nice, if you know what I mean.'

'So what did he say about her?'

' "One day I'll be back." That's what he said. He said he'd see her again. He said, "Gary, one day I'll be back." '

'What d'you think he meant by that?'

'Listen, I'd have been scared if I was her. Ever seen a smoke bubble? You need washing-up liquid and a cigarette. Either of you got a cigarette? No? That's a pity. That's a good one, that is.'

George Macrae was wheeling a supermarket trolley. It was not the first time he had done this. There had been times when his first wife, Linda, had managed to get him into a supermarket – these were when she was pregnant – and the same thing had happened when Mandy, his second wife, was pregnant.

He had rationalized that they were what might be termed mercy missions.

But he had never gone into a supermarket alone and wheeled a trolley and he had never wheeled one with Frenchy. He was wheeling one now with Tammy walking beside him and he kept his head down and wheeled it along the aisles and prayed that he would not bump into anyone from Cannon Row or who had known him in the Flying Squad or the Murder Squad in the old days.

He and Leo had returned to Cannon Row after seeing the Phantom Regurgitator in Southsea and Macrae had been on his way to Wilson's office when a call had come in for him. It was Tammy.

'I'm at your house,' she had said.

'Oh?'

'I'm sorry to do this to you at work but I'm phoning to tell you I can't get on with what we agreed.'

'Why not?'

'There's nothing here to clean with.'

'There must be something. Of course there is.'

'There's an old plastic mop that's gone hard, and there's an empty Ajax package and that's about it. I've come all the way across London to clean your house and I can't do it.'

'There's a big supermarket two streets away. Can't you go there and buy what you need?'

'George, I'm flat broke until I can get my cheque tomorrow. Haven't got a penny.'

He told her where the supermarket was and said he'd meet her there. Which is how he came to be pushing a trolley.

'What about food?' she said. 'You don't seem to have much. I looked in the fridge and there's a piece of cheese that expired last month.'

'All right, let's buy some.'

'We'll have to get the basics, too.'

And so the trolley was getting fuller and fuller and Macrae thought it didn't seem possible that all jythis was for one person.

Tammy had walked the couple of streets to the supermarket so he had to drive her back and when they reached the house she asked if he'd had anything to eat and when he said he hadn't she said she had bought some ham and why didn't she make him a couple of sandwiches and then he could go back to Cannon Row? He had those and very good they were and then she made some coffee, real coffee from a newly opened packet, and imperceptibly work seemed to become less important for Macrae. He said if she was going to do any work now he'd go back to the station, do what he had to do and then come back.

And she said, 'You mean I'm a cleaner . . . plus?'

'Well?'

'I don't think so, George.'

He drove back to Cannon Row feeling irritated and somewhat confused.

He wasn't supposed to push trolleys around in the late afternoon and then not be recompensed. He'd always been recompensed before.

Chapter Sixteen

The winter sun came in through the living-room windows of Highlands House and made patterns on the blue carpet. Jane had never liked blue as a furnishing colour and she would have chosen yellow to pick up the sunlight more warmly. She wandered to the windows and looked out over the Downs. Michael was just beyond them, in Portsmouth. She had given him his breakfast an hour before and seen him go off in the Porsche.

In London she hardly ever made his breakfast. He fed on the run between his study and the kitchen. But this morning he had sat down in the big farmhouse kitchen with the warmth of the Aga making it welcoming and had eaten bacon and eggs.

Now she was alone. The memories of the dark cellar were still with her and her terror at the sudden falling of her old panda. But these, she told herself, were no more than childhood terrors of the dark.

She had to make a start on clearing the house some time and it might as well be now. She went to her mother's room. Already she had laid out some of her clothes on the bed and she would have to sort out everything to take into the Oxfam charity shop in Winchester.

She went to her mother's heavy old mahogany chest of drawers and made piles of underclothes and jerseys on the bed and on the floor near the windows. Later, she would pack them into big black plastic bags.

As she worked she thought about the house. At one time she had wondered if she should keep it rather than sell it, but she'd never really liked it enough for that. It was a gaunt, flint house perched on uncomfortably high land. It didn't feel like her home any more than the house in Hampstead was hers. That was Michael's home, which had been set up by the first Mrs Stone. In Highlands, even her own rooms had been arranged by her mother and step-father. They comprised a small flat which her mother had created for her when she remarried. A bribe to keep Jane happy.

She wandered along the upstairs passage and let herself into them. There were two rooms and a bathroom. One of the rooms, which had been her bedroom, was relatively small, but the other was large. She went into it and the sun streaming in through the big casement windows gave her the feeling she had never left it.

Against one wall was the wooden structure her father had built for her in the old house before he died. 'Jane's Magic World', he had called it. It was a

large playhouse, a Wendy house her mother had
called it, which he had added to over the years until
it was big enough for her to sleep in and in which
she had created her own world. It could be whatever she wanted: one day a cave, another a country
house.

The phone rang. It was Michael.

'You OK?' That was his regular question now.

'Yes. I'm about to start thinking about your
dinner tonight. Any preferences?'

'That's what I'm phoning about. I'm going to be
very late. The defence team wants me to have a
working dinner with them and God knows how long
it'll be.'

'Oh.'

'I'm sorry, but there's nothing else I can do.'

'Yes, of course. Any idea when you *will* be home?'

'Before midnight, I hope, but don't wait up.'

She put the phone down, aware now that clouds
were obscuring the sun.

*Don't wait up. Wait for the dark. Darkness. Decay.
Her mother's dead body.*

Leo put his head round Macrae's door. 'We're getting
there, guv'nor. I've just spoken to the doctor's secretary down at Loxton. She thought we had the
manuscript written by Underdown. I had to argue
with her. She said it was with the papers she'd given
us, I said it wasn't. She went off in a huff but she's

just phoned me back. It was in the photocopier. She thinks it had been borrowed.'

'Borrowed? By the Hampshire police?'

'No. By Dr Stone. He went down and got copies of the reports and he must have taken this too. She's faxing it to – hang on, that might be it coming through now . . .'

Report 8 MSU/SM

Dear Dr Michaelson,

I'm writing this as a letter because I don't know how else to write it. The last thing I ever wrote was an essay on Malthus at college. I don't want to write it at all but you go on at me. You tell me to call you Sidney. I can't do that. Not on paper.

I'm not going to write about Jane if that's what you think. I'm also not going to write about my mother. She didn't want to see me and I don't want to see her now and I don't want to talk about her or write about her.

It's really my step-father's death you're interested in. My grandmother was always talking about sins of omission and commission and I think that's what you are after. Finding out things like that.

I didn't like him and he didn't like me. He wanted my mother and I was part of the contract. He had to take me as well.

She was always going off in her job. By that time it wasn't what she had done at the beginning. She used to go to places like Nairobi and Bombay, but after she married Stokes she couldn't get the best jobs any more.

She wasn't young enough. She didn't work for BOAC then but for a charter company and they flew to the Canaries and back.

I told you that when my real father was alive and at sea, and my mother was away, I was looked after by my grandmother. But she died after my mother married Harold Stokes and so he was supposed to look after me.

He was much older than her, I suppose about fifty-something and he'd had a farm or a ranch out in Zimbabwe and then he'd come back and bought this farm in Hampshire and he was breeding cattle. They were red and white cattle called Herefords. The problem was that all the subsidies from Europe were for crops and he didn't like growing crops. He wanted to grow cattle. So he was going downhill and drinking heavily. He was big. Bigger than me then, with a big gut and a big round head and he wore one of those African hats with the leopard skin round them.

He hit me a lot. He was always telling my mother it was for my own good. He had a retriever called Boy and he used to say that Boy had grown up into a perfect dog because he had been hard on him as a pup. And that's what he was doing with me. My mother never cared much. She used to say sometimes, 'Don't be too severe on the lad, Harold.' But that was about all.

He used to take my trousers down and smack me on the bottom with his hand. First he'd feel my skin and say, 'This is where I'm going to hit you, Malcolm,' and he'd feel it for a time and then he'd hit. It was sore. The first time I cried. He said no one but a ninny cried so after that I never cried and he didn't like that. He wanted me to cry so he could say that about the ninny. But I used to go out and leave the house and sometimes when my mother was away I wouldn't come back for a whole day. Sometimes I didn't go to school and stayed on the farm, but not where he could see me.

At first I had a little garden shed. He hadn't done anything about the garden for years and it was a wilderness. I didn't like the shed because it was too near the house and the old felt roof leaked but it was better than being in the house with him.

There were field-mice and rats and some voles down there and I tried to make friends with them but they were too shy. I shot some with a catapult and I also shot a pigeon with a bow and arrow and it flew off with the arrow still in its chest.

My step-father told me he didn't want me playing in the shed so I moved away. In the old days there had been a sand-pit in one part of the farm and I went there. It was all overgrown and the track to it was overgrown too but if you forced your way through you could get to the pit. It was the size of a couple of tennis courts and went down about thirty feet. On one side there was a little building. I suppose in the old days when the men came to load sand they needed a place to get out of the rain.

It was made of brick walls and about the size of a bedroom. It had no roof and the window was gone.

I mended it. I took wood from the farmyard and felt off the shed roof and bits and pieces from old barns that were not in use any more and made it OK. When it rained the rain came in a bit but mostly it was OK.

I suppose I was about fourteen then and big for my age. Stokes said where was I going to all the time and what had I done with the felt from the shed and things like that and I wouldn't tell him. One day he said take down your trousers and I said no and he hit me in the face and I had a piece of rope in my hand and I hit him back, not once but ten or twelve times and the blood came.

He fell over against a chair and on to the floor and held his hands over his head and shouted at me to stop hitting him. Then he said he was going to kill me, then that he was going to tell my mother and also the police, and I said if he told the police I'd tell them he was always making me take my trousers off and touching me, so he never called the police and I don't think he told my mother because when she came back from one of her flights she didn't say anything to me.

So I had my little house and Stokes left me alone. I think he was a bit frightened of me then because he was so overweight and he had a heart problem and he was drinking heavily when my mother was away.

My sand-house, which is what I called it, was the first thing I ever owned. And just about the only thing.

I didn't really own it, it was Stokes', but it was so difficult to get to because of the dense trees and bushes you had to force your way through, that nobody ever went there except me because by that time the farm-workers had been fired.

I used to spend whole days there, from early morning to late at night, specially in the school holidays. No one cared, really. They were just pleased I wasn't in the house.

My mother had started to drink then too. She'd be at home three or four days at a time and for most of it she was drinking and so was he. The house was filthy and horrible and the farm was run down and the cattle were not being replaced when they were sold. I don't know how Stokes managed anything at all.

I made friends with some of the animals in the sand-pit. There was a squirrel that had a broken leg and I fixed that with a splint and fed it nuts. And I had a pet rat in a cage and I fed it grasshoppers and things like that. There were pheasants too and they would often feed right up to the sand-house door. I sometimes shot one with my catapult and cooked it over a small fire in the sand-house. Those were the best times I had.

My step-father died when my mother was on a flight. This is what you said you wanted to know about.

It was a school day in winter. It was cold and the house was cold when I got back to it in the late afternoon. There was a bus that brought us along the lane but I had to walk half a mile from there and it had been raining the day before and the road was muddy. When I reached the house he said I was to take off my shoes. He didn't really care but it was something he could say to me and I said I was going to anyway. And he said I wasn't to talk to him like that.

This was the kind of conversation we used to have. Arguments about little things. But that day it started small and ended pretty big.

When I went to my room I switched on the central-heating and he came and switched it off. So I switched it on again and when he came to my room the next time he had a stick in his hand.

I supposed he'd been drinking all day, he usually did, and he said I wasn't to touch the central-heating and I said I would and he hit me with the stick.

He was so drunk I could hardly feel it, but I didn't like being hit. Then he hit me again and I grabbed the stick and pulled it out of his hands and said if he was going to go on I'd hit him.

So he left my room and went back to the sitting-room and I heard him give a kind of cry and when I went in he had fallen down and was choking.

He was heaving and choking and vomiting and I asked him what he wanted me to do. I know now this was stupid but I really didn't know what to do. I tried to lift him on to a chair but he was so heavy I couldn't, so I got a pillow and put it under his head and then phoned for the ambulance.

They took twenty minutes to get to the farm. I tried to stay with him but he was dying and I was only a kid so I went outside and waited there.

That's what happened to my step-father. I suppose I should be sorry but I'm not really.

Malcolm.

Note by SM
This is highly decorated and departs from what he originally told the police. We have checked his story and found that the ambulance attendant said the body was nearly cold by the time they reached the farm. The central-heating was not on – Malcolm makes this point – but it means that Stokes was dead at least a couple of hours before Malcolm phoned for help. Originally he told the police that he had come home from school and found the body. Now we have a different story. My own view is that he knew what was happening and did nothing for too long, hoping that Stokes would die.

Wilson, who had come in a minute after the faxes arrived, read them over Macrae's shoulder.

'There's nothing much in that,' he said. 'Sounds

just like I thought he was. Mad as a hatter. What do you think of the doc's note, George?'

'If Stokes had been feeling my bottom and bashing me as much as Underdown says he did, I'd have watched him die, too.'

'What about all this animals stuff?'

'He had no one else to play with,' Macrae said. 'Same thing happened to me when I was a kid. We lived out on the Findhorn miles from anywhere. What I did was fish. You don't have to have friends to fish, specially if you're poaching salmon.'

'I don't want to hear about that, George.' But Wilson said it lightly.

Macrae said, 'What annoys me is Dr Stone wanting to see all this stuff.'

'Wouldn't you?' Wilson said. 'I mean, if she was your wife who was threatened.'

'Course I would, but if I was Stone I would have got in touch with us about it, wouldn't you?'

'Not necessarily.'

'Why the hell not? Are you suggesting that if you are a forensic psychiatrist and your wife is threatened by a bloody madman you would try and do the investigation yourself? Come on, Les!'

'I'm saying I'd have tried to get all the information I could, that's all.'

'And when you'd got it? I mean, he hasn't even asked if *we* have got it.'

'Well, why don't you ask him?'

'Aye, that's just what I'm going to do.'

Chapter Seventeen

Michael stood in Tammy's doorway for a few seconds, allowing the dramatic silence to reach out then went forward into her living-room. His face was devoid of expression, his eyes cold and his lips compressed. He was about the same height as she but next to her full body he seemed smaller.

'Don't be cross, Michael,' she said. 'I had to talk to you.'

'*Don't, Michael*?' he repeated. 'Is that how we greet?'

'Please. Not now.'

He smiled. 'I can come in, can't I?' The smile under the thatch of white hair was slightly crooked and Tammy knew it of old.

'I've been waiting for you. Look, have a drink. I've got some Krug.'

He raised his eyebrows. 'The cooking business doing well? I'm flattered.'

He sat down and she gave him a glass of champagne.

'Why do you always drink champagne?' she said.

'Is there anything else?'

'How's Jane?'

'She's fine.'

'Fine?'

'Now you're asking questions. That's good. I like it when you don't say things like "Not now, Michael".'

He raised his glass and she could see him controlling his hand. There was a shake she had seen once or twice before when he had been angry.

'Jane's down at the Hampshire house,' he said. 'We both are.'

'I know, you said you were going. How is it?'

'I never liked the place. You know it, of course.'

'I haven't been there since we were at college. It's very remote. I'm a city girl.'

He finished the champagne in one long swallow and she rose from her chair and filled his glass.

'So talk,' he said. 'That's what you wanted, isn't it? Let me guess. It's about Jane?'

'Of course it's about Jane. What else is there?'

'And you're unhappy.'

'Very. I mean I feel I'm being—'

'Disloyal?'

'Of course. I'm her friend. I should be doing something.'

'Let's take that in parts.' His voice was silky.

'No! No! Let's not bloody analyse everything.'

'Why don't you want to analyse? Are you afraid of what you'd find out?'

'Of course I'm afraid. The more you analyse, the more afraid I get. It's always been like that.'

'No, it hasn't. Listen to me. You're supposed to be Jane's friend, right? But where were you when she needed you after Edward was killed?'

'You've got no right to say such a thing!'

'Where were you? You weren't with Jane. So isn't it a little late to start the disloyalty thing?'

'I wasn't with Jane because you were. You had taken over. You were running the psychological show.'

'And if I hadn't? Have you any idea how traumatized she was? No, of course you haven't.'

'Don't you think I felt a shit? But how was I going to get near her with you keeping everyone away? The thing is I feel a bigger shit now. I mean I'm not doing anything for her. She should be here or I should be there with her!'

'Jesus, I've explained at length the whole business of spousal dependency and—'

'Oh, God, there you go again with the long words and the jargon.'

'It's just as well someone knows what they mean and is able to use them. We've got a mentally unbalanced killer running about loose. With any luck he'll be caught before he harms anyone else – and that includes Jane – and he'll be put back in a special hospital. That shouldn't take too long. Every police force in the south of England will be on the lookout for him by now. But what happens then to Jane?

What legacy does all this leave in her? Do you want her to be a half person? Someone who cannot ever make a decision? Someone who won't go out of doors? Who will only sleep with the lights on? Because that's what will happen if we give in now.'

'But, Michael, you don't know. She might become more traumatized by what's happening to her now.'

'You know about these things do you?'

'Of course I—'

'You've studied reactions like this?'

'No, no. You—'

'Well, for Christ's sake do me the favour of not playing the parlour psychiatrist.'

'For God's sake. This is something I feel deeply about.'

'Ah, it's intuition. I see.'

'Listen, she needs me at the moment. Or if not me then someone. But she doesn't know anyone else because you've kept her so locked away and—'

'Don't go on! You're going to say something you'll regret.' He stood up and walked slowly round the large room. 'There's something I think you should know. It'll explain part of the way I feel about this. I'm going to get a divorce.'

'What!'

'I should have done it a long time ago. Jane and I have been drifting apart for some time. We haven't slept together for weeks.'

'Oh, God, Michael.'

'This isn't the time to talk about it but I wanted you to know.'

Tammy had risen too, and now she sat down as though the wind was knocked from her body.

'Michael . . .'

'No, not now. I've got to go. I don't want to leave her alone at this time of night. But just think about that.'

'It makes it worse in a way. How do you think I'm going to feel about a) making her miserable by not going to her, and b) then watching her come apart in a divorce?'

The phone rang.

'Let it ring,' Michael said.

'I can't do that. It might be Jane or someone with an order. It might be my mother.'

He sat back nursing his glass as she answered.

'Yes,' she said. 'Well . . . not really . . . oh, I see. Yes, I suppose so. Give me five minutes.'

She put the phone down. 'The police,' she said. 'That was a call from their car. They're only a few streets away. I said to give me five minutes.'

'Oh, Christ! I didn't want to get into this with you because I'm not certain, but I think I know where Underdown could be. If I can find him, I might be able to bring him in. If the police find him, they'll probably have to kill him. If I do find him, there's just a chance he'll come. He trusted me before and he must be getting desperate now.'

'You're crazy. He's bloody dangerous!'

'No, I'm not crazy. It's possible. And if I do, it solves the dilemma about Jane. Neither of us has to feel guilty, or at least no more guilty than in any ordinary marriage break-up. The whole Underdown problem vanishes.'

She let him kiss her on the cheek and then he was gone. She heard him going down the stairs and heard the front door slam, then the engine of the Porsche come to life. She went to the window and saw the car drive away and its red tail lights flicker as he accelerated down the street at high speed.

It was also seen by Macrae. He was standing on the opposite side of the road. Unable to find his way to her flat by car, he had left it a couple of streets away and walked. He frowned as he watched the Porsche whip round the bend at the end of the road and disappear from view.

He went up the stairs and Tammy was at her door. Her face was flushed and there was also a flush on her neck. She looked as though she had been under strain.

Macrae held up a couple of keys on a piece of string. 'You left these and I was passing. I thought I'd drop them in.'

She frowned. 'I've got your keys, George.'

'These were the ones I gave you. On the string. I found them in the kitchen.'

She scrabbled through her bag and brought out a similar set, also on string. 'No, I've got them.'

'Oh, well, it was an excuse to see you.'

She smiled and seemed to relax. 'You wouldn't like a glass of champagne, would you?'

'I don't much like champagne.'

'Nor do I. I've still got some of your whisky. I'll get that.' She picked up the champagne bottle and the two glasses and took them to the kitchen. He followed.

He said, 'Whoever that was, he went off at a hell of a rate.'

'What?'

'The Porsche. He came from here, didn't he?'

'Oh, yes. Yes, he does drive fast.'

Macrae waited.

After a moment she said, 'It was Dr Stone. He came in to tell me about Jane.'

'How is she?'

'They're in the country now. He says she's fine.'

'Fine?'

'That was my line. But that's what he said.'

Macrae took the whisky from her. She touched his hand. 'I'm glad you've come. Can you stay?'

'For a while. I'm on duty tonight.'

'I thought the police went home at five o'clock these days.'

'Not all of us.'

'I'm only joking, George.'

He began walking up and down as Michael had done and she watched his big frame. The two men were very different, she thought. Each aggressive in his own way.

REPORT 9/MSU/SM (2 enc)

ENC. 1

From: LOXTON HOSPITAL
TO: Director of Social and Community Services
       Winchester
       Hampshire

CONFIDENTIAL

re: **Malcolm Stephen Underdown**

The above-named patient will shortly be appearing
before a Mental Health Review Tribunal. The Mental
Health Review Tribunal Rules, 1983, require an
account of the facilities available for the care of the
patient if the authority for detention were discharged.

The Tribunal requires information on:

1 The patient's home and family circumstances
including the attitude of the nearest relative as defined
in the Mental Health Act, 1983.

2 (a) The opportunity for employment or occupation
and housing or accommodation facilities that would
be available to the patient if discharged.
   (b) The availability of community support and
relevant facilities.

The patient's nearest relative is Donna Elizabeth
Stokes of 'Donna's Place', North Meon, Hampshire.

Your attention is drawn to the Mental Health Tribunal

Rules, 1983, Part III, Section 12, 'discourses of documents'. This allows for the patient to receive copies of all reports unless a specific request is made for them to be withheld.

The information should be addressed to the Medical Records Office.

Yours faithfully,

T S HAXTON
Senior Social Worker
Loxton Hospital

ENC. 2

WINCHESTER SOCIAL AND COMMUNITY SERVICES DEPARTMENT
REPORT FOR MENTAL HEALTH TRIBUNAL

re: Your request concerning Malcolm Stephen Underdown.

SOCIAL CIRCUMSTANCES REPORT

Malcolm Stephen Underdown has no home of his own to which he can return, and so far he has no offers of accommodation in the event of his discharge.

At the time of his offence, which led to his admission to Loxton Hospital, he was living rough, either in London or the country.

His nearest relative is his mother, who lives in Hampshire. I visited her to discuss her son's application to the Tribunal. She is unsupportive of her son. She would not like to see him discharged.

On my visit to his mother, I formed the opinion that she would like him to be kept in Loxton for the foreseeable future. I gained the impression that this was as much for her sake as for his. She believes he has disrupted her life to a point where she no longer wishes to see him. The simplest way this could happen would be if he was kept in special hospitals. I do not think the mother's opinion therefore has any bearing on his future life and behaviour.

His mother appears to be living with a much younger partner and my view would be that it would not be helpful to Malcolm Underdown to be part of such a household in the unlikely event that his mother would have him.

MARGARET PROUT
Senior Social Worker
Winchester Social and Community Services

Note by SM
I agree with this. I have seen a letter which his mother wrote to the prison authorities while he was on remand saying she did not wish to visit him. She wrote a similar letter to Underdown's lawyers.

So far his treatment has been successful and his chances of rejoining the community good. I am worried about an attack on a fellow patient. It was believed it was by Underdown but we have been unable to substantiate this. A special watch on him was set but his behaviour remained good.

He is unfortunate in having no family support. I think it would be prudent for the current plan of transfer to Rakesbury Hospital to be implemented as an intermediate stage in his rehabilitation.

Chapter Eighteen

Leo Silver made it his practice to watch Scales carefully when they were having what the deputy commander called a 'conference'. It was as if he was watching someone with a nervous disease. Scales tapped his hair, clicked his pen, nibbled at its end, moved in his seat, opened and closed desk drawers . . . and the reason Leo watched him so closely was that he hoped never to become like him. Better be a piano teacher like his father than a deputy commander like Scales if this was what being a deputy commander did to you.

'Nothing . . . that's all I can say? Nothing?' Scales clicked his pen at the two other men in the room, Detective Chief Superintendent Wilson and Detective Superintendent Macrae. 'So I just tell a deputy commissioner that we have nothing about the Pimlico murder. Don't ring us, we'll ring you. Is that what you're saying?'

Click . . . click . . . went the pen.

'No, that's not what we're saying at all,' Wilson said. 'We know or at least we're bloody sure who did it and it's a question of finding him and we'll do that in the next couple of days. The Hampshire force is making it a priority but he lived all over the place and it's not easy to track back and find out where.'

'Easy or not, it had better be done or I will want to know why.'

That was the sort of remark from Scales which Leo knew made Macrae even crosser than he normally was when they were 'in conference'. Now Macrae reached into his pocket, took out his packet of small cigars and began to play with it. On the wall behind Scales was the big 'No Smoking' sign and Leo could see how agitated he was becoming at the very thought that Macrae might light up.

'We have a woman murdered in her own flat in the middle of London and we know who did it and we can't make an arrest! You want me to release a statement like that to the media?'

Macrae said, 'I wouldn't do that. The deputy commissioner won't like it.'

'Oh, thank you, George. I was wondering whether you were going to grace us with an opinion.'

'I don't have opinions,' Macrae said, staring at the packet of cigars. 'I like to deal in facts. And we have a few facts, not many, and I'll stay with those.'

'A few facts!' Scales tapped copies of the Loxton Special Hospital reports on his desk. 'There are hundreds of facts here. Hundreds.'

Wilson said, 'But the main fact is that Underdown's a nutter and when you deal with nutters you can't think logically because they don't.'

'Oh, for God's sake, Les, don't give me the philosophy of policing, just do the policing. I want a breakthrough on this. I want us to be able to hold up our heads again and—'

'And give some nice news to the deputy commissioner,' Macrae said.

'Why not? We're not all bolshie like you, Macrae.'

It had happened. The name had switched from George to Macrae and Leo knew that this was when Scales was fishing for something he could use against Macrae. Hastily he said, 'Sir, I was talking to Mr Macrae a little earlier. Jane Stone, that's the woman—'

'I know who she is,' Scales said. Click . . . click . . .

'Well, she's gone down to her country house. Mr Macrae and I thought we'd go down and see her again, generally look around.'

Scales threw down his pen. 'For God's sake, do that then! Do something!'

They left Scales' office a few minutes later and in the corridor Wilson said, 'You always irritate him, George. That makes things worse for everyone.'

'Not for you, Les. By comparison with me, it makes you look good.'

Macrae and Silver went into Macrae's office and closed the door.

'So we talked about going down there, did we?' Macrae said.

'I thought if we showed willing he'd end the conference.'

'Aye, I suppose you're right. But I wanted to talk to you anyway. There are one or two things. The main is, I'm not happy about this bugger Stone. I go back to what we were talking about: why is he investigating all this? The chief super thinks it's reasonable. I don't. Ordinary people don't investigate, except in the pictures. And there's another thing. I went out to see Mrs Weston about something last night . . .' He was aware of the questioning expression on Leo's face but plunged on regardless. 'When I was in the street outside her place Stone came down from her flat and got into his car. Didn't see me. Drove away like the clappers. And knew without thinking which way to turn at the end of the street and which way to turn after that because I could hear the note of the car engine and it didn't drop. Now I've been to the flat a couple of times and I still couldn't find my way through the barriers and had to park streets away.'

Leo had been watching Macrae as he had watched Scales. Here was a different person, one who didn't fidget even though he was blatantly lying. He said, 'I remember Mrs Weston saying she had difficulty in finding her way.'

'Dr Stone didn't have any trouble. And I'm asking the question, why?'

'Practice makes perfect as that regurgitator said.'

'Right. And what does that mean, laddie?'

'It means he's been to her place quite a bit. Guv'nor, are you thinking what I think you're thinking: that he's got his leg over?'

'Could be.'

'But Jane Stone is her best friend.'

'That's where it happens most, to best friends.'

His voice was harsh and Leo had a sudden thought. Frenchy had been gone for months. Macrae liked women, especially women of Tammy Weston's build. He had visited the flat a couple of times. Did *he* have a leg over?

Macrae said, 'The point is that he's not been very frank with us, and I don't like people not being frank with us.'

'You mean those reports from Loxton? You think he's looking for something?'

'How the hell do I know? But there's certainly one way of finding out. We bloody well ask him what he's up to. Go and see if you can raise him. He's at the Portsmouth Crown Court. Ring the Clerk and ask him to give Stone a message to call us. In the meantime, let's see if we can find his ex-wife. She should know him backwards.'

The object of these inquiries was lying on his stomach at the top of a small land hummock about two hundred yards from a country lane. He'd driven into a field and parked the Porsche behind a tall hawthorn hedge and had walked up the hill to the top of the rise and put down a rug. He had done this several times and knew the area now.

He made himself comfortable and took a powerful pair of binoculars from their case and checked their focus. He was looking downhill to a patch of secondary forest about ten acres in extent. There were beech trees and elms, heavily bushed by silver birches and wild willow, brambles and stinging nettles.

It had taken Michael Stone several hours of exploring different fields and locations before he had found a place from which he could see into the wood. The wood itself had taken him several days to find. But once he had the Loxton reports and Underdown's own manuscript it had not been difficult to add two and two and come to the conclusion that the old sand pit was where he might have taken refuge. Once he had come to that conclusion he'd had to find out where the farm was. The *Winchester Times*, which had carried detailed reports of Underdown's trial, had identified the place where Malcolm Stephen Underdown had grown up.

Michael had come to the area looking for one identifying mark: the old road that went into the sand pit. He had found it and now he used the zoom on the binoculars and brought the small hut into close-up.

He could only see it through a tangle of branches but even so it was sharp enough for him to make out that recent work had been done on the roof. Cut branches had ben laid over it with black plastic silage bags across them, kept in place by large stones. The hut was small and obviously in poor repair, but it seemed a reasonable haven for a man on the run.

Michael settled down to wait. It was a dry, chilly day but he was dressed in a fleece-lined leather coat and fleece-lined boots and did not feel the cold.

He kept his eyes glued to the binoculars. Then he saw smoke which, if he hadn't been looking at the area in close detail, would have been lost among the trees. It rose from a stone fireplace on the far side of the hut.

There was a movement in the trees and, for the first time in more than four years, he saw Underdown. He came out of the underbrush, a large man in a heavy overcoat with a woollen cap on his head. Even at that distance Michael could see that he had grown his hair longer than he remembered, for it hung below the cap. He held something in his hands and when he crouched down and began to cut it with a knife Michael realized it must be a rabbit or a squirrel which he might have snared or gathered from the surface of a country road.

Underdown and animals. This was a part of the reports which had particularly interested Michael. What had been fascinating was the sentimental attachment one moment and the cold killing the next.

Underdown spitted the small pink carcass and took it to the fire. He bent and blew on the coals and soon there was enough heat for him to start cooking his mcal. There was almost no smoke now and Michael realized he must be using very dry wood.

Should he go down now? Or would it be better to wait until Underdown had eaten? He decided on the latter, for just going near the man would be dangerous. Michael's fingers touched the small pistol which lay in the pocket of his coat. Not that he wanted to shoot Underdown. That was the last thing he wanted. No, he wanted to talk, to see if he couldn't bring him out of this country fastness.

It took Underdown about half an hour to cook his meal and then, like some primitive tribesman, he tore at the carcass with his teeth. It was obvious that he was ravenous.

Suddenly he threw down the animal bones and strode off into the wood. Michael followed him as best he could through the glasses then, a few minutes later, saw him going up the opposite slope to the one on which he was lying. Underdown paused at a hedgerow and pulled a bicycle from its covering leaves. He went through a gate on to a lane from which the lorries had come to the sand pit in the old days. His figure was briefly silhouetted against the sky, then he was gone.

Michael did not hesitate. He trotted down to the wood and into the hut. It was dark and fetid but he could see newspapers and plastic sheets and a pile of old clothing and blankets. You would have to know how to live like a tramp to exist here, he thought. But then, that was what Underdown had become. A tramp. A fugitive, always on the move.

He went out to the fire. There were a few bones, not many, in the surrounding grass. He was not eating much.

How long would he stay here, Michael wondered. How long could anyone stay in a place like this?

The piles of clothing in her mother's bedroom were growing by the day and Jane was not looking forward to taking them into Winchester. She wondered if Oxfam would collect them and decided to phone them and ask.

She was about to pick up the receiver when the telephone rang under her outstretched hand. She jerked involuntarily and stepped back. The phone had rung only once or twice since they had come to Highlands and the calls had been from Michael. This was probably another. She picked up the receiver and for a moment, just listened. That was their arrangement. She would not say anything and he would identify himself. But a woman's voice said, 'Hello . . . hello . . . anyone there?'

'Who's that?'

'Jane?'

'Who is it?'

'This is Deborah.'

In the background Jane could hear a child crying and she visualized Deborah Broadbent in the untidy house in the tree-lined street. She said, 'Sorry. But I didn't want to give my name in case it was . . . well, you know.'

'Of course I bloody know.' The voice was icy and at the same time charged with anger and hatred. 'Why shouldn't I know? He was your boyfriend after all.'

Jane was confused. Why was she angry? Who was she talking about?

'I'm sorry, I don't—'

'Your bloody ex-boyfriend has attacked Charlie!'

'What?' She felt her legs go to rubber.

'He must have followed you and—'

'That's not true. How could he have followed me? I didn't know I was coming to your house until the last moment and I'd been driving all night.'

'Well, it seems like it. You come one day and a few days later, *he* comes.'

Jane tried to get to grips with her emotions. 'What about Charlie? Is he all right?'

'Charlie's in hospital with a wired-up jaw because of that bastard.'

'Deborah, I'm so sorry! Can you tell me what happened?'

'Charlie thought he was that tramp at the dust-bins again and when he went out into the street it was—'

'Don't say the name.'

'Why the hell not?'

'I don't know, it just makes me uneasy.'

'Uneasy! My God, listen to you. I'm telling you what happened to *us*!'

'I'm sorry. Please go on.'

'He must have wanted your address otherwise he wouldn't have come. We'll know that soon. At the moment Charlie's wired-up and sedated and isn't talking or writing.'

'I'll come and—'

'No! No! Don't come near us. Not ever again. I'm taking Mark to my mother's house. We're not budging until all this is over.'

After a pause, Jane said, 'Can I ask you how you got this number?'

'From Charlie's telephone book, of course.'

There was a loud wail from a baby and Deborah said, 'Mark, do shut up!' Then, into the phone, 'I've got to go now. Don't try to contact us and don't contact Charlie in the hospital. OK?' She put down the receiver.

Jane was left in the empty house feeling hurt and humiliated and scared. It wasn't her fault. She hadn't – absolutely had not – been followed there by Malcolm. He must have done exactly what he had done in London. He had tracked down Charlie in Guildford – not difficult since all his friends at college had known he lived there and Broadbent wasn't all that common a name.

She began to walk along the corridors and in and

out of rooms, hardly knowing where she was. The
picture of what had happened was vividly in her
mind. She could see Charlie going out to remonstrate
with the man he thought was the tramp. She could
see the big figure of Malcolm grab him and ask him
questions and then the blows and the collapsing
body.

Oh, God, what a terrible thing to have happened!
Was it her fault? Was it?

She found herself in her old playroom. She had
a doll in her arms and was holding it tightly for
comfort.

Chapter Nineteen

The offices of Computer Studies Ltd lay in a small cul-de-sac on the west side of the Edgware Road where Paddington becomes Maida Vale. It occupied the large ground floor of what had once been offices of a different sort – there were still the remains of an estate agent's logo on the wall – but the windows were covered by venetian blinds and the computer services sign was in elegant black on white.

Leo and Macrae looked at the building from Leo's car.

Macrae said, 'There's a parking space over there.'

'Residents only.'

'To hell with that.'

Macrae was in a dark mood. Leo had recognized its onset when Macrae had mentioned seeing Michael Stone coming out of Tammy's house and driving away in that over-familiar way. He guessed now that this visit to Dr Stone's ex-wife had little to do with Underdown, a lot to do with Tammy Weston and what Macrae thought might be going on between her and Stone. In other words, the bugger was jealous.

Well, he might have reason to be, Leo thought.

Computer Studies front office was smartly furnished in greys and whites and blacks, with a large black table behind which a receptionist would normally sit. There was no receptionist.

They heard voices from behind a door and Macrae opened it, letting them into a large room in which there were eight or ten desks, each with its own computer screen flickering and glowing in the strip lighting.

About half the desks were occupied. An elegant woman in a black skirt and white blouse was bending over a desk at which a young man was sitting.

'Look,' she was saying. 'You hold the mouse firmly so the pointer doesn't flick around the screen and remember that when you go to File Manager, it's a double click.'

One of the other students said, 'Mrs Stokes, there's someone here.'

She turned and saw the two detectives. They saw an attractive, professional-looking woman with short dark hair, greying at the temples, and a face with features that were too sharp for beauty.

Macrae identified himself and Leo. Frowning, she led them into a rear office, just as clinically furnished in black and white as the rest of the suite. 'How may I help you?' she said. Her voice's metallic ring suited the offices.

'You're Mrs Pamela Stone, Dr Michael Stone's former wife?' Macrae said.

'Has something happened?'

'Not to him. What we've come about is something that happened some years ago.'

They sat. The chairs were black mock-leather on steel frames. Pamela Stone sat behind her desk.

Macrae filled her in about Underdown.

'Yes, I read that in the paper.' Her voice was not precisely hostile, but chilly. 'There's nothing I can tell you about him, though.'

'Nothing?'

'No.'

Macrae said, 'Do you mind if I smoke?'

'If you have to.'

He lit a thin panatella. 'You see, Mrs Stone, you might know something you don't know you know.'

'Mr . . . Macrae, is it? Mr Macrae, I'm running this place without help. My assistant is ill today. I haven't time to delve into the mysteries of the past as they apply to someone like this person Underdown.'

'This person Underdown killed a man called Edward Craig and your husband was a defence witness. This person went to Loxton Special Hospital, then to a regional unit, then to a hostel, then he walked out of that and we think he has killed again.' Macrae was staring at her over the grey ash of his cigar and she shifted under the impact. 'This person Underdown may kill again, Mrs Stone, which is why

we have come to you to see if there is anything you
can remember about him that may lead us to him.'

'You make me sound very callous.' She smiled.
'I'm not really. Would you like a coffee?'

She poured three mugs from a Cona jug and
said, 'Some people think anyone who deals with
computers is turned into a cypher. I'm not that,
either. It's just that I don't like digging up the past.
It's taken me a long time to escape from it.'

Leo said, 'We really do need any information you
might have.'

'Well, it's not something I'd forget. Here's a man
who murders someone and the someone's girlfriend
ends up marrying the defence psychiatrist. My
husband.'

'Did your husband talk to you about the case?'

'My *former* husband never talked to me about his
work. In fact, when I come to think of it, he never
talked to me about anything very much. He was
always talking to other people and listening to other
people – his patients or clients, or whatever they
were – and he didn't feel much like talking when he
got home. That's why I took up computers. They
didn't talk to me either but at least I could talk to
them.'

'Didn't you get on with your husband?' Macrae
said.

'Yes, I got on with him. I loved him very much.
At the beginning, that is. I knew him at university.
He was the proto-typical scholarship boy. Working

like a dog and with ambitions as high as the moon. You've only got to know his background to realize why. He came from nowhere. Father was a plough-man, mother did cleaning jobs. I only met them once and that was by chance. They simply turned up at college one day. He never even told them we were getting married. They didn't come to the wedding. I don't think he wanted my parents to meet them although he didn't say that. And then he cut all contacts with them.'

'Why wouldn't he have wanted your parents not to meet them?'

'Michael is the world's biggest snob. And that means a money-snob as well as a social snob. My parents were well-off. Not fantastically rich but well-heeled, and they supported Michael through the early years when he was struggling. But that's enough about me and Michael. You wanted to know about Underdown. Well, Underdown means only one thing to me and it's of no help to you. His name means that Michael started to have an affair with Jane, which meant the end of our marriage.'

Leo said, 'Did he ever say anything to you about Underdown's background, his home, where he lived? Something that you might have forgotten?'

She shook her head. 'No. As I said, Michael didn't bring his work home.'

'Was your husband having affairs with other women?' Macrae said. It was so pointed and abrupt that Leo winced. Pamela Stone's face hardened.

'I think that's enough, Mr Macrae. You'll have to excuse me.' She rose and waited for them to file out of her office.

In the street outside Leo, irritated, said, 'Well, we didn't get much from her, guv'nor.'

'That's what you think, laddie.'

As they spoke Leo's phone rang.

It was Wilson for Macrae. 'George, there's been a development in the Underdown case. The Surrey police have been in touch. They think he's attacked someone in Guildford.'

'Have they got him?'

'No, only the victim. He's in North Surrey General. If you've got Silver with you, why don't you get down there and see him.'

Macrae took down details and said, 'Right, Les, we'll go and have a look.'

The house was as alive as the house in London, and Jane was aware of noises all around her. There was the creaking of the old timbers, the ticking of the clocks. These worried her more than anything else, especially the grandfather clock in the hall. Michael had wound it and he had also wound the strike. So now she had to close her ears with her fingers or count backwards, so she did not count the strokes correctly. Once, lying in bed when she was a child and they had first moved into the house, she had heard the clock, at midnight, strike thirteen. It had terrified her. She did not know whether she had counted incorrectly or whether the clock itself had been wrong, but she had taken it as a bad omen. After that she did not count the number of strokes in case it ever did that again.

She told herself she should not even be thinking of things like that. She still had a huge amount of work to do in the house before she could bring the cleaners in. She had almost finished her mother's wardrobes and drawers but then there was the kitchen and all those cupboards and her own room and the playroom. What was she going to do with the play-house? It was huge and would not be able to be brought out whole. Was it worth taking it to pieces and having it put together again? Would anyone want something of that size?

And all the time she was thinking of what she had to do, she was hearing the movement of the house.

What if Malcolm did come, she thought? What if he came while she was here alone?

The thought was too terrible to dwell on. She tried to focus on something else, but couldn't. She began to see other pictures: the tramp who wasn't a tramp, the collapsing body of Charlie, the hospital bed, the wiring of his jaw.

Poor Charlie, injured by Malcolm for the second time. And all because of her.

She had phoned the hospital immediately after Deborah had called her. They had given her the normal bromide: as well as can be expected. She had wanted to get into her car and go to Guildford at once, but even if Deborah wasn't there, she might have left instructions that Jane was not to be admitted to Charlie's room.

She needed Michael to take some of this load, but she knew that she should not phone him. That was part of their unwritten agreement, never to phone him at court. Not only was it wrong, he said, to try and phone a witness, but it would also interrupt his concentration. So she hadn't. But shouldn't he know about Malcolm's new violence?

After she had come back from her walkabout, as Michael had described it, to Charlie's house in Guildford, he had said, 'You know I'm only a phone call away if you need me.'

But that did not mean at court. She didn't even have the name of the lawyers who were acting for the accused. That was something she could do! She could phone the court, get their names and leave a message with them to ask Michael to call her as soon as possible.

She telephoned Portsmouth Crown Court. An abrupt woman said no, she couldn't help. It wasn't her job to search for solicitors, she was far too busy for that. When Jane asked whose job it was, she became angry and said she didn't have time to talk any longer. Jane could come down to the court and consult the lists of cases like anyone else.

She felt helpless. She needed Michael and he wasn't around.

But the police in Guildford would know about Charlie. What about Macrae and Silver? Shouldn't they be told? Would the Guildford police tell them? Should she phone Cannon Row?

It wouldn't do any harm. If they knew, they knew. If they didn't, they should.

Neither Macrae nor Silver was in the station, she was told. She left a message with her number, asking one of them to telephone her.

That was all she could do.

She wandered about the house again. How could she protect herself? The gun? She went to her room and looked at it. Tammy had tried to explain how it worked but her mind had refused to take it in. Just looking at it made her frightened, and not this time of Malcolm. She hated guns. She would never use it. Never. She put it in the bottom of a drawer under her clothing.

What else was there? What could she use to defend herself? Knives? God, no! Sticks?

She thought of simpler and non-violent weapons: mace, but she didn't have any; pepper, she would look for some; hairspray, perhaps; keys held in the hand, useless.

If only Michael would come home.

Chapter Twenty

The afternoon was dry and cold but Michael Stone, dressed in leather and wool, was able to lie on the hard ground without becoming frozen. His heavy gloves held the binoculars. Every few minutes he would begin the sweep. Starting at the hedge which ran along the opposite road, he would come slowly down the slope to the woodland. Using the zoom, he would bring up the hut and the fireplace next to it, the door, the windows with their partial glazing.

Everything was still.

He could see a cock pheasant in the opposite field, he could see rooks and ravens in the bare branches of the trees. The day before he had seen a fox, and the day before that two roe deer.

What he was waiting for now was Underdown.

His glasses went back to the hut. No smoke rose from the fireplace. Was he still asleep? Sick? Dead? Or had he vanished to new surroundings?

Michael didn't believe any of these alternatives. This place was so remote, so enclosed by its hedges and trees and folds of the ground, that there could hardly have been a safer hiding place. He remembered how much store Malcolm had set by it. *His* place. That's how he had thought of it. The place where he had escaped from his step-father; the place he had used as a playground, with animals as his friends. As with any relationship, he was kind to some and not so kind to others. And not so kind with Underdown had meant killing them. Well, now he was killing as many of his friends as he could, killing them and eating them. Even so, he must be starving.

There he was!

Michael swung up to the opposite road and zoomed in on the pedalling figure. He could just see it above the hedge. Underdown stopped at the heavy gate, brought the bike through and hid it in the hedge, as Michael had thought he would.

He held him in the lenses as he came down the slope towards the wood. He vanished into the trees and Michael played the glasses over them. There he was again, like a huge shadow. His coat flapped and his big arms flapped and his feet seemed to flap – and here he came, down the path through the undergrowth, and stopped.

Michael tried to get a clearer picture of him but the thin branches created a veil. Underdown was examining the hut and the surroundings. When he was satisfied, he began a tour of the area, head bent, and Michael, who had seen him do this before, knew he was looking for tracks.

But the past couple of days had been dry and there was no mud or soft earth. Anyway, Michael had been very careful. Very careful indeed.

Slowly, Underdown came round by the front of the hut and gently pushed the door. It swung open. He stood back, and then, reassured that it was empty, he went in.

That was when he would see it, sitting there in the middle of the floor, a large brown paper bag with an envelope stuck on the top.

Michael came quickly down the slope and, keeping low, made for the front of the hut. By now Underdown should have at least read the note. Michael was pleased with the note, it had taken some thought. *'Dear Malcolm,'* he had written. *'You must be hungry. This is the best I could do for you. When you've opened the bag and had a taste, come to the window and look out. You'll see me. I mean you no harm and have only come here for your own good. Please believe that. Your friend, Michael.'*

He had wanted an understated, undramatic note which dealt in basic instincts like hunger and fear and happiness. Food meant relief from hunger and relief from hunger and fear meant happiness. Once these primitive functions had been attended to Underdown would probably be receptive to more sophisticated emotions.

For a second he thought he saw a movement behind the filthy glass of the window. The door of the hut had been half open and now it was slammed shut and Michael could hear something being man-handled against it.

He walked slowly towards the hut.

'Malcolm,' he called. 'It's Michael Stone. I'm sure you remember me. We talked so much.'

Again there was a movement behind the window.

'Look.' Michael held up his hands. 'No weapon, nothing. And I don't want to come in. I'll stay here.' There was a tree stump near the fireplace and he sat down on it. 'I mean you no harm,' he called. 'I hope you understand that.'

Another movement by the window. This time it was followed by a shape. The shape became a head, a face. The face was covered in hair, the mouth was invisible. Only the eyes, dark sockets amid the hair, belied that this was an animal. Michael felt he could have been looking at Robinson Crusoe.

'Eat something,' he said. 'You'll feel better then.'

Part of the window had been broken and Underdown had covered the hole with a piece of cloth. This was now pulled aside and Michael was surprised that the fingers he saw were not covered in long hair but were the ordinary fingers of a large hand.

A voice from inside the hut spoke. It was the first time he had heard Underdown's voice for nearly five years and he was unprepared for it. The lips, below the hair, had moved, must have moved, but he had been unable to see them.

'I can't hear you, Malcolm. Can you say that again?'

'Poison! You want to bloody poison me!' The voice was a hoarse monotone.

'That's the last thing I'd do. I want to help you. Listen—'

'You bloody liar!'

'Malcolm, listen to me. You're hungry. I brought this food for you. I know what you've been eating. I've seen you eat. Yesterday it was a rabbit I think, and you cooked it over here on the fire. If I'd wanted to harm you I'd have brought the police days ago.'

'I don't trust you.'

'If you think I want to poison you, pass some of the food to me. I'll taste it for you.'

'Why are you doing this?'

'Because you're my responsibility. We worked together and you said you liked me.'

'That was before I went to Loxton. I'm not going back to that place.'

'OK, Malcolm.'

'Never!'

'Right. But you're going to need support. That's why I've come.'

'Bullshit. You've come because . . . because . . .'

'Why, Malcolm?'

'Because you interfere, that's why!'

'OK, I interfere, but only with people who are important to me. You're important to me.'

'I don't want to talk to you.'

'You're going to have to talk to someone, you know. If I could find you, the police will find you, then things will be different.'

The head suddenly disappeared from the window.

'Malcolm . . . did you hear what I said?'

The face reappeared and a hand was thrust out of the broken part of the window. It held a cold chicken leg. Michael moved forward and took it, bit off a mouthful, chewed it and swallowed. 'OK?'

He handed the drumstick back.

Now he heard movement. Paper being torn. A bottle of lemonade being opened.

'Enjoy it,' he said. 'There isn't a thing there that will do you any harm.'

The hand came out again, this time with a packet of potato crisps. Michael opened it, took a couple, chewed, swallowed, passed it back.

So it went on. Small pieces of food, paper cups of lemonade, all to be tasted and passed back. Then, without warning, the door was pulled back and Underdown was standing there.

Michael had forgotten how big he was. He was about six-foot-five with broad, square shoulders, made to seem even larger by the heavy coat he wore. It was a tweed overcoat that reached mid-calf and had seen better years. Beneath it he seemed to be wearing three or four shirts. He had on torn jeans – not fashionably torn, just torn – and workmen's heavy boots on his feet. But it was his face that was

memorable, if not frightening. Now he could see it
more clearly it reminded Michael not so much of
Crusoe but of old black-and-white movies of
werewolves.

'Hello, Malcolm,' he said.

Then he saw the knife. It was a large kitchen
knife with a blade about seven inches long. It
seemed to grow out of Underdown's right sleeve as
though it was part of his body.

Michael noted it but did not feel afraid. Once,
he had dominated Underdown and he had not the
slightest doubt that he could do so again. Underdown
had, on several occasions in the prison, ended their
dialogues in tears. He was big in body but not,
Michael thought, in spirit.

'I hope you're not going to use that knife on me,
Malcolm. That would be very unfair since I haven't
done anything to harm you. We have to talk. We
talked before, remember, and talking did you a lot
of good.'

'You put me in Loxton!'

'I didn't. That was the system. I explained to
you that it was either going to be that or gaol and
remember, we thought that Loxton might be the
better of the two. Why don't you sit down on the log?'

Underdown ignored him and Michael said, 'You
won't mind if I do, then.' He sat down and was now
well below Underdown's level. But since Underdown
was so huge he was below his level even standing
and now seemed to gain a dominance from the fact

that he was sitting down and Malcolm was still standing. There was a kind of schoolmaster–pupil effect.

'Is there any more food?' Underdown said.

'I'm sorry, but that's all I could bring.'

'You got a cigarette?'

Michael dug into his pocket and came up with a pack of twenty. He held it in his hand close to his body so that Malcolm had to bend towards him.

Again there was something of the master and the mendicant in the exchange.

'I've come to help you,' Michael said. 'And goodness knows, you need it.'

Underdown had leant against the wall of the hut. He smoked the cigarette, holding it in his left hand. The knife was still in his right.

'Don't you think so, Malcolm?'

'Don't I think what?'

'That you need help.'

'That's what you said before. When they sent me to Loxton.'

'But they did help you. It's not five years since you were in court and you've been to Loxton and then come through the system to Rakesbury and the hostel in Winchester. Why did you walk away from it? You wouldn't have had to spend much time there and then they would have found you accommodation in the community and your life would have been your own again.'

'You think *your* life is your own?'

'In most ways.'

'You've never done anything wrong?'

'Some things.'

'But you never got punished as I did.'

'It wasn't punishment, Malcolm, it was treatment. You were ill.'

'*Were*. You used the word *were*. What about now?'

'That's a bit more difficult. You'd have to see the experts again. Go back on medication and—'

'I don't want to go back on that stuff! Christ, it turned me into a zombie.'

'You're off it now, Malcolm, and see what's happened.'

'What d'you mean?'

'I'm talking about the woman in London. The one you put in the cupboard.'

Underdown lit another cigarette from the one he had almost finished and Michael could see that his hand was shaking.

'You want to tell me about that, Malcolm?'

'What?'

'About the woman.'

'What woman?'

'The one in London.' Again there was a pause. 'You know what I'm talking about, don't you? Look, the sooner we talk, the sooner I can help you. Don't you realize what's happening? I've found you. The police are interested in you. The reason I found you first is that I got your reports first and I remembered our talks so I knew how much store you set by this place.'

Suddenly Underdown ground out his cigarette in the dirt and said, 'What are they going to do to me?'

'It depends on how you let me handle this. It depends how we talk. But I think I can save you a lot of strife. The future may not be as dark as you think it is. Tell me, have you been feeling very depressed?'

Underdown's face crumpled and tears ran down his cheeks. He mumbled something and Michael said, 'Sorry?'

'I can't help it. I just can't help it. There's something inside me. A force. I just can't help it . . .'

'I know, Malcolm . . . I know. And I think I know where that force comes from. The point is, I don't think what's happened is your fault. We can't control forces sometimes, not when they assault us as this force assaults you.'

Underdown stared at him. He had stopped crying and what could be seen of his face was anguished.

'How do you know?' he said.

'It's my job to know. You're not unique, Malcolm, only in terms of the force itself. It affects you. It doesn't affect anyone else. Other forces affect other people. That was something that was never brought out properly at the trial.'

'But you think . . .'

'Sit down. Let's talk about this. I think there are things we can work out together.'

Underdown came slowly forward and then

lowered himself on to a log. His beard was wet with his tears. 'What things?' he said.

The North Surrey General Hospital lay on a hill overlooking Guildford. It was an old building, partly Victorian, with modern additions.

Macrae and Silver were seen by one of its management team who explained that Charlie Broadbent had a compound fracture of the mandible. 'Our maxillo-facial people have been looking after him,' he said, and Macrae had a feeling he used the jargon only because it sounded impressive.

A nurse led them along a corridor to a private room. Before they went in she said, 'There are wires so that we get the correct alignment on his teeth and he has a tube. Please don't let him see you think it looks nasty. OK?'

'Right,' Leo said.

'Hello, Mr Broadbent,' she said cheerfully as she led them into the room. 'I've got some visitors for you. And this is Mrs Broadbent.'

A heavily pregnant woman was sitting beside the bed.

Macrae identified himself and Silver and said, 'The Surrey police notified us of the assault, Mrs Broadbent. We're very sorry it happened.'

Leo tried to keep his eyes off Charlie Broadbent's head. With the bandages and wires and the tube in his mouth he looked like someone dressed for the part of victim in a medical soap on TV.

Deborah said, 'It wouldn't have happened at all if that bloody woman hadn't come to our house.'

'Which woman?' Macrae said.

'Jane Stone.'

'You mean Dr Stone's wife?'

'Of course I mean Dr Stone's wife. She came a few days ago and—'

There was a gurgling sound from the bed. Deborah stopped talking. It came again, more of a mumble, and she said, 'Charlie doesn't think she had anything to do with it. But what the hell did she come for? She just panicked and came to him.'

'Can you tell me a little more about that?' Macrae said.

In a tight, cold voice Deborah told him about Jane's visit. Occasionally Charlie mumbled something, but she took no notice. When she had finished Macrae said, 'How would Underdown have known she was coming to your house?'

'He might have seen her in the street. He might have followed her from London for all we know.'

'We don't think he has a car.'

Charlie began to mumble more loudly and it was accompanied by hisses as he tried to form words through his lips, which were held together by the wires.

'Can he tell us anything about his meeting with Underdown?' Macrae said. 'Has he told you?'

'Of course he's told me. It happened—'

'Can he tell us?' Macrae turned away from her. 'Will you try, Mr Broadbent?'

There were sounds of whistling and gurgling and hissing but slowly the words came out and Macrae began to piece together a scenario.

It had happened when Charlie came home from work. Underdown had been waiting for him near his house in the tree-lined street. He had caught him by the throat and started to shake him.

'I thought . . . he was . . . the . . . old tramp . . . from before . . .' Charlie mumbled. 'Then . . . I saw . . . who . . . it was.'

There was a pause and Leo said gently, 'And then?'

'He wanted . . . to know . . . where Jane was.'

'Do you know her London address?'

'Not offhand.'

'And her house in the country?'

'Her mother's house. I knew the village.'

'Is that what he wanted to know?'

'All he was . . . doing . . . was shaking me and saying . . . and saying where was she . . .'

'And you didn't tell him?' Macrae said.

'No . . . he was holding my neck . . . and then he began to hit me . . . and a couple of . . . men . . . in the street . . . ran up and he went off on . . . a bike . . .'

'He was very brave – and she doesn't bloody well deserve it,' Deborah said.

*

The afternoon was dying. Again, as the word came into Jane's mind, it was followed by the thought of death and decay. She fought the words as she fought the silence of the house, as she fought the ticking of the clocks.

She had finished sorting her mother's clothes and all that remained was a load of black plastic sacks which she had carried downstairs and put into the garage. She had started on her own rooms but things were going slowly. How could she throw away her panda or the large diary of a trip to America, written when she was seven? And if she didn't throw them away, what did she do with them?

But all this had become secondary to the tension and the fear which the house created. She had thought this house would be less frightening than being alone in the London house; that its familiarity would help her. But she had not bargained with her discovery of the attack on Charlie.

She went down to the kitchen and dialled Tammy's number once again. She waited for the answering machine to switch on as it had already done three times that day.

Instead, Tammy answered. 'Hi, I've just got in and I was about to phone you,' she said.

'Is your mother sick?'

'No . . . I mean, well, she's been better the last couple of days.'

'I wondered if you'd been with her.'

'Never mind me. How are *you*?'

She told Tammy about Deborah's call.

'Oh, Lord, that's bad. Poor Charlie!'

'And Guildford's not too far from here.'

'But Malcolm clearly doesn't know your address otherwise he wouldn't have attacked Charlie, so you're safe. Safer than you would be in London.'

'That's what Michael says.'

'He all right?'

'I wish I knew. I can't get hold of him to tell him. He's supposed to be at the Portsmouth Crown Court but I can't get any sense out of the Crown Prosecution Service down there. They seem to think I want them to run messages for me. But I think Michael should be warned about what happened to Charlie, don't you?'

Tammy paused, then said, 'Yes, I suppose so. But if Malcolm tries to find Michael he'll be caught quicker. I mean, everyone knows Michael was his forensic psychiatrist at the trial. One call from Malcolm and they'll be alerted and, of course, he'd never show his face at court. He's not that stupid.'

'He may not be stupid, but he's mad.'

'That's true.'

'And being mad means you don't know your own behaviour pattern, yes?'

'Yes.'

'And that means no one else does either unless you're on your medication and Malcolm isn't. Am I right?' Her voice had been steadily rising.

'Hang on . . . hang on. Listen, you've been marvellous so far. Don't crack now. Darling, they're going to pick him up. Christ, he's enormous. He can't go down a street without people noticing him. Just hang on.'

'Hang on. That's it, is it? Hang on?'

'What else can I say? You could go to Mongolia or Iceland and wait there until he's caught. Have you thought of that?'

'Michael doesn't want me to go away. And after the fuss I made about coming down here and getting him his meals and all that, I don't suppose I want to either. The trouble is he's never here to eat his meals. He gets back late at night and is gone early in the morning. You couldn't come down, could you?'

'Jane, I've this work to do and—'

'I'd pay you. I'd pay your fares and a salary for being here and—'

'Darling, I just can't. My mother—'

'But you said your mother was all right.'

'Well ... yes, she is, at the moment, but that could change. And it isn't only her. I've got a job.' She told her about Macrae.

'Cleaning?'

'Not cleaning exactly. It's more house-keeping. He can't cope. And he's paying me quite well. Not a fortune, but I told you the cooking business was going down, so it's coming in very handy.'

'I could have let you have money. You know that.'

'Thanks, but I'm a big girl now and I've got to look after myself.'

'You all right?'

'Why?'

'You sounded . . . I don't know, your voice sounded funny.'

'I'm tired and I've had a couple of glasses of wine and you know how I get. But never mind me. You haven't told me how you are.'

'Lonely. Scared. House-bound. Or shouldn't I say things like that? Should I be brave like Michael wants me to be? Tammy, I'd pay your fares and a salary for being here if you don't want to take a loan.'

'Don't be bloody silly. I wouldn't take money from a friend. But, darling, I just can't. I said I'd get his place right and he's depending on me. Oh, God, I know this sounds bad, but if I could, I would, you know that. It's just that I think . . . well, I think you're exaggerating the danger. Malcolm doesn't know where you are. Anyway, you've got money to stay in a hotel if you want to. Have you thought of that? It's what I'd do. I'd go down to be near Michael and I'd stay in a hotel.'

'OK, Tammy, don't worry.'

'Of course I'll worry.'

'I have to go now.'

'Don't ring off!'

'I must. I want to try Michael again. 'Bye. See you.'

'Listen, darling—'

But the line went dead.

Chapter Twenty-one

'That's better, isn't it?' Michael said as Underdown folded his big body into the Porsche. 'Move the seat back. Listen, don't worry about anything. I said we weren't going anywhere and we're not. We're just sitting, talking. And you must admit that it's warmer and more comfortable than the hut. That might be all right in summer, but it can't be too good in winter.'

The light was going fast. There was a drizzle on the wind that had strengthened from the south-west.

'I like it.' It was said as if Underdown was replying automatically and without much thought. Michael believed this was a symptom of his depression and it had become more noticeable in the past hour.

'Do you like music?' Michael switched on the radio and the car was filled with the soft notes of a Mozart piano sonata. 'I haven't had anyone else in the car, except a girl I know, for longer than I can remember. She loved it, but she's always loved expensive things. Didn't you find that with Jane?'

Underdown's head swung round and for a second Michael thought he had gone too far.

'I don't want to talk about Jane!' His voice was loud in the confined space.

'Fine, Malcolm. I know how you're feeling. It's depression, isn't it? Comes out of the blue? I've got stuff for that. I can help you to overcome it. We have to talk about it.'

'What?'

'Your depression. I'll tell you something. Talking about it is the best possible medicine because it's worse when people don't talk about what's worrying them, when they're not being open about their innermost thoughts. And that's what's happening to you. You haven't been open.'

'About what?' His emotional upsurge had retreated, the antagonism had gone, but now there was only this wooden apathy. Michael wanted to dispel it and bring back his earlier mood, even though it might be dangerous.

'At the trial it was said that everything goes back to that evening in Pimlico with Edward and Jane. I think it goes back a good deal further than that. We talked about it then, remember? But you didn't want to talk much. My view is that you must talk about the affair you were having with Jane. Confront it. Confront what happened during it, and what happened after it was over.'

'I don't want to talk any more,' Underdown said. 'And I'm not going to take any more medication and I'm not going back to that fucking place.'

By the dashboard lights Michael could see the

clenching and unclenching of his big hands. He
wasn't holding the knife any longer. It was back in
one of his coat pockets. Michael hadn't asked him
to put it away, hadn't commented on it after that
first moment. When they had been talking for a
while, it had just disappeared.

'I agree. I don't think you should go back to that
place. And as far as medication is concerned, there's
a new drug which has been developed in Sweden
which will make you feel a lot better and won't turn
you into a zombie.'

The hands unclenched.

'They've carried out trials in Sweden and
Denmark and people with your problem have been
helped wonderfully.'

'Why didn't they give it to me then?' Underdown
said.

'Things don't work out sometimes the way we
would want them to. If you let me look after you I
can promise that you'll never be given any of the
drugs you had before.'

'I'm not going back again.'

'Did I say you were? Not at all. When I suggested
you come to sit in the car it was just to make us
more comfortable. If you want to go to the hut, fine.'

The hands clenched again.

'Listen, we have to talk about the police. I've told
them nothing, but they're going to get around to
looking for you in these parts and they'll find you
and then I won't be able to help you. If you're going

to come in at all, it'll be much better for you to come in with me. No . . . no . . . don't answer, don't simply react. Leave it in your mind. Think about it, that's all I ask.'

Underdown said nothing and Michael paused while his mind reviewed what he was doing and what he wanted to say next. He also reviewed his own danger. The knife was in a pocket. Provided he could see Underdown's hands, he was safe. One of his own hands was lightly touching the pistol which lay on the floor of the car between the driving seat and the door. It was better placed there, he thought, than in his pocket where it had lodged most of the day.

'Do you trust me, Malcolm?'

Underdown did not speak.

'I worked very hard for you at the time of your trial. You could have gone to prison. You realize that, don't you?'

'It would have been better than Loxton.'

'No, it wouldn't. You still have a chance to go before a mental health tribunal in a few years' time and who knows what they may decide. But if you'd gone to prison and escaped and done what you did, you could kiss goodbye to the rest of your life. That's why we have to be honest with each other and why you have to trust me. You see that, don't you?'

The hands, which had been lying like two white rodents on his lap, twitched.

'You loved Jane very much, didn't you?'

'Yes.' It was little more than a hiss.

'Do you know what happened to her?'

The big head moved from side to side.

'She married. I found out all about her. She could have married you, you know. You wanted to, didn't you?'

This time the head nodded slowly.

'And she wanted to, I'm sure, early on, didn't she?'

'She loved me. She said she loved me. She told me.'

'Was she your first, Malcolm?'

'First what?'

'Girlfriend . . . lover . . . however you phrase it. Was she the first woman you'd ever had sex with?'

'I don't want to talk to you about this!'

'We have to talk about it. It's the most important part of your problem. If we can get to the root of this, then you won't be so depressed.'

'I don't want to fucking talk about it!'

'Do you trust me, Malcolm?'

Silence.

'Do you?'

'I don't know.'

'OK. Look, we've got to talk about Jane and then I'm going to help you. It was a kind of contract, wasn't it? She loved you, you loved her, you were going to share the rest of your lives. Isn't that so?'

'Yes!' This time the hiss was explosive.

'Malcolm, I want to give you a proper meal. You

haven't had very much, I'm afraid. You're still hungry, aren't you?'

'Yeah.'

'OK, let me give you a proper meal and then we can go on talking. I'm not going to take you back to Loxton unless you ask me to. But I've got the drug that will take away your depression, and when you've had a meal and I've given you the drug, I'll bring you back here if that's what you want me to do. Do you understand that?'

Underdown did not reply and Michael said, 'You must say something. "Yes" and I'll help you. "No" and I'll leave you and you can go back to that hut. What's it going to be? The short drive? The help?'

'You try anything and I'll kill you,' Underdown said.

'I know that. I know you've got the knife. I'll take the chance.'

Suddenly the knife was in his hand, the knuckles shining whitely in the dim light. But it wasn't pointed towards Michael and he knew that the worst was over. The weapon now was not so much the knife, but Underdown himself.

He turned the ignition key and the car came to life.

'Portsmouth Crown Court,' the telephone said.

'My name is Jane Stone. I called earlier to check

if my husband was in court but I think I was put through to the wrong department.'

'Is your husband a solicitor or a barrister?'

'Neither. He's a witness. I was put through to the Crown Prosecution Service.'

'I'll connect you with the Witness Service.'

A woman answered and Jane explained that she was trying to contact her husband.

'We don't usually deal with that kind of inquiry.' The woman had a well-educated, friendly voice. 'Our job is to help witnesses who haven't been to court before. Show them the court-rooms, so they feel less worried and tense.'

'It's very important,' Jane said. 'He's an expert witness, a forensic psychiatrist.'

'I'm not sure—'

'The Crown Prosecution Service wasn't any help at all. The person there sounded very brusque.'

The woman laughed. 'No, they wouldn't be much help. Give me your number. I'll try to trace your husband and phone you back. What case is it?'

Jane explained that she didn't know what case Michael was appearing in and then sat in the kitchen and waited. When the phone rang it came as a shock, even though she was expecting it.

'Mrs Stone? I've checked as well as I can, but there's no record of your husband being down for any of the cases here. Are you sure you have the right court? It could be Winchester, you know.'

'He said it was Portsmouth.'

'Well, I'm sorry, but there doesn't seem to be a witness here called Dr Stone.'

'Have you checked thoroughly?'

'As thoroughly as I can.' The friendliness had gone out of her voice and it was impatient.

'Would you check again? I've got to tell him something very important.'

'I'm sorry, but I can't do anything more. In any case, the courts are closing up and most people are going home. Goodbye, Mrs Stone.'

Jane sat staring at the telephone for some minutes. Why was it so difficult to achieve a simple thing like getting a message to Michael?

It was already dark and, with a vague plan already in her mind, she decided she had to do something to protect herself, although it meant leaving the house for a short time. She put on more lights and went out to the car.

The village shop was less than a mile away and it was like a beacon in the darkness. It was the furthest she had ventured from the house since she and Michael had come to the country.

Mrs Prewett was behind the counter and when Jane asked for six cans of hairspray she glanced at her hair and said, with surprise, 'Six?'

'Yes, please, six.'

'Right-ho, but I don't know if I've got six. I'll look.' After a search she put four on the counter. 'That's all I have. Something wrong, love?' Mrs Prewett was

large, plump and well past middle-age. She had
known Jane since she was a child.

'Nothing's wrong. What other sprays are there?'
Jane was tense and didn't want conversation. 'Oven
cleaner. That's a spray, isn't it?'

Mrs Prewett bent her ample bottom to peer into
a low shelf and came up with a can. 'One,' she said.

'Give me that. And I'll take an insecticide as
well!'

She paid for the six cans and took them out to
the car.

In Guildford at the same time, Macrae had been
phoning her. He'd heard from Cannon Row that Jane
Stone had left a message for him to call her. He let
the telephone ring and ring and finally gave up.
Then he dialled Tammy's number in London. That
only brought on her answering machine so he took
a chance and telephoned his own number in Battersea. After a moment the receiver was lifted and a
cool voice said, 'Yes?'

He identified himself. 'Do you know where Mrs
Stone is?'

'At Highlands House, of course.'

'She's not answering the phone.'

'I spoke to her there not too long ago. She said
she never left the house.'

'Oh, Christ. We can't be too far. Tell me how
to get there.' Macrae jotted down her fragmentary

instructions. Then he said to Leo, 'Dr Stone never rang back, did he?'

'No. And no one seemed to know anything about him.'

'Shit! Listen, I want to check on Jane Stone. I'll have the map, laddie, and you go like hell.'

Jane pulled into the drive. The house blazed with lights. She carried the spray cans into the kitchen.

The telephone rang. She thought: I must answer. I must.

It was Tammy. 'I had to phone. I'm working at Macrae's house and he's just been trying to get hold of you. No one was answering. He called here to see if I knew where you were.'

'I was at the shop.'

'Thank God for that. Anyway, he's coming to see you, to make sure you're OK.'

'Where's he coming from?'

'He didn't say, except that he wasn't far. He was on a mobile.'

Jane heard a car engine in the drive. 'That's him now,' she said.

Chapter Twenty-two

'Look, Malcolm, all the lights are on. That's a waste of electricity, isn't it?'

Michael drove the Porsche around to the back of the house. There was a full moon which shone from time to time in the cloud breaks and he could see that Underdown's hands were knotted together.

'Where are we?' Underdown said. 'I don't want to be here.'

'I swore to you that I wasn't going to do anything you didn't want me to do, remember? And you said you trusted me. Listen, trust me for another few minutes. Once you've had a steak and I've given you the new Swedish drug you're going to feel a different person. Half an hour, that's all, and then back to your hut if you want to go. All right?'

'You're having me on! You've got people in the house! You'll let them take me!' His voice had risen and Michael knew he was becoming increasingly unstable.

'Malcolm, if I was going to try to trap someone, would I leave the house with all the lights on, would

I leave the gate open? If there were police or anyone else here, they would grab you now, in the car. You've got a knife. Hold it to my throat if you like. Then you know I won't harm you.'

Michael got out of the car. He went round to the passenger side and opened the door. Malcolm stayed where he was. 'Come on, you must be hungry as hell.'

'But whose house is this?'

'Mine, of course. Whose did you think it was? That's why I know everything we need is there.'

'The Swedish stuff?'

Michael straightened up. 'Of course.'

Slowly, like some vast orang-utan, Underdown clambered from the car.

'We'll go in the back way,' Michael said. 'That door over there.'

Jane couldn't see the car. She had heard it. She had told Tammy it was there. Now she couldn't see it. She went from the drawing-room to the spare room to the bathroom, but it was nowhere.

Fear, now, was part of her personality. She went to the windows of another room and there, in a place she had not expected to see it, was the Porsche. Her heart lifted. A surge of happiness hit her. 'Michael,' she said out loud. 'Oh, Michael, you're back!'

She ran down the broad staircase. 'Michael,' she called. 'Where are you?'

'Here! In the kitchen.'

She ran along the passage and threw open the kitchen door.

There, standing in the middle of the room, was Malcolm Underdown.

For a moment, she thought she was hallucinating.

There was no Michael, only Malcolm. Before she could turn and run he had closed the gap between them and was standing in front of the kitchen door.

'Jane,' he said.

The word spilled out through his beard as though some phantasmagoric creature had learned to talk. The voice was low and Jane remembered its timbre well.

She tried to speak but her jaw seemed locked. She noticed that he was trembling.

At last her jaw loosened. 'Michael?' she said again. It was no more than a whisper.

Had it been Michael's voice saying 'Here! In the kitchen,' a few moments before? Of course it had. She had called and he had answered.

The huge figure in front of her held out a hand and took her arm.

'Don't,' she said. 'Please don't, Malcolm.' It was like talking to one of the great apes.

He held her gently and said, 'I told you I'd come back.'

Suddenly he seemed a different person. The trembling was not so noticeable. Apart from the facial hair, he seemed more of the Malcolm she had once known.

'Yes, you did,' she said.

'You've waited,' he said.

'Waited?'

'You knew I'd come back. Did you think I wouldn't?'

'I didn't know what you meant.'

'Didn't I always say we would never part?'

His eyes had grown larger. The beanie held back his tangled hair and the eyes shone out of the face like flickering night lights.

Some of the fear left her. This wasn't the Malcolm she had expected, the animal-like figure bent on revenge. This was a man she knew, a man she had gone to bed with more than once.

Suddenly she realized that the phrase 'I'll come back' had not been a threat, but a promise.

'We're together,' Malcolm said.

'Yes, together.'

'And I'm never going back. Never!'

Michael came out from behind the scullery door. 'That's true,' he said. 'You're never going back.' And he shot Underdown twice with a small-calibre hand-gun. Once in the shoulder and once in the stomach.

Underdown lurched against the wall and stared at him as a wounded ape might stare at a hunter. There was shock, bewilderment and anger in the look and he pushed himself away from the wall, dropping Jane's arm and forcing himself upright.

Jane said, 'Oh, God, Michael, he wasn't doing anything! He wasn't *going* to do anything.'

'That's the problem,' Michael said.

Jane, who had been half-crouching in Underdown's grip, straightened. She said, 'What are you saying? You've nearly killed him!'

'I brought him here to do something and he didn't do it. That was always a possibility. I wasn't sure of the scenario but it was worth taking the chance. It would have saved me so much trouble.'

His face in the bright kitchen light was shiny with sweat and his silver fox hair hung down untidily. Jane would hardly have recognized him.

What he said made no sense to her and she did not want to believe what she had just seen.

Underdown groaned. Blood was running along the vinyl-tiled floor under the table. Michael bent over him, felt in his pockets, then shot him again.

'Stop it, Michael! Stop it!' Jane shouted. 'He hasn't harmed me! It was not a threat that he was coming back. It was a *promise!*'

'He was a weapon. That's how I thought of him. "*I'll come back!*" That's what he said. And it sounds like a threat, doesn't it? So I thought, why not see if I can use him?'

The fear, so long a ghostly presence, had left her and been replaced by something she had not felt for a long time – anger. 'I don't know what the hell you're talking about! Why have you done this? He's dying!' She bent over Malcolm, who now was nothing more to her than a severely damaged human being, needing her help.

Michael was talking again but she hardly heard him. There was a spreading red stain on Malcolm's chest. Blood was oozing from his mouth.

'I'm going to call an ambulance.' She reached for the phone.

Michael picked it up and cut the cord. He had put the gun in his pocket. He was wearing gloves and now there was a knife in his hand.

'This is Malcolm's,' he said, holding up the knife. 'With his fingerprints all over it. That's what they're going to find.'

And then, just as if he had told her what he was proposing, she knew. It came into her mind as a single volcanic thought: he wanted her dead.

'Oh, God,' she said, more to herself than to him. 'Why?'

'Humiliation. There is always a simple reason. Mine is humiliation. I have debts. Debts so large they hardly bear thinking about. Remember Lloyd's? How I was going to get rich beyond my wildest dreams? No, of course you don't for we never discussed it. I remember you saying once that I never discussed my work with you. Well, there were other things I never discussed. Money was one. There was never enough. And now, with the Lloyd's crash, it's all gone. And the end of that road is humiliation.'

'I have money! I have all this. The house and what Mother's left me in cash.'

'Oh, yes I know. That's what this is all about. But you see, your way I'd have to have you. And that's the problem. With the house and the money she left you – I make it that the two will fetch something over a million – I can pay what I owe and have something left. But not if there are two of us. Not even you would be generous enough to let me have everything.' His tone was bitter. 'Jesus, you wouldn't know what it's like to need money. You've always had as much as you needed. More!' He moved away from her to the middle of the room, taking care not to step in the blood.

She realized that his love for her must have died a long time before. That's if he had ever loved her. She could only hear the hatred that was left.

To her right was the fuse box and below it, within reach, the electricity control buttons. Michael was standing by the kitchen table, some way from her.

'Michael, I beg you, don't do this!' She spread her arms to give her words more meaning. 'Please!' Her raised right hand grazed the buttons, then she punched the biggest one and the lights went out. She ducked down expecting a shot, but it didn't come. She wrenched open the door and ran along the passage. She knew the front door was a mass of locks and chains and would take precious seconds to open, so she made for the stairs.

She heard him come out of the kitchen. She fled

through her bedroom into her old playroom and ran to open the window, which led out to the roof of the porch.

It was a sash window. She slid aside the double-glazing and grabbed the lower window to raise it. She heaved. It did not move a fraction of an inch and she realized that the paint was holding it.

She heard Michael in the upstairs passage. He was trying the doors of the other rooms. But in her anxiety about being left alone in the house, she had locked them all. And there was no way she could get to another room because her only exit was through the bedroom. In the playroom was her big play-house. One wall was loose and she managed to pull it out a little bit more. She got down on her stomach and slowly she began to work herself into it. She stopped moving and listened. Michael was in her bedroom. She heard him opening her hanging cupboard.

Her clothing caught on pieces of wood. Her blouse ripped. Slowly she twisted and turned until her whole body was inside the house. She was lying on her right side with her head on the floor and her eyes to one of the small windows.

'Jane?'

Michael came into the room. In the moonlight she could see him clearly.

He had the knife in his hand, and she knew then why he had not attempted to shoot her. He wanted her to die as Malcolm might have killed her, by the knife.

'Jane?'

He stood in the doorway and looked around the room. She knew he was seeing her old panda, which she had brought up from the cellar, and piles of books. She had moved everything else downstairs for packing.

The knife had been held by his side. Now he raised it and moonlight glinted on the blade.

'It's no use,' he said. 'You've got to be here. The other rooms are locked. So . . . you've got to be . . .' He went down on his haunches. 'Yes, there you are!' He was staring through the glass pane. His face was distorted, manic, his voice was high. 'I can see your eyes. And part of your mouth. It's not much of a hiding place, Jane. I wish this didn't have to happen! I wish Malcolm had done what he was supposed to do. How much simpler that would have been.'

She did not speak. Held her breath. What could she do? She thought of the hairspray down in the kitchen. She thought of the pistol in her drawer. Here she had nothing.

Then he said, 'This changes the scenario. Let's see . . . Underdown found where you lived as he found the others. You ran from him and hid here in the play-house. And he found you here. What would he do? He'd tear it apart, wouldn't he?' He put the knife in his pocket and took hold of one of the walls

of the Wendy house. 'Oh, yes . . . he'd tear it apart!'
There was a ripping noise and it came away,
uncovering her feet. 'Now the roof! Tear it apart!'
He pulled and pushed and the thin plywood broke.
In a moment he had half the roof in his hands. He
threw it down. 'Now the top storey!'

He grabbed the flooring that separated the top
floor from the ground and as it came away some of
the small pieces of doll's furniture fell on her.

Another section of the house was torn away.
There was only the section now that covered her
head. He walked to the left side of the house and
began pulling this away from where it had been
screwed to the wall. Plaster fell on her face. A long
screw fell. She grasped it and held it like a knife. It
wasn't much, but it was something.

The play-house was in ruins. She came up on
her knees, then stood. He had a knife. She had a
long wood-screw.

'Now what would Underdown do?' Michael said.

She raised herself on to the balls of her feet. She
would use the screw to slash at his face.

He came towards her.

She saw a shadow by the door that didn't belong
there. Then the moon, breaking through one of the
racing clouds, showed her that it wasn't a shadow. It
was Malcolm. His head was bent and he was holding
himself up against the door-frame.

'Oh, Christ!' Michael said.

Underdown moved away from the door-frame in

slow motion. He was like someone walking in heavy sand. Michael ran at him, the knife held low. He began to drive upwards towards Underdown's stomach. But the two great hands went out and gripped him around the neck.

Jane picked up a piece of heavy plywood and began to belabour Michael. But it was like belabouring someone with a feather. He simply did not seem to feel it. She broke away and ran. She heard Malcolm give a great cry and then she was on the staircase and running through the kitchen to the back door. It was locked and the key was gone. Michael, she thought.

She heard a noise behind her.

'It's no use, Jane,' Michael said. She heard him fumbling with the switches and the lights burst into brightness.

He was like some nightmare figure: hair awry, blood on his arms and face, eyes wild and mad. In one hand he held the knife.

She ran to the scullery and tried to close the door but it was old and warped and had never closed properly. She leaned against it but as he pushed she could feel her feet sliding along the stone-flagged floor. She fell. Then, as though the building itself was crashing to the ground, the kitchen windows burst in and the huge figure of Macrae landed like an unexploded bomb. Michael whirled with the knife and stabbed once, twice. And then Macrae hit him.

He caught the blow on the side of his head and

its power caused him to fall backwards. His arms flailed as he tried to regain his balance. Then a foot landed in the pool of Underdown's blood. He slipped and slid and went down with a thudding fall as his head hit the wall.

At the same moment, Leo came through the smashed window with a tyre lever in his hand.

They heard Jane crying in the scullery. Macrae went to her and comforted her as he might his own daughter. 'Cry as much as you can, lassie,' he said. 'It's all over now.'

And it was all over.

Leo looked down at the forensic psychiatrist. He was lying on his back and his head seemed to be growing out of his left shoulder.

Chapter Twenty-three

'Growing out of his left shoulder?' Zoe said.

'Broken neck.' Leo was standing in the shower and Zoe was holding his towel, waiting for him. 'Dead as a doornail.'

'How does Macrae feel?'

'How should he feel?'

'He caused Stone's death, didn't he?'

'Would you rather he'd stood aside and let Stone cut Jane to pieces? Anyway, it was Underdown's blood that made the floor slippery. So you could say Stone caused his own death.'

'Leo, are you sure *you're* all right?' she said.

'I'm fine. I'm just pleased we got there. We don't always get to places in time. Jane Stone can thank Macrae for that. If he hadn't been screwing Tammy he'd never have seen Stone drive away like that and wouldn't have been suspicious.'

'Suspicious? He didn't even know what he was suspicious about.'

'Macrae's suspicious of everything. Even if he gets it wrong he gets it right, if you see what I mean.'

302

He took the towel and began to dry himself. 'I must say I felt a bit sorry for Underdown. It took him thirty-six hours to die and some of that time he was talking to us. He was quite gentle, you know. That's what several people said about him.'

'Some way to be gentle! What about that poor woman he killed round the corner?'

'That's the trouble with madmen. Gentle one moment, violent the next.'

He put on his dressing-gown and wandered upstairs to the sitting-room. It was the first time he had been home for two days.

'When did he die?' Zoe said.

'Today. Macrae and I went out for a beer and a sandwich and he died during the lunch hour. He and Jane were in the same hospital, you know. We were going from one to the other, Jane Stone one minute and Underdown the next. Trouble is, Jane's pretty shocked and she couldn't tell us much but she did say her husband had played everything very cleverly. He'd let *her* think of coming down to the country.'

'If I'd been her I'd have stayed with Tamsin, or whatever her name is.'

'Tamara. Stone had told her not to let Jane stay with her. Said she was in danger of developing "spousal dependency". We checked with the Home Office psychiatrist. There's no such thing. Stone had promised Underdown a new miracle drug and that didn't exist either. He made it all up. But the psychiatrist told us one interesting thing. Underdown was probably suffering from De Clerambault's Syndrome.'

'What the hell is that?' Zoe said. 'You come home and use these big words and I know you've only just learned them.'

He went to the bedroom and came back with a sheet of paper. 'Listen to this. I copied it from one of the books in the hospital. "*De Clerambault's Syndrome is named after the French physician who first identified it. A variant of the disorder known as erotomania, in which usually a woman, but not always, believes that a man, unrealistically attainable, is passionately in love with her.*" You see, we have our reports too. And I want you to remember that part about it being the woman who is usually after the man. Sort of reminds me of us.'

'You say things like that, Sunshine, and I'm going to take this knife and—'

'Don't make jokes like that. Not after what happened.' He touched wood and so did she.

She said, 'You've got me doing all your Jewish superstitions! Next thing we know, people will start interfering with you at concerts.'

'Get tickets, get tickets!'

She waved a dismissive hand. 'Now that I come to think of it, maybe not. But listen, Leo, what about Dr Stone? You said he was after her money. Was she as rich as all that?'

'The house is valued at three-quarters-of-a-million. There are ten acres as well. And there's over half-a-million in blue-chip shares. The thing about Stone was that he had to pay his losses within the next few weeks. He'd done a bloody stupid thing. He was always apparently a bit of a gambler, the horses, but nothing serious. But when the Lloyd's syndicate went down he went down too, for hundreds of thousands. To try and recoup he began gambling in a big way. Borrowed money from not very nice people and lost it too. It became like a downward spiral. And when people like that want it back and don't get it back they breaks things like arms and legs and knee caps. And then they give you a fatal accident.'

'And while all this was happening he was having it off with Tamara whatsit. Busy man.'

'Anyway he must have seen Underdown's escape as a gift from the gods. According to his wife he had tried to turn him into a weapon, had actually brought him to the house to kill her. What he hadn't realized, just like everybody else, was that after Underdown had murdered Edward Craig he hadn't meant that he'd come back to kill Jane. What he'd meant was "I'll be back *for* you". And there was something else: Stone had seen all the reports on Underdown and there was one which was about some symposium or other on dangerousness. In it was the warning that Underdown was a threat to any man he saw in the company of Jane. Either Stone had forgotten it or perhaps he was just too bloody arrogant to accept it applied to him. The irony was, he had written the report himself.'

South of the River Thames, that alien land from which Manfred Silver had thought never to return – or at least never with his private parts undamaged – Macrae was parking his car. He had come up from Guildford earlier that evening and had gone to the pub. Now he had a couple of stiff whiskies inside him and was carrying a bottle of Glenmorangie. He did not necessarily want to make an evening of it, for he was tired, but it gave him a feeling of security.

He walked along his street and saw that the lights were on in his house. His spirits rose. It was a sight he had not seen for too long and he thought: Frenchy's back!

But she wasn't. As he entered the house, Tammy was standing in the kitchen doorway. They had spoken on the phone earlier – she had wanted to come down to see Jane but the doctors had refused permission – and she had said she would see him later. He had not realized she'd meant later that evening.

'Hello, George. I thought I'd cook you something. You must be in need of a hot meal.'

He decided that neither altruism nor love was the real reason she was there and he waited to discover what was.

She had made him steak and kidney pie and it

was better than any he had had before. But she was tense, picking bits of bread to pieces as she sat and watched him eat.

When he had almost finished she said, 'Tell me about Jane. Is she all right?'

' "All right" is a comparative term,' Macrae said.

'You know what I mean.'

'She's all right, I suppose, the poor thing. But it'll take a long time before she's really recovered.'

'I'll help her,' Tammy said.

'Aye. You do that.'

'I'll go down the moment they say I can and I'll help her to clear the house. I know I wouldn't want to live in either of them after what happened. Would you?'

'Probably not.'

'Do you like the steak and kidney?'

'It's no' bad at all.'

'That's praise in Scotland, is it?'

He did not reply and she went on talking in a hasty, rather nervous manner. 'What she needs is something to do,' she said. 'Some work of some kind, something to keep her mind off what happened. Thank God it's all over now. I mean, it is, isn't it?'

Abruptly, Macrae said, 'You were having it off with Stone.'

'What?'

'Don't give me the innocent. You were having an affair with him, weren't you?'

'Why do you say things like that, George?'

'Because they're bloody true.'

'You patronizing bastard! You don't know what you're talking about!'

'Listen, I'm a policeman. When policemen get suspicious about something, they check up. I saw Stone coming out of your flat. He drove his car away that night like he'd done it time and time again. It's bloody difficult to remember where the road barriers are. I know because I couldn't. I said to myself, how does he know the place so well? And it was bloody obvious. So I asked Jane about Paul, your ex, the man who's supposed to be making your life a misery with his phone calls, and she told me he's happily married and living in Bath. See? It's not all that difficult.'

She started to cry and he said, 'Oh, for God's sake!'

She said, 'You're such a shit! Can't you understand how guilty I feel? How do you think Jane's going to feel when she finds out?'

'Haven't thought about it.'

'It just happened! I was lonely and he said there were problems between himself and Jane. That it wouldn't hurt her if she didn't know. But I finished it. I told him the other night it was over. And then he goes down and tries to kill her!'

'Don't flatter yourself he was trying to kill her because of you. It was about money.'

After a moment she said, 'George, can I ask you something?'

'Go ahead.'

'Does Jane have to know? I mean, she's all I've got now.'

'I'm not going to tell her. It won't go in any report. So unless you tell her, she won't know.'

She nodded. 'Thank you. I won't tell her.'

She stood up and began clearing the dishes. He lit a cigar and watched her. She was good-looking, there was no denying that.

She said, 'You could really do something with this house, you know. It's in a street on the way up.'

He looked at her in surprise. The self-pity had gone from her voice. It was as though the discussion about her feelings of guilt had not taken place.

'I like it as it is,' he said.

'So do I. But I meant the kitchen. You could do with a new kitchen . . . and a new bathroom . . .' She went through the house room by room, suggesting improvements. He sat there, pulling on his cigar and half listening. Then she said, 'George, can I say something else?'

'What?'

'You want me to work for you and you want me to sleep with you, and that's fine. I want to, too. But would you do something for me in return?'

'What?'

'Put your clothes away. You take them off and throw them down. I had all this with my ex. That's why he became my ex. Would you just put them away in your cupboards or in the laundry basket? Would you mind?'

That's what did it. The 'would-you-mind?' It wasn't so much a question, more a statement of a relationship.

Macrae rose and phoned for a mini-cab.

'What's the matter, George? Have I said something?'

'I've just remembered. I've got to go into the office.'

'Now? Whatever for?'

'I've got to write a report.'

He saw her into the mini-cab then came back to the empty sitting-room and poured himself another glass of Glenmorangie. He wondered if he had been too hasty. She was good in bed. But the payment was too high. It wasn't so much the money, he could manage that, but the would-you-minds. He wouldn't be able to stand those.

He felt suddenly free and released and went upstairs to have a shower. He dropped his clothes on the floor and stirred them around with his feet.

Then, on the bedside table, he saw an envelope which he hadn't noticed before. Tammy must have put it there for him. The writing was familiar. He opened it and inside there was a card. It said, 'Happy birthday, George. Love, your Frenchy.'

He hadn't remembered his birthday and now,

standing in his bedroom, half dressed, the feeling of freedom and release faded. Once again he was just the old George Macrae he had always been: the man who didn't know when he was well off.

All Pan Books are available at your local bookshop or newsagent, or can be ordered direct from the publisher. Indicate the number of copies required and fill in the form below.

Send to: Macmillan General Books C.S.
             Book Service By Post
             PO Box 29, Douglas I-O-M
             IM99 1BQ

or phone: 01624 675137, quoting title, author and credit card number.

or fax: 01624 670923, quoting title, author, and credit card number.

or Internet: http://www.bookpost.co.uk

Please enclose a remittance* to the value of the cover price plus 75 pence per book for post and packing. Overseas customers please allow £1.00 per copy for post and packing.

*Payment may be made in sterling by UK personal cheque, Eurocheque, postal order, sterling draft or international money order, made payable to Book Service By Post.

Alternatively by Access/Visa/MasterCard

Card No.   ☐☐☐☐☐☐☐☐☐☐☐☐☐☐☐☐☐☐

Expiry Date   ☐☐☐☐☐☐☐☐☐☐☐☐☐☐☐☐☐☐

Signature   _____

Applicable only in the UK and BFPO addresses.

While every effort is made to keep prices low, it is sometimes necessary to increase prices at short notice. Pan Books reserve the right to show on covers and charge new retail prices which may differ from those advertised in the text or elsewhere.

NAME AND ADDRESS IN BLOCK CAPITAL LETTERS PLEASE

Name _____

Address _____

_____

_____

_____

8/95

Please allow 28 days for delivery.
Please tick box if you do not wish to receive any additional information. ☐